Emily Kerr has been scribblin
since she learnt how to write.
is based in Yorkshire.

She can generally be foun
hunched up over her laptop
been known to venture outside every so often to take part in
various running-based activities.

Her novel *Take a Chance on Greece* won the Jane Wenham-
Jones Romantic Comedy award at the Romantic Novelists'
Association Awards in 2023.

www.emilykerrwrites.com

twitter.com/EmilyKerrWrites
facebook.com/emilykerrwrites

Also by Emily Kerr

Duvet Day

Meet Me Under the Northern Lights

Take a Chance on Greece

HER FIXER UPPER

EMILY KERR

One More Chapter
a division of HarperCollins*Publishers* Ltd
1 London Bridge Street
London SE1 9GF
www.harpercollins.co.uk
HarperCollins*Publishers*
Macken House, 39/40 Mayor Street Upper,
Dublin 1, D01 C9W8

This paperback edition 2023

1

First published in Great Britain in ebook format
by HarperCollins*Publishers* 2023
Copyright © Emily Kerr 2023
Emily Kerr asserts the moral right to be identified
as the author of this work

A catalogue record of this book is available from the British Library

ISBN: 978-0-00-854303-7

Printed and bound in the UK using 100% Renewable Electricity
by CPI Group (UK) Ltd

To all my little cousins

Chapter One

'This isn't an all-inclusive resort, you know,' barked the dinner supervisor as she caught me attempting to smuggle a couple of extra bread rolls into my handbag from the stack at the end of the counter.

'They're for a lesson on the Irish famine.' I attempted to style it out, painfully aware that our exchange was attracting the attention of a gaggle of sniggering Year Eleven boys. I'd never live it down if they found out that this was a particularly pathetic attempt at economising as part of my mission to boost the funds in my savings account, which was optimistically labelled 'House deposit'. The introduction of free meals for teachers had been the school's way of compensating us for the fact that we'd not had a pay rise in three years. Naturally, we'd all have preferred the pay rise, but if free food was on offer, I was determined to make the most of it. Unfortunately, it seemed that the dinner supervisor had other ideas.

She looked back at me, the withering expression in her eyes enough to make the boldest sixth former want their mum. When she was certain that I was pinned to the spot by her gaze, she glanced across at the counter, making it clear what she wanted me to do.

'Sorry,' I muttered, putting the bread rolls back, and scurrying away to the teachers' table at the far end of the canteen, the laugher of the Year Elevens following me across the room.

'Surely living on stale bread from school isn't going to make that much difference to you getting on the property ladder, Freya?' said Leila, grinning at my sheepish expression as I sat down opposite her.

I tried to signal to my work bestie to stop, but it was already too late. Her comment had been overheard by my head of department, Mr Rhys, a man who had an opinion on absolutely everything and liked to give it, even if he hadn't been asked. When he was around, I lived in a confusing state of fear and irritation, which didn't exactly make for a relaxing working environment.

'Still struggling to buy a place, Miss Hutchinson?' he said, the words muffled by the cottage pie which he was chewing. 'Perhaps if you gave up the avocado toast and fancy coffees you wouldn't find it such a challenge. Young people these days have all their priorities wrong. I was onto my second property by the time I was your age.' He shook his fork in my direction as he emphasised his point, bits of half-chewed mince dropping from his mouth onto the table as he spoke.

2

I fought so hard to stop my eyes rolling at his comment that they went watery. Had he seen house prices nowadays? By my calculations, it would take me approximately twenty-seven years of no coffees to get a deposit together by that means alone, by which time, of course, the goalposts would have changed again. And had he any idea how difficult it was saving anything at all when most of my wages went on overpriced rent and bills?

'I'm allergic to avocados,' I said in lieu of the angry speech I was too cowardly to deliver.

'How's your wife, Mr Rhys? And her family? They own that soft furnishings chain, don't they?' said Leila, sending the ghost of a wink in my direction.

'She's very well, thank you for asking,' replied my boss, apparently unable to put two and two together to realise that the main reason he'd been onto his second property at the same stage in life as me was because he'd married an heiress. He then went on to tell us in great detail about his latest trip to the holiday home they owned on the coast. It seemed spectacularly unfair that some people had more than one property when I was still struggling to graduate beyond a rented room in a shared house.

I concentrated hard on my food so I didn't say something I'd regret later. Overbearing as my boss was, I had to keep him on side. He kept dropping hints about creating a new role of Deputy Head of Department, a position I sometimes let myself daydream about in more confident moments. I probably didn't stand a chance of getting it, but it would be good to have the recognition of my hard work, and the very modest pay rise which would go along with the title.

Mr Rhys carried on pontificating about his favourite theme of the falling standards of youth as he moved onto his second course of jelly and ice cream, both of which were such lurid colours that it didn't bode well for the hyperactivity levels of our pupils this afternoon. Then at last he finished his meal and went off to supervise detention, leaving Leila and me with the table to ourselves.

'I thought you were going to pour your water over his head when he started going on about "young people these day",' said Leila with a laugh. 'Does he realise that he's a walking, talking cliché?'

'He's never been particularly good at reading between the lines. He genuinely thinks it's as easy as going to a mortgage adviser, asking for a loan, then collecting the keys of your dream home, whereas the last appointment I had, the guy struggled to keep a straight face while he was reviewing my application. Apparently I'm a "risk". Never mind that I pay nearly twice in rent what I would on a mortgage, my lack of a megabucks deposit means that they don't think I could afford one. It's so frustrating. I spend all my time urging the kids to dream big, and telling them that if they work hard, they can achieve whatever they want. But I'm beginning to feel like I'm lying to them.'

'You'll get there one day,' said Leila, unconvincingly.

'Yes, but will it be before it's time for me to move into a care home? That's the real question. I swear every time I search on Rightmove, they add another zero on the end of the prices. I'm just grateful the school Wi-Fi won't let me on the site anymore as it's getting too depressing for words.'

Leila scraped some of her excess chips onto my plate.

'Have these to cheer you up. You know what you need? Something to take your mind off it all. When it's meant to be, it will happen, trust me. And in the meantime, why don't you allow yourself to have some fun and join me and the gang for the pub quiz tonight? We're celebrating surviving the first week back.'

I ate one of the chips and winced at the amount of vinegar Leila had doused it in.

'I really shouldn't,' I said, the smug mortgage adviser's face appearing before me as I remembered how high his eyebrows had risen as he'd read through my bank statements. It had been humiliating having to justify every tiny transaction, and he'd not even cracked a smile when I'd hastily explained that some money which Leila had transferred to me under the jokey reference 'Hookers and poor decisions' had actually been dosh she owed me for a Boxercise class we'd mistakenly signed up for. He had strongly implied that I needed to rein in my spending still further, which was going to be tough given that I spent most of my life behaving like a miserly hermit. But if I kept on turning down invitations to social events, people would eventually stop issuing them. I couldn't sacrifice everything in my life for a potentially unattainable dream.

Leila caught the note of hesitancy in my voice. 'Come on, it'll do you good to get out. And it's a decent prize – a free meal – so it's practically an investment. Besides, we could do with your expertise on the team. We're got music and sport covered, but your general trivia knowledge will be a great help.'

'And there was me thinking it was my company you were after.' I laughed. 'Go on then, anything to delay returning to my current hovel. The pub will be heated, right?'

'Tell me you're not rationing the heating too? I know it costs a bloody fortune and you might as well be burning actual money for warmth, but it was minus two this morning, Freya. You'll only make yourself ill if you don't put it on.'

I sighed. 'For once, this wasn't my decision. Our landlord has the thermostat in his part of the house, and he's seemingly completely impervious to the cold. He wandered into the kitchen the other morning dressed only in shorts and asked why the rest of us all had three jumpers on apiece. I'm seriously considering starting to wear a woolly hat indoors.'

Leila pulled a face. 'I imagine semi-naked Steve was enough to put everyone off their breakfast.' She checked her watch. 'Right, I'm going to have to love you and leave you. The Year Seven netball tournament is calling. Pray for me. See you at The Taps later.'

I had my own challenge to face in the form of the Year Nine boys, who'd clearly all been given cans of extremely pungent body spray for Christmas and had applied it liberally. I made a mental note to warn my colleagues in the Chemistry department. If they lit a Bunsen burner around these lads, the whole school would be going up in smoke. The boys were in their usual ebullient mood, sniggering at in-jokes and trying to wind me up by moving their desks forward an inch every time I turned my back on them to write on the whiteboard. I pretended to be oblivious of their tricks and distracted them with a lively discussion on women's suffrage. When the bell eventually rang to mark the end of the day, there were several more Emmeline Pankhurst fans in the room, but I was exhausted from the effort and fantasising about collapsing in a heap in a darkened room.

Leila caught me trying to sneak from the staff room to the bicycle racks so I could ride straight home.

'Oh no you don't,' she said. 'All work and no play makes Freya's friends sad for her. Come on. You'll feel better once we've beaten the team from the posh PR firm down the road. I swear I spotted them using Google at the last quiz. It's time they faced their comeuppance.'

She looped her arm through mine and marched me around the corner to The Taps, the perfect venue for our little gang of teachers because it was too close to school for the sixth formers to dare venture in, and too new for the more traditional members of staff to bother with.

She waved cheerily at the barman. 'G&Ts all round, please, Rog. And make them doubles. We deserve it after the week we've had. My treat,' she insisted as I started to protest.

The quiz turned out to be a lot harder than I'd expected and it definitely brought out my competitive side. Our team hunched together in the corner, fierce whispers going back and forth as the answer paper filled up and the pile of empty glasses grew larger.

While we were in the middle of a passionate debate over whether it was the first or second Harry Potter book where Harry and Ron crashed a car into a Whomping Willow, Leila seized my arm and pointed at the next table.

'The PR posh boys are at it again. Look at that guy on the bar stool Googling away on his mobile phone. Could he be any more obvious? Pathetic.'

'I'll go and have a word,' I said, the combination of a double gin and tonic with a day of dealing with naughty schoolkids giving me an unaccustomed sense of self-confidence. I was in no mood to mess around.

'Freya, don't…' hissed Leila as I strode across.

I stood in front of the man and cleared my throat. 'Hand it over,' I said, fully in teacher mode. In fact, I only just managed to stop myself from telling him he should do his top button up and comb his hair so he didn't look like he'd just got out of bed.

He was so startled he started to do as instructed, before he caught himself.

'I beg your pardon? Are you accusing me of cheating in the quiz? Because I certainly was not. I was checking my emails and…oh my goodness, Hutch, is it you?'

He rose from his seat, his face breaking into a huge grin. The smile was unmistakable, even though the last time I'd seen it its owner had been a gangly pre-teen, certainly not the stubbly, broad-shouldered man who stood before me now. But there was still that slight awkwardness in his tall frame, and his brown eyes were as warm and sparkling as they used to be – eyes full of mischief, our teachers always used to say, generally followed by an indulgent smile. Always mischief, never malice.

'Charlie Humphries, I don't believe it!' There was a catch in my voice when I greeted him. It had been far too long since we'd spoken, and it was strange to hear my childhood nickname spoken in a resonant bass when the last time I'd heard him call me it his voice had been a ringing treble. I fought the urge to reach out and grasp his hand to check that he was real, and not a figment of my imagination. 'What are you doing here? I thought you got a job in London after you finished travelling.'

I felt a pang of nostalgia for the rose-tinted past when the pair of us had been so inseparable that I was frequently mistaken for his actual twin sister. When I'd had to move away because my mum got a new job, it had felt like the end of the world, but despite our grand vows to remain best friends no matter what, the pressures of distance and new friendship groups had meant we'd drifted apart, until as adults we'd become mere acquaintances who only kept in touch by following each other on social media. Our interactions on there were so rare that the algorithms didn't even bother showing me updates about him anymore.

'London? No thanks,' said Charlie. 'That's my sister's domain. I love visiting her there, but I'm always happy to jump back on the train to Yorkshire. Having done more than my fair share of country hopping, I can confidently say there's no place like God's own county. What are you up to nowadays? How have things been?'

I laughed. 'I think I'd probably be better off answering the first question rather than the second. If you're wanting the full lowdown on how things have been since we were kids, we might be here all night. I'm teaching history, and working at the school down the road. My folks moved back too when they took early retirement. How about you? Are you working in PR now?'

Charlie looked confused.

I gestured at the blokes who were braying with laughter at the table near him, slapping each other on the back with pleasure at the dodgy addition one of them had scrawled on the photo of some poor woman in the picture round.

Charlie pulled a face. 'You think I'm with those guys? Thankfully not. I didn't realise when I came in here to drown my sorrows that it was quiz night and by the time I did, I'd already got a drink, and this was the only place left to sit. No, I run my own agency, doing all the social media for various local businesses. I suppose it's PR of a sort, but I like to think it's a different art, more about engaging with customers on their level, and helping them to see the real people behind the brands. I can be creative and have some fun with it.'

'Wow, good for you. How amazing to run your own business and be your own boss.'

'You'd think,' he said, looking suddenly downcast. I thought of his throwaway comment that he'd come in here to drown his sorrows and wondered if I should ask him more. But before I could say anything, Leila came across waving the answer sheet towards us.

'Hello hello, who's this then? And why is he distracting you from the serious task of winning our dinner?'

Charlie held his hand out. 'I'm Charlie, and I used to be Freya's partner in crime. We were next to each other in the register at primary school thanks to our surnames, and we became known as Hutch and Humph...'

'...The Terrible Twosome,' I finished off for him with a laugh.

Leila raised an eyebrow. 'Freya as part of a "Terrible Twosome"? Now that I would love to hear more about. You must come and join us, Humph, and tell us all Freya's dark secrets so we can use them to blackmail her when she eventually becomes headteacher.'

I pulled a face at my friend's generous ambition for me. Leila swiped her hand in the air as if brushing away my doubts. 'She's going to get there one day, sooner than she believes,' she told Charlie. 'Right, you look like the kind of guy who could contribute some useful knowledge to a quiz team. Ringers are always welcome. Better than Googling like the PR poshos, anyway.'

'I don't want to intrude,' said Charlie.

'You wouldn't be intruding,' I hurried to reassure him, not wanting him to disappear off so soon after we had been reunited. 'It would be nice to catch up. And trust me, once Leila's got an idea into her head, there's no saying no to her.'

'Hello, Pot, this is the Kettle calling you black,' retorted

Leila. 'Come on, Charlie, I think your speciality might be the music round, and that's up next.'

We settled back around our table and as Leila had predicted, Charlie turned out to have an excellent ear for song artists and an encyclopaedic knowledge of the years in which certain singles were hits. But although he seemed to be enjoying himself, I couldn't help worrying about his reason for coming to the pub in the first place. It might be several years since we'd last spent time together, but I still cared for my old friend and wanted him to be happy.

When the last round had been marked and the results announced – despite Leila's protestations that they'd been cheating, we missed out on first place to the PR boys – I finally had the opportunity to ask Charlie what was up.

'Penny for 'em,' I said, echoing the phrase we had adopted as children from my grandfather, Arthur. He'd encountered us looking glum once while we were staring at our maths homework wondering why we had to learn how to do long division. We'd perked up no end when we thought he'd been offering us actual money for our thoughts, and bless him, he had then proved his status as Best Granddad Ever by giving us a shining pound coin each as he chuckled and told us not to worry too much about long division, we'd either get there eventually or a calculator would help us out in a mathematical crisis.

Charlie smiled as I reminded him of the story. 'Maybe if I'd saved that pound instead of spending it on sweets, then it would have started a habit which would hold me in good stead now. It's nothing serious, definitely not life or death, but I guess it's the death of a dream I've been nurturing.' He sighed. 'I was turned down for a loan today. Well, a mortgage actually. I've done everything I should have; I've moved back home with my parents so I could save a deposit, I have more than two years of books from my business proving that I have a regular income, but apparently it's not enough. The guy actually had the cheek to say it would be easier to get a mortgage if I was applying for it as part of a couple. Let me tell you, it's a bit harder to become part of a couple when you're living at home and your mum and dad are there quizzing a date about her prospects and ambitions over breakfast.'

'Tell me about it. I'm in a similar position, not living at home but...'

'Don't let her get started again,' said Leila. 'Freya, I love you very much, but you'll admit it yourself that you can be a bit of a stuck record about the house thing. Don't encourage her, Charlie.'

'I know exactly how Freya feels,' said Charlie. 'It's a tough situation to be in. It makes me feel like I've stalled somewhere along the route to being a proper grown-up.'

I nodded in agreement.

'You should be like me and acquire some relatives with more money than emotional intelligence so they try to purchase your affection in the form of a grace-and-favour one-bedroom flat,' said Leila. 'Not that I'm bitter about my family's complete indifference to me as a human being, of course. Or failing that, do what that mortgage bloke told you, Charlie,' she suggested. 'You used to be the Terrible

Twosome, why don't you and Freya buy a house together? Cheers.' And with that, she clinked her very full glass against our empty ones, downed her drink and disappeared off to the loo.

'I think Leila might have had a few extra shots in between rounds,' I said quietly to Charlie.

'We did get married in the playground at school. Maybe it's not such a foolish suggestion.' He paused, keeping his expression completely straight. Then I saw the corner of his mouth twitching and he winked at me, making it very clear that he was joking.

We both laughed at the idea. Charlie checked his watch. 'Right, I should probably be going. It may not be a school night for you, but it is for me. I've got a side hustle showing people around houses for a local estate agent. It helps the savings, plus it means I get to hear about properties I won't be able to buy before they even come on the market.'

He leaned forward and kissed me on the cheek. 'See you later, Hutch. It's been great catching up. Let's not leave it so long next time, eh?'

Chapter Two

By the time I'd got Leila safely back home – it took all of my persuasive abilities to stop her singing en route – and cycled back to my house, it was well past midnight. I cursed as I tried to get my key in the lock, the struggle more due to the fact that the outside light was broken again than to the G&Ts I'd consumed earlier in the evening. Although our landlord Steve lived on the premises, and was personally affected by the things which needed fixing, he still never went ahead and actually sorted them out. I'd even gone so far as to present him with a neatly itemised list, the required fixes colour-coded in order of priority, but he'd spilled his tea on it, probably deliberately, and that was the last of that.

I went into the kitchen and cursed yet again as I realised that one of my housemates had left the sink full of washing up and the fridge door wide open. I fought the urge to tidy up. Although I was itching to make everything spick and span, if I carried on doing it, everyone else would be even less likely to bother pulling their weight. It was about time the rest of the household stopped assuming it was my responsibility because I was the only female.

I heaved my heavy bag of marking into my bedroom and started getting ready for bed. It had been a long day and I was more than ready to crash out. As I brushed my hair I thought about the encounter with Charlie. It had been good to see him again. And it was reassuring to know that I wasn't the only person in this situation. He was lucky that he could move back home to save up. My parents had downsized into a development exclusively for over-55s, and it was quite a while until I'd fulfil that criteria.

I turned off the main light and then got into bed, pulling my two duvets up and hugging my three hot water bottles to me in the vain hope that my nest would remain cosy enough for me to get a good night's sleep. Steve was too stingy for double-glazing, and the only place my bed could fit in the room was right underneath the windowsill, exactly where the worst of the draughts were. But despite the unwanted air-conditioning, I still managed to fall asleep pretty quickly thanks to the sheer exhaustion which came from a long day dealing with unruly teenagers.

I woke with a start a couple of hours later to the terrifying realisation that I was no longer alone in my room. Despite the light from the street lamps which was seeping through the thin curtains, I couldn't make out whose silhouette I could see against my wardrobe doors. But I could hear the sound of their heavy breathing, and I could smell the thick stench of their body odour mixed with a beery vapour. I lay frozen in position, too terrified to even draw breath. What should I do? I knew I'd locked the front door when I came in, but the guys weren't always diligent about it. The house was in a studenty area of Leeds, slightly cheaper to rent because of it, but it meant that it was an attractive prospect for burglars looking for easy pickings and rooms full of gadgets and expensive tech. We'd avoided any incidents so far, but now it seemed our luck had run out. Was my room their first target? Or had they already ransacked the rest of the house?

The floor creaked as the intruder moved a step closer to the bed. And that's when my imagination went into overdrive. What if this wasn't a thief after a laptop, but an attacker after something much worse? However thick my duvets might be, they wouldn't do much good against someone armed with a weapon. If I screamed, would any of my housemates pay attention to it? And if they did, would they have time to react before the intruder lunged towards me? Were they even at home to hear my call for help? My phone was on the other side of the room, plugged in to charge, so there was no way I could dial 999, even if I could remember what you're meant to do on a silent call to alert the authorities that you're not a prankster but actually someone in need of help.

The intruder took another step closer, then the mattress

groaned as he sat down on the end of the bed. I swallowed the bile which was rising in my throat. Every receptor in my body was on high alert, my limbs clenched in horrified reaction. I knew I needed to move, to get away and find safety, but sheer terror paralysed me, the stuff of nightmares come to life in horrifying reality. In slow motion I saw the shadow of his arm as he reached towards me, rough fingers pulling at the duvets which I was gripping up to my chin.

'Freya,' said the intruder, his slurry voice growing closer as he started to lean towards me.

The proximity of his face to mine finally gave me the impetus to get moving. With a strangled yelp I let go of the duvets and thrust the base of my hand upwards. I'm not sure what it came into contact with, but it gave him enough of a shock to make him let out a cry and move a vital inch back. I leaped up and grabbed the nearest thing to hand which happened to be one of my hot water bottles and thumped it against my attacker's back before I thudded to the floor and stumbled over to the door.

'Freya, whadyadoin, isssme, Theve,' groaned the intruder.

I jabbed my elbow against the light switch, my hand on the doorknob ready to make my escape. As light flooded the room, my eyes processed what my ears had failed to register. My landlord Steve was sprawled on the bed, his hand pressed against his cheek, which if I'm not very much mistaken had the imprint of my palm on it.

'What the hell do you think you're doing, Steve?' I

yelled, my fear morphing from stranger danger into a different kind of horror.

'Sorry, wrong room,' he stuttered.

'Wrong room? Do you really expect me to fall for that blatant lie?' I yelled, the adrenalin giving an unexpected power to my voice. 'Your room is on the top floor and funnily enough is way nicer than my ground-floor dive. There's no way you could mistake the two.'

He let out an indeterminable jumble of sounds, none of which sounded like an apology. He was obviously completely rat-arsed, but that was still no excuse for what he'd done. He wasn't saying it, but I could add together the late-night visit to my room and his attempt to sit on my bed for what it was – a booze-inspired attempt at a booty call. And that was putting it nicely. I wracked my brains trying to remember if I'd done anything at all that might have given him the wrong impression that I might be the vaguest bit interested in him that way. And then I gave myself a stern telling off for allowing my mind to go in that direction. Even if I'd been playing the ultra-flirt the entire time I'd lived in his house, it still gave him no right to come into my bedroom uninvited and try something on. It was disgusting, predatory behaviour, and I was well within my rights to summon the police. I told him as much, summoning the confidence of my inner teacher to keep the wobble out of my voice. It had an instantly sobering effect on him.

'Please don't, Frey-Frey,' he pleaded. If he thought he was going to win his way back into my good books by abbreviating my name in a ridiculous manner, he was very much mistaken. Then he added something which made my heart start beating even faster. 'Not again.'

So this wasn't the first time he'd played a trick like this.

'Get. Out.' I over-enunciated the words, so that even his booze-addled brain could understand them, then I pulled the door wide open and gestured to him to be gone.

He staggered across the room and stepped into the hallway. I was about to heave a sigh of relief when he turned back towards me. He slipped the tip of his tongue out of the corner of his mouth as he eyeballed me, and then his gaze wandered downwards. Even though I was wearing the thickest, baggiest flannel pyjamas imaginable, I felt as exposed as if I was naked.

'I knew you'd be fiery with that hair of yours. One for the memory bank,' he said. Then he hauled himself upstairs.

I gripped the door frame to try to stop the trembling in my hands. I felt violated and utterly vulnerable. This was meant to be my home, the place where I could feel completely safe and relaxed. Instead, I was standing here shaking, a normally calm and poised woman reduced to a quivering mess. I tried to pull myself to my senses and retreated into my room, dragging the chest of drawers behind the door so that Steve couldn't get in if he decided he was in the mood for round two. I was shivering with shock. I wanted to wrap my duvets around me and hide myself in their comforting warm folds, but they were tainted by Steve's touch. I would rather burn them. I tore my pyjamas off – they too would be going in the recycling pile – and then once I'd got a comfy tracksuit on, I started haphazardly throwing my possessions into bags. I could not live here a single moment longer.

But where could I go? After tonight's horrifying experience, I'd never feel safe renting a room in a shared house again. And if I tried to push the boat out and rent a place by myself, it would be a struggle, and my dreams of home ownership would become even more unattainable. I knew Leila would happily offer me her sofa to sleep on, but that was only a short-term fix. I needed a long-term solution.

Suddenly Leila's jokey comment about Charlie and me buying a house together came back into my mind. We'd both laughed it off, but was it actually all that laughable an idea? Charlie and I were in the same boat, wanting to buy, but not being able to do it by ourselves. And who better to buy a house with than my best friend? Well, he had been my best friend when we were eleven, but from last night's brief encounter I didn't think the Charlie of today was all that different from the Charlie of old. As a child he had been a loyal and completely trustworthy friend. I couldn't imagine those characteristics would have faded with age. The still-surging adrenalin was making my brain run at a million miles an hour, and the idea developed rapidly. What if we were to find a place that needed a bit of fixing up, fresh paint, new flooring, that kind of thing, complete the work together, and then sell it on for enough of a profit to enable both of us to get deposits for our own separate places? We'd been turned down for mortgages as individuals, but Charlie himself had said that the adviser had told him he'd have a better chance as part of a pair. And with two incomes rather than one, there was double the opportunity to find somewhere affordable. It would be the best of both worlds. We'd both achieve our dream without being tied into a long-term house-sharing commitment.

I forced myself to take a moment before I got carried away with the idea. I knew I was in a state of high emotion, never the best frame of mind in which to be making a big decision. I needed to take a breath and think about this logically, really assessing the practicalities of the plan. I threw on an extra hoody and then sat down on the floor, my back against the chest of drawers. I put my glasses on, pulled a notepad out of my school bag and then used my marking pens to draw up a list, green ink for the pros, red for the cons. But I soon realised that things weren't quite as clear-cut as that. My first potential pro was getting on the property ladder at last, but did doing it tied to another person make it more of a con? On the other hand, fifty per cent of something was better than one hundred per cent of nothing.

Another massive pro was that I would no longer be at the mercy of predatory landlords like Steve. Though I also needed to be honest with myself and admit that I was considering living with a man whom I'd last known properly before puberty struck. Sure, he'd probably moved on from his childhood Indiana Jones obsession, but what was adult Charlie really like? We wouldn't only be living with each other; we'd be financially tied together. Commitments didn't get much bigger than that. My red pen faltered on the page. And then I heard a creak from the hallway outside my room, and I knew without doubt that anything was better than staying here.

Chapter Three

To give Leila her due, she didn't bat an eyelid when I buzzed the intercom on her flat at four-thirty in the morning, even though when she opened the door to me she had the appearance of someone who was about to experience a massive hangover kicking in. She took one look at the hold-all and pile of bin bags full of my worldly possessions, which I'd somehow managed to hook onto my bike and wheel over to her place, and opened her arms. I sobbed noisily on her shoulder until one of her neighbours rapped on the wall to remind us that most people were still in bed and trying to sleep at this uncivilised hour. Then she helped me carry the bags upstairs to her tiny but beautifully appointed flat, and set about making me a cup of very hot, very sweet tea while she gently prised the full story out of me. When I got to the part where Steve had tried to pull my duvets down, she picked up her phone and started dialling.

'I'm calling Nim, he used to be on the sex crimes squad. He'll sort the bastard.'

I lunged for the phone. 'Please don't. I really don't want the police involved.'

'Nim doesn't count, he's my ex. Sort of.'

'Yes, but he's still a copper, and if we involve him, he'll have to make it official. Besides, I don't want to be held responsible for you having to get in touch with your ex again.'

'He's only an occasional ex, as you well know. We're still friends with benefits and involving him in this situation would very much be a benefit.'

'I'm not sure Nim would agree with that,' I muttered.

'Don't distract me. Are you saying we shouldn't involve the authorities because you've got another form of punishment in mind?'

I pulled a face at Leila. 'Um, hello. Have you ever met me? Just because my pervy landlord decided to try it on, it doesn't mean I'm going to go Liam Neeson rogue and start taking matters into my own hands. No, quite the opposite. I merely want to put the entire episode behind me and forget the whole thing ever happened.'

Leila dropped another spoonful of sugar into my tea, then reached out and gripped my hand. 'Drink up, hon, and we'll discuss this further. I know this is only the shock talking, because we are both very aware that unless someone makes a stand against creeps like him, they will carry on with the same pattern of dangerous behaviour. I totally understand why you want to forget it ever happened, but what if it had been one of our sixth formers that had been in your position?'

She'd got me there and she knew it. With a groan, I gave her permission to drop Nim a message. Even if the only thing that happened was that Nim went round and had a quiet word, maybe that would make Steve think twice before he did anything similar with his next female tenant. Leila was right. He needed stopping. I finished the cup of disgusting tea, and felt an overwhelming wave of tiredness hit me, perhaps a delayed reaction to the drama of the night.

Noticing my yawns, Leila made up the sofa bed for me, then, sensing that I wasn't quite ready to be alone yet, she sat stroking my hair like a parent looking after a sick child and told me silly stories about the kids at school which she knew I'd heard a hundred times before and were therefore comforting in their familiarity. My last waking thought was that I must tell her about my decision to buy a house with Charlie, but before I could put the right words together to explain it to her, I drifted off to sleep.

I woke to the sound of Leila giggling. If I wasn't very much mistaken, Nim had responded to her message by paying a personal visit. I wrapped a blanket around me like a cape of protection and padded into the kitchen to join them. Nim was leaning against the countertop sketching a caricature of Leila on the back of an envelope while she sat on the worksurface next to him, casually resting her arm along his shoulders as she cheerfully critiqued his artwork. It was as if they'd never been apart. I hesitated on the threshold, feeling like an intruder.

'Hey, Freya, are you okay?' asked Nim, switching from flirting with Leila to professional police mode in an instant. 'I'm so sorry about what happened to you. What a scumbag. Do you feel up to talking about it?' He gestured for me to sit at the kitchen table, and sat down opposite me, watching my expression closely while Leila quickly rustled up some coffee for us all.

'I'm feeling a bit better now I've had some sleep. Thanks for coming round. I feel silly wasting your time with this. I kind of want to forget the whole thing ever happened, but as Leila says, if someone doesn't stop him, he'll carry on trying it on with other people.'

'You're most definitely not wasting my time. Now I'll totally be guided by what you want to do, but I think I've found a way of dealing with the situation without dragging it out too much, if that sounds good?' He waited for me to nod, then continued. 'It might interest you to know that I've done a little digging, and our Stevie boy doesn't have an HMO licence, so I will point that out to him when I pay a visit later today to warn him of the error of his ways. House in multiple occupation licence,' he clarified, catching the confused expression on Leila's face and mine. 'It means that he's not technically allowed to have as many tenants as he does. It's a poor substitute for arresting him, which I'm happy to try, if you want me to, but the burden of proof is a bastard when it comes to this kind of thing, and being completely honest with you, sadly I'm not sure it would get much further than an arrest.' He pulled a face. 'It winds me up no end, but that's the judicial system for you. Don't worry, I will be having a stern word, making Steve very aware that if he even thinks about trying something like this ever again, I will track him down and throw the book at him.'

He jabbed his finger on the table for emphasis as he gave me a sneak preview of the cold anger which Steve was soon going to be on the receiving end of. I felt grateful that he was on my side, even if I was slightly dubious about how good an idea it was for Leila to have him back in her life longer term.

'Thanks, Nim, I appreciate your support.'

'Happy to do my civic duty. Sex pests like him need to learn the error of their ways.' He put his mug down on the counter. 'Right, ladies, I'll leave you to it. Let me know if there's anything else you want, Freya. Maybe see you around some time soon, Leila?'

'Sure,' she said, in such an affectedly casual manner that I knew she was already calculating how soon she could get away with arranging it without seeming too keen.

'Ex? As if. You were blatantly checking out his bum,' I teased her as the door closed behind him. 'What happened to the "ex is hexed"?' But while I was desperate to keep the conversation light so that things felt more normal, I knew I had to say something. 'Although I'm glad he's fighting my corner, maybe take a breath or two before you rush into something with Nim and go through all that heartache again, eh? Remember what happened before. I hated seeing you so upset when he kept on cancelling dates and not being there for you.'

Leila shrugged. 'Not every ex is like your ex, Freya. What can I say? It's the nature of Nim's job, and he's been here this morning when I needed him. Yes, we had our issues, but he's a very fine specimen of the male species, who also happens to be a pretty decent human being most of the time. It's a rare combination and I think he's worth taking another chance on. Sometimes you have to go with your gut, and trust that it'll be worth it. Besides, it would be rude not to admire the wonders of creation.' Her eyes twinkled. 'Speaking of which, it was nice to meet that old friend of yours last night before Evil Stevil overshadowed the whole evening.'

I could tell she was trying to distract me, but I decided to let her and seized the opportunity to tell her about my plan.

'Ah yes, I meant to talk to you about Charlie,' I said. I took a deep breath, wondering how best to phrase what I was about to say. And then I decided to stop overthinking and just come out with it. 'Given everything that's happened, I've realised that your suggestion was an excellent one, and I'm going to visit him today to see if I can persuade him to agree with me.'

Leila looked confused. 'While I'm always happy to take credit for excellent suggestions, you'll have to remind me exactly which one you're referring to as I don't have a clue what you're talking about. My memory of last night is a little hazy. I think the tonic water was off.'

'Or maybe it was the gin you kept on insisting they add to it,' I teased her. 'You said Charlie and I should buy a house together. And I've analysed the pros and cons, and the former definitely outweigh the latter.' I quickly explained my idea to flip the property for a tidy profit, leaving both of us in a much-improved position.

Leila started laughing. 'And you think *I'm* being impulsive wanting to get back with Nim? You don't do things by halves, do you? It's been quite the twenty-four hours in the life of Freya Hutchinson. From coming second in the pub quiz to embarking on a new adventure in the world of housing. You go, girl. Why not? But I must warn you that I'm quite the connoisseur of property porn, and these fixer upper dreams always have more than their fair share of nightmarish scenarios. Never underestimate how challenging it could be.' She paused, and then put her arm around my shoulders, giving me a reassuring squeeze. 'But if anyone can do it, you can. For as long as we've been friends, you've always succeeded in whatever you've put your mind to. As for Charlie, your partner in crime, well, I can't really comment as I don't know him. But then again, neither do you, really, do you? It's an interesting situation. You'll probably end up killing each other. Either that or kissing each other. Both are messy in their own way.'

Her laughter grew even more uproarious.

'Thanks for the vote of confidence. And don't worry, this is very much a decision based on cold, hard logic. I've thought about it carefully and I've already considered every eventuality. Not that kissing Charlie is a realistic eventuality at all,' I added hastily. 'We're practically brother and sister. Or at least, we were. I'm going to write The Rules, a list of clear boundaries and guidelines for behaviour that we can agree to so we know exactly where we stand. We're both grown-ups. With a joint mortgage at stake, we neither of us could afford for things to get messy.'

'Hmm,' said Leila. 'If you think that will work, then who am I to disagree? But I will say this one thing. Real life isn't like being in the school environment where the rules are simple and the consequences for breaking them are obvious.'

I experienced a pang of misgiving which I firmly stamped down on. I had no other alternative. This plan had to work.

'And what does Charlie think about The Rules?' she asked. 'No wait, when would you even have had the time to ask him?'

'As you pointed out, it's been quite the twenty-four hours so I haven't had the opportunity to run the plan by him yet. He mentioned last night that he's working for an estate agent today, showing around clients. I thought I'd go and find him there. This is probably the kind of conversation which should be done in person.'

'Oh, I should say so,' said Leila. 'Well, I guess I'd better let you use the bathroom first. I'll be crossing my fingers for you, though you know you're more than welcome to stay here as long as you want.'

'And get in the way of you and Nim? No fear,' I said. 'The walls of your flat are definitely not thick enough.'

I wondered if I'd change my mind once a shower and breakfast had clarified my thought processes, but the more I considered the idea, the better it seemed. I was sick and tired of living in limbo, always being at the mercy of the precarious rental market and the dodgy characters who took advantage of it. It was time to move on and start positive action. Hopefully Charlie would agree. I sat for a couple of hours compiling The Rules, wracking my brains to make sure that I covered every eventuality that could occur in joint home ownership. As I always told my pupils when they were meant to be revising, if you fail to prepare, then prepare to fail.

Once I was satisfied that I'd created a clear set of guidelines with absolutely no room for error, I set about tracking down Charlie. A bit of rudimentary research on social media helped me to find the agency that he was doing shifts for, a rather glossy-looking place in leafy Harrogate. He probably got to show people around a lot of gorgeous but unattainable properties in that highly sought-after area. Charlie and I were born in the Yorkshire Dales, and Harrogate was the town we were first allowed to visit by ourselves in what felt like a massive childhood rite of passage. I'd always thought it would be a nice place to live – lots of lovely Victorian buildings, plenty of cafés serving seriously scrummy food, plus it had a vibrant social scene with amazing book festivals. I was starting to sound like an estate agent myself.

I wondered if Charlie would have the same taste in housing as me. I stamped down on the voice at the back of my head that told me that this was another issue I hadn't properly considered. What if Charlie had completely different ideas about where he wanted to be based? But I wouldn't find out until I asked him.

Armed with my list of The Rules for reassurance, I hopped on the train and made my way to Harrogate, rehearsing how best to explain the rationale behind my proposal the whole way there.

'How can I help you?' The estate agent's voice was studiously neutral and distinctly lacking in enthusiasm. I wondered if he'd done a quick assessment of my appearance and decided that I was clearly not likely to be a rich prospective client who was worth cultivating. The undercurrent of snootiness made me panic slightly, which was why I said what I did.

'I'm expecting to meet Charles Humphries. We have an appointment. He's due to show me around The Glades.' I named a house which I'd happened to see in the window as I'd come in. Of course, the reason it had stood out was that it was one of their 'Premium listings' displayed on gold paper with the price not even listed, a clue that it couldn't have been more out of my league. The man's attitude changed in an instant from complete indifference to vomit-inducing obsequiousness.

'Certainly, madam, would you like to come and take a seat in our lounge? I'm sure Charles will be with you in the blink of an eye. I can only apologise that he's not already here ready to meet with you. May I offer you a beverage while you wait?'

He practically bowed as he ushered me into a room full of plush upholstery, mood music playing quietly in the background. It even smelled expensive.

'An Americano would be lovely, thank you,' I said, deciding I might as well take advantage of his offer of hospitality, even if it was elicited under false pretences. The instant coffee from the communal jar in the staffroom created a drink more like dishwater, and contrary to what Mr Rhys thought, I did not spend all my spare cash buying fancy drinks from expensive shops.

'Certainly, right away, madam,' the estate agent said, hurrying off to the no doubt posh coffee machine to fix my drink.

I tried to look relaxed, aware that I might well be under the scrutiny of CCTV, but I felt very out of place, expecting to be asked to leave at any moment. I heard the shop doorbell tinkle, then the distinctive sound of Charlie's voice greeting his colleagues cheerily. He received a curt response. I hoped he wasn't being told off for not letting them know about a fictional appointment to show somebody around The Glades. The last thing I wanted was for my arrival to cause difficulties for him. I sat up straighter, gripping the piece of paper with The Rules written on as if it was a talisman. Now that the moment had arrived to present the proposal to Charlie, I felt incredibly nervous. What if he said no? For once in my life, I didn't have a back-up plan.

The estate agent reappeared, drink in one hand, ushering Charlie along with the other.

'Charles, this is…' He hesitated, suddenly realising that he'd failed to get my name.

'Miss Hutchinson,' I replied, figuring he was the kind of man who would appreciate a bit of formality. I stared at Charlie, hoping to telegraph the message that we weren't meant to know each other. Fortunately, Charlie caught on straightaway.

'Ah, Miss Hutchinson, lovely to see you,' he said, making an excellent show of sounding convincing.

'Not at all, Mr Humphries. I'm very much looking forward to our tour of The Glades. In fact, I'm eager to set off now. If you wouldn't mind?'

I'd happily sacrifice the nice coffee if it meant being able to put my plan to Charlie without any further delay.

Charlie glanced at his boss quickly, seeking his permission.

'Go, go,' he responded, nearly falling over himself in his eagerness for me to be given the guided tour. He was going to be disappointed when Charlie returned without an offer being presented.

'Let me get a brochure,' said Charlie, 'and then we'll be on our way.'

We left the shop and walked all the way down the road together keeping up the pretence of estate agent and client until we were safely around the corner and out of sight. And then Charlie loosened his tie and leaned against the wall, fixing me with a quizzical expression.

'We don't see each other in years, and then it's twice in two days. To what do I owe the honour?' he asked.

Now that the moment had come, I felt quite sick, suddenly very aware of the utterly ludicrous nature of my plan. I realised how presumptuous I was being, reappearing in his life after a gap of so many years and asking him to team up with me, essentially a stranger, for one of the biggest rites of passage there was. Sure, he'd joked about it in the pub, but that was all it had been. A joke.

'Maybe I do want to see The Glades,' I prevaricated.

Charlie pursed his lips. 'It's well worth a look, especially if gold-plated toilets are your thing. But unless you've won the lottery since we were chatting last night, I'm afraid it's rather out of your league. If you wanted to meet up again, you only had to ask, no need to go to all this effort at subterfuge.'

'There was a particular reason I wanted to see you again. Not that I need a particular reason, of course...unless I do?' I was digging myself deeper into a hole. I firmly told myself to get my act together and speak to him as I'd rehearsed in my head. 'I've been having a think since we met, and I'd like to suggest an idea to you. It's probably best that you hear me out in full, and then once you know exactly what I'm talking about, I'd love to know what you think about it.'

'You're talking in riddles, Freya,' said Charlie. 'If you're after an agreement that I won't interrupt you, that's fine, you say what you need to and I'll keep quiet.'

I steeled myself for the inevitable rejection and set about explaining my idea – well, Leila's drunken idea – and how I saw it working in practical terms. 'It's the perfect solution for both of us. We get on the property ladder together, and if we work hard, in eighteen months or so, we could be looking for our own places by ourselves. And so you know that I'm taking this very seriously, I've written a set of guidelines for both of us to follow as house co-owners. If you agree to this document,' I waved The Rules at him, 'then we'll both know exactly where we stand, what our obligations are towards each other, and we'll have the perfect house partnership.'

Charlie stared at me, apparently stupefied by my plan. I dropped my gaze, unable to bear seeing his expression when he rejected the idea out of hand. Perhaps, I wondered, I should have told him what had happened with Steve to help convince him why it was such a good idea, then I reminded myself why I had decided not to go down that route. It wouldn't be fair to the guy to use emotional blackmail to get him to agree. If he said no, fine, that was absolutely his right. I'd always have Leila's sofa bed, so I wouldn't be homeless. But it would be the death of my dreams and I didn't have a clue what I would do next.

'I think it's a great idea,' said Charlie suddenly. Only I was so startled by his positive response that I had to get him to repeat what he'd said.

'Really? I mean, you don't think it's totally unworkable

and stupid?' I said, then mentally berated myself for challenging him when he was obviously in agreement. The last thing I needed was for me to talk him out of it.

Charlie shrugged. 'What's the worst that can happen?' he said. 'I believe most things happen for a reason. We were obviously meant to bump into each other last night. We have a shared goal, and this can help us achieve it. It's a good solution for both of us.'

'And what about The Rules?' I pushed, still not believing my luck.

He grinned. 'Despite you being one half of the Terrible Twosome, you were always a secret stickler for rules. I prefer to live life on my own terms, if you don't mind. Let's just say that I accept the principle that we should be respectful of each other's space and we'll go from there.'

'But there's so much more to The Rules than that. I'd really prefer it if you read them for yourself,' I said, thrusting the piece of paper towards him.

'If it matters so much to you, why don't you read them to me?' he said. 'Can I suggest you do it while we're in the car? It's freezing out here, and I'm not going to be much use on the home renovation front if I lose my limbs to frostbite.'

'Sure,' I said, automatically following him as he started striding down the street again. 'Hold on, why are we getting in the car?'

'Because I think I know the perfect property for us, and I'd like to show it to you,' he called back over his shoulder.

Chapter Four

Charlie's car turned out to be a battered old Land Rover, apparently held together by rust, complete with bits of straw all over the seats.

'Apologies, the old girl could do with a wash,' he said, casually swiping the worst of the countryside detritus off the passenger seat and moving a guitar into the boot. 'I've been helping my dad out on the farm in return for my bed and board.'

I tried to surreptitiously wind the window down, figuring that the sub-zero temperatures of outside were a better option than the aroma of *eau de* farmyard. But the whistling of the wind combined with the rattling din of the engine meant that it was impossible to hear what Charlie was saying, so I settled for trying to breathe through the fabric of my scarf instead.

'So let me read The Rules to you,' I said. But Charlie had other ideas.

'Yes, yes, all in good time. First I'd like to tell you about where we're going. I think it would be the perfect property for us.'

'But we've not even discussed what we're looking for in a house,' I protested. 'That's one of the things I cover in The Rules. We both have to agree on where we live. If one of us has any doubts, it's a no from both of us.'

'Sounds reasonable,' said Charlie.

'Oh. Well, that's good,' I said, surprised at his immediate agreement. I hoped he consented to the rest of my guidelines with equal ease.

'I know you're going to love this place,' he said. 'It's very well situated, has two bedrooms, a lovely garden which will be a proper sun trap in the summer, and the whole place has a really good energy. You'll feel it at soon as you step foot over the boundary. It's a place guaranteed to put a smile on your face. And this isn't me speaking in estate agent mode, this is me telling you about it from my personal perspective.'

'You sound very confident,' I said, vowing to reserve my judgement about his assessment of the property. It was all well and good talking about a house making you smile, but it seemed sensible to deal in facts, rather than feelings. 'Perhaps eleven-year-old me would have loved it, but that's no guarantee that adult me will like it. I might be completely different from the girl you remember.'

Just like he could be completely different from the boy I knew then, although I tried to quash that thought.

'Hmm, the outer appearance may have developed somewhat, but I reckon you're still the same old Freya.'

There was an awkward pause.

'"The outer appearance may have developed somewhat"?' I repeated back to him.

He glanced away from the road briefly to send me an apologetic smile. 'Sorry, that was horribly phrased and I'm only going to make it worse if I try to backtrack, so perhaps we should pretend I didn't say it, and move on.'

'Probably a good idea,' I said, unable to stop myself from grinning back at him. Adult Charlie might still put his foot in his mouth like juvenile Charlie had, but at least he unashamedly owned it.

As he indicated and turned the car off the main road, I stared out of the window, trying to glean from the road signs where he was taking me.

'Have you worked it out yet?' he asked, a note of amusement in his voice.

'I see your old mind-reading trick is still working. I've narrowed it down to a few villages, but surely there's no way there's anywhere in this area that we could buy. I mean, I'm making a complete assumption about your income – yet another practicality we've not got into yet – but you know as well as I do that despite what most people think about the north having cheaper houses, that sweeping statement does not apply to this particular area. I'd be lucky to aspire to a shed in this postcode. Anything remotely affordable will have already been snapped up by the buy-to-let gang or people wanting holiday cottages.'

'Trust me,' he said. 'While you're right that the majority of places around here are priced for people at a very different stage in life to us, this house is the exception. I'm showing it to you because it is the perfect fixer upper. It's been on the market for absolutely ages, the decor is dated to say the least, and most people can't see past the work that needs doing. And I'll be straight with you, there is *a lot* of work that needs doing. But I know you've got a good imagination and you'll be able to see it for what it could be, like me. It's a little gem. And as it's been on the market for a fair while, I have a strong feeling that the current owner will be prepared to listen to a cheeky offer. He tried to put in for planning permission to knock it down and build flats, but it was resoundingly rejected, and now he's so pissed off with the villagers who objected to the plans, he's desperate to get shot of the place and not have to deal with them anymore.'

'Is it a good idea to be considering a place where the neighbours have already shown themselves to be difficult?' I questioned. 'And while I'm not averse to painting and basic remodelling, I draw the line at structural work. Unless there's something you've not told me, neither of us have a clue what we're doing when it comes to actual building work.'

'I don't think the fixing will be beyond our capabilities,' said Charlie in a casual manner. 'And as for the neighbours, they only objected to the flats. As would any right-minded person. Destroy a period property for identikit apartments? I don't think so. I've done my research, and they won't cause a problem for the right owner with the right, sympathetic restoration plan up their sleeve.'

'Hmm, you're so knowledgeable about this place that it sounds like you've already tried putting in a cheeky offer but the small matter of not being able to get a mortgage got in your way,' I said. It was a guess, but it was a good one.

'You've got me there. I'll admit that's exactly what happened. It was love at first sight. I knew it was out of my league by myself, but I had to try, and of course, it didn't work, hence my disappointment-fuelled trip to The Taps last night. But with two of us in the game, it could be a whole different story. I don't want that to make you feel obliged, though,' he added hastily. 'I promise if you don't like it, we'll look elsewhere. But I know you will like it,' he repeated, as if by saying it enough times he would make it true.

'I still think we should agree on the practicalities before we view anywhere,' I muttered. Things were moving a lot faster than I'd anticipated. It was less than half an hour since I'd presented him with the plan. I should probably be delighted that Charlie was so enthusiastic about my idea, but I would have felt better if he'd bombarded me with questions about the details rather than being so relaxed about everything.

But it was too late for that. We bumped down a narrow country lane, turned a corner and there at the side of the road was a faded 'For Sale' sign leaning lopsidedly towards a cottage built of honey-coloured stone. At least, I think that's what it was constructed with, but it was hard to tell as most of the stonework was covered with a tangle of wiry stems from a plant which seemed to be doing its best to smother the entire building. The windows were so thick with grime it was like they were deliberately protecting the privacy of the cottage's interior. I half expected to see Red Riding Hood's grandmother looking down on us from the upper floor. I peered at the roof. There appeared to be a few loose tiles here and there, but to my untrained eye, the disrepair on the roof line seemed to be superficial, although the same couldn't be said for the chimney stack, which was balancing precariously at one end of the building. I made a mental note to give that part of the house a wide berth when we looked round. It looked like one puff of wind would send it crashing to the ground.

'What do you think?' asked Charlie eagerly as we got out of the car. 'If you ignore the plants that have gone wild. And perhaps overlook the front door and the steps leading up to it.'

I hadn't noticed before, but now he mentioned it, the front door looked ancient enough to have been around in the Viking era, the woodwork managing to appear like it was swollen into position while simultaneously having massive gaps between the frame and the hinges. And it was perhaps rather generous to refer to the steps as steps, because the treads mostly consisted of hazardous-looking holes.

'When I said we should look for a fixer upper, I wasn't envisaging a project on quite this scale,' I said, my head spinning at the thought of how much work it would take to transform the place from a wreck into something vaguely habitable.

'I'll admit from this angle it doesn't look its best. But it's been standing for centuries, so I don't think it's in any danger of actually falling down, and I promise you, it's oozing potential,' said Charlie. 'If we could do it up properly, we'd be sitting on a gold mine. You could take your pick of dream homes after that.'

I crossed to the other side of the lane so I could stand back and get a better perspective on the house as a whole. Although Charlie had referred to neighbours, it stood alone with the nearest buildings at least half a mile up the road, closer to the centre of the village. The lane seemed to be quiet and narrowed into a footpath just beyond the cottage. No danger of people racing past and using it as a rat run then. But how did I feel about the idea of living in such a rural location? The house couldn't be further from the clean, modern place in town that I'd been picturing for my own. It had been fun living in the countryside when I was a child, but I was an adult now. I had to think sensibly about stuff like the job I needed to get to, preferably without an epic commute.

Charlie came over to join me. 'What do you think about the windows? Aren't they beautiful? Call me fanciful, but they're like eyes on a friendly face. It's a place full of good vibes, it only takes the right people to see it.'

I spluttered with laughter. 'Fanciful is one way of putting it. So what you're saying is that the cottage is like

Sleeping Beauty, waiting for a prince to come along, wake it up, and give it a new lease of life?'

'If you want to put it like that, yes. We could be the perfect people for that job, I know it. I'll admit it's a lot to take in. But hold off on your final verdict until you've looked around inside.'

Reluctantly, I gestured for him to show me the way. Charlie punched the air triumphantly. 'I knew you'd feel the same as me.'

'I haven't said a word, and good vibes or not, my head is ringing with alarm bells.'

'Trust me, once you've seen exactly how much potential this place has, you'll be sold, and then we can talk practicalities, if you really insist.'

'Charlie, if we're going to buy together, you're going to have to accept that I will put a great emphasis on the practicalities. Boring it may be, but you'll be grateful for it in the long term.' I knew I sounded like I was back in class, but I felt it was important to say it. 'And speaking of practicalities, how are we going to look around inside? You had no idea I was going to visit you and suggest this, so there's no way you've managed to get an appointment for us to be shown round.'

'There's no need for us to have an appointment. Follow me,' he said mysteriously.

He tried to push open the big gate at the side of the house, but the hinges seemed to be rusted into position.

'You still any good at climbing over obstacles, Freya?'

Charlie led the way. I instantly regretted my decision to

dress smartly for my meeting with him. But I wasn't going to let a pair of high heels and a trouser suit stop me demonstrating that I was still the capable girl he used to know.

The wood of the gate felt spongy underneath my grip, and I briefly wondered how good an idea it was for both of us to be attempting to climb over it at the same time. How would I explain to Mr Rhys if I injured myself trying to break into an abandoned building? It was the kind of offence that would get parents writing in asking for me to be fired. Fortunately, the gate was tougher than it looked and although it let out a few ominous creaks when we were straddling it, it held fast.

'This is the driveway,' said Charlie, as we waded through weeds that were nearly waist high. I stumbled slightly as my foot got caught in a loop of brambles, and he reached out to steady me. 'Are you okay?'

I leaned down and rolled my trouser leg up to check. 'Skin unbroken, but it gave me a bit of a shock. Maybe this is the house's way of saying we shouldn't go any further.'

'The house is shy about revealing its secrets,' he said with a smile. 'A bit of elbow grease and we'll soon get rid of these things. Anyway, weeds are just flowers that happen to be growing in a place where they shouldn't be. There's still gravel beneath the undergrowth so we wouldn't have to go to the trouble of laying a new driveway, and there's more than enough room for one car to park, perhaps even two if one of them is only small.'

'As I don't have a car, it's not really a problem. But that

is an important factor for us to consider. I think we'd be too far out from Leeds here for me to be cycling into work, especially in the winter. The house seems rather isolated, if I'm being completely honest.'

'I'm glad you mentioned transport links,' said Charlie, his face lighting up as he seized the opportunity to expand on the cottage's virtues. 'This is where I would do the hard sell if I were showing you around the house in an official capacity. Contrary to its sleepy appearance, the village has a regular bus service to both Leeds and Harrogate, and the stop is only a couple of hundred yards away from here. The buses run early enough for you to get to school, and finish late enough to see a play at the theatre and not have to worry about being stranded in town. I did the research because while I mostly run my business from home, I have to be able to get out and about to meet clients, and sometimes it's easier to do public transport so I don't have to worry about parking. The bus even has USB charging points for your phone, and fold-down desks if you wanted to do some marking during your commute.'

I nodded. 'You sound like you've got shares in the bus company. Fair enough, the bus is a big positive, USB charging points or no. There's no point in living in a beautiful countryside location if we're stranded in it. But what happens if there's a strike, or the weather is bad and the buses get stopped? I have to be able to get into school, come what may.'

'Ah, so you admit it's a beautiful countryside location,' said Charlie. 'Better and better. Wait until you see the view from upstairs. And if there's a strike, or it's snowing, I'll drive you into work myself, I promise. Or you can borrow my car. Now, would you like to look around the rest of the garden or shall we explore inside?'

He seemed to have answers for everything, and although I wasn't completely convinced how realistic they were, against my better judgement, I found myself starting to get swept up in his enthusiasm. I glanced around at the wilderness which didn't really deserve the name of 'garden', although I'll admit it was a decent-sized plot of land.

'I'm not sure I'm suitably clothed for trekking through the jungle and unfortunately I left my machete at home. I've seen enough to get an overall impression and the massive task which would face us.'

'But all very doable,' said Charlie, the eternal optimist. 'I've got loads of relatives and friends I could bribe into helping us. You'll forgive me if I once again put my estate agent hat on and point out the tree over there after which the cottage is named.'

The tree looked ancient with its huge trunk and sprawling bare branches taking up a sizeable corner of the garden. I tried to picture what it would look like in summer. It would probably cast a huge shadow over the garden, and in autumn it would shed leaves all over the place. But despite my determination to be sensible, I started to picture a swing hanging off one of the broad, horizontal branches, a swing big enough for an adult to relax on with a good book, with only birdsong interrupting the peace and quiet.

'Forgive me but I'm a history teacher, not a biologist. What kind of tree is it?'

'An oak tree.'

'So this is…'

'Oak Tree Cottage. I'm not convinced it was always called that because according to local folklore the tree is only around two hundred years old, whereas the cottage was built in the early Georgian era. Though you being a historian, I'm sure you'd already worked that one out for yourself.'

'The tree is a relative baby then,' I said, not liking to admit that I hadn't had the first clue of the house's age. It was hard to get a proper sense of its structure and design given how much detritus there was on the walls, I told myself.

'Shall we have a look inside?'

Charlie led the way to the back door, and then scrabbled around underneath a cracked flowerpot which looked like it had been in situ for as long as the tree had.

'Aha, here we go,' he said, brandishing a heavy key which looked like something out of a period drama.

'Wow, it really is like being back in the village we grew up in, keeping a spare key hidden underneath a flowerpot. But even though it's there, I'm not sure we should be using it to let ourselves in. It feels like we're breaking and entering.' I glanced around, half expecting a member of the local neighbourhood watch to leap out from behind a bush and accuse us of just that.

'I won't tell if you don't,' said Charlie with a grin that immediately transported me back to when he used to persuade me to sneak into the neighbour's barn with him to play with the sheepdog who he thought must be lonely having to live out there by himself. 'Besides,' he continued, 'when I booked an official appointment to look around here myself the other week, the vendor told me to do exactly what we're doing right now. I think he's so long given up on selling it that he can't even be bothered to show people round. It's a family property that he inherited from a relative that he'd never met, so he has zero sentimental connection with the place.'

'Either that, or he's not wanting to risk his life by stepping foot in the house,' I said cynically.

'Have a bit of faith, Freya. Would I do anything that would get us into trouble?'

'I don't know, would you?' I asked, in all seriousness. Charlie laughed.

Now that I knew the situation with the seller, I felt slightly less guilty about what we were about to do, although I'll admit that I still expected an alarm to sound when Charlie put the key in the lock and finally turned it, after some effort.

'A dab of oil and it'll work sweet as anything,' he said.

'The first thing any sensible buyer should do on moving into a house is change the locks,' I said, thinking about scenarios such as my recent unfortunate encounter with Steve.

Charlie looked rather surprised by the passion in my

voice. I could tell he wanted to ask more, but I distracted him by taking the initiative and leading the way inside.

The interior was so dim it was difficult to see anything at all, though whether it was because of the shadows cast by the oak tree, or the thick layer of dirt on the windows, it was difficult to tell. Gradually my eyes became accustomed to the gloom, and I started to be able to make out the shape of cabinets along the wall.

'I'm guessing this is the kitchen,' I said.

'Yes, let me find the torch on my phone and we can take a proper look,' said Charlie. 'But before I do that, I must warn you that the decor is, well, interesting.'

'That sounds ominous.'

It was an understatement. The beam of the torch lit up mucky walls and cabinets which were so thickly covered in lacquer that they looked bright orange, while the worktops appeared to be made of roughly cut sheets of plywood tacked into place with industrial sized staples. The look was finished off by a thick sticky carpet which might have been lime green in a former life before several thousand insects and goodness knows what else apparently curled up and died on it.

'Prison chic meets 70s horror show,' I said, blanching at the sheer state of the place.

'Obviously everything in here needs to be ripped out and preferably burned. But if you ignore the dodgy fittings and the terrible carpet, the room has good bones. It's a decent size, and those windows are something else. Look at how deep the sills are. Perfect for window seats.

Imagine how the room will look when it's flooded with light...'

'A range against that wall, blue and white tiles creating a splash-back above a butler sink by the window, a scrubbed pine table with a bench and a couple of chairs,' I continued dreamily, the decor appearing in my imagination as I slowly turned on the spot. I knew I shouldn't be getting carried away like this, let alone saying what I was thinking out loud, but Charlie was right, the room had serious potential despite its current state.

'Exactly. But perhaps we could go bottle green and cream for the tiles,' said Charlie. 'Bringing the sense of the garden inside. Just a suggestion. Anyway, I'm glad you can see beyond the hideousness.' He walked over to the internal wall and started knocking it. 'This is a load-bearing wall, but I don't think it's an insurmountable problem, because it would be great to be able to knock through into the dining room at some stage.' As he said the words, he opened a door with a flourish and led me through what seemed to be a cupboard and then into the next room.

The stench nearly sent me staggering backwards.

'What is that?' I asked, gagging.

'I don't know. I think it's coming from the chimney. Something to add to the list of things to be investigated,' replied Charlie, sounding remarkably calm given the smell, which was thick enough to taste.

'I'm not sure there's enough paper in the world for the list we'd have to make of things in this cottage which need investigating or fixing.' I turned to face him, arms folded.

'Look, while we can talk as much as we like about its potential and how we could redecorate it, there's no point in getting carried away until we know for certain that it's not going to fall down around our heads. We neither of us are building experts. I don't have the first clue about finding out the structural integrity of this place, but I think I know someone who could help.'

Chapter Five

Granddad Arthur answered my FaceTime call on the first ring. Despite being closer to ninety than eighty, he was determined not to get left behind when it came to technology and had even set up a TikTok account for his dog, Ted, which is more than I had ever achieved on that platform. I tried to avoid interacting on most social media, leaving that Wild West domain to my pupils.

'Freya, my dear, how is this lovely Saturday treating you?' Granddad always referred to weekend days as lovely, even if the January weather was far from it, saying he'd worked too many Saturdays not to appreciate them now he was retired.

I angled the phone so that he could see my companion.

'Now is that who I think it is? There's a lad I've not seen in a while. Charlie, my boy, how is life treating you?'

'I'm very good, Arthur. Great to see you again.'

Granddad's face pixelated suddenly as I tried to move the phone to a more comfortable position.

'Patchy signal then,' I said with a pointed glance at Charlie, once again reminding him not to get carried away.

'Nothing a Wi-Fi booster won't combat,' he responded. 'As my business depends on being connected, it's not something I'd mess around with.'

'What are you two up to? Are you on a date?' Granddad interrupted our discussion.

'No, of course not,' we chorused very quickly. We caught each other's gaze and pulled equally surprised faces.

'Forgive an old fogey with a fondness for romances. The local library does a wonderful line in large-print Mills and Boons, and they've got me seeing sexual tension everywhere I look,' said Granddad with a twinkle in his eyes.

I didn't know whether to be amused or appalled at the idea of my sweet grandfather devouring raunchy novels.

'Anyway, you didn't call me to discuss my book club choices. Unless you've got a strange background filter on, you're calling me from a building site.'

'It might as well be,' I said, quickly explaining the joint house-buying idea. Granddad nodded his head in approval which made me feel a whole lot better.

'That sounds like an excellent plan,' he said. 'And let me guess, you're touring a prospective property and you'd like my expert opinion? Remember that my eyesight isn't what it was, and there's only so much I can tell through a phone screen. I would still advise you to get a proper survey done, the best one you can afford.'

'Don't worry, that's the very top of my list.' I once again waved The Rules at Charlie, reminding him that he was yet to read and agree to them.

'You have a look around the rest of the house with Arthur, and I'll go and investigate the outbuilding. I think it would make a perfect office for me,' said Charlie.

I was grateful that he was offering me the opportunity to explore by myself. It would be too easy to get caught up in his infectious excitement and allow myself to get carried away.

'Now then, love, let's start with the downstairs and we'll work our way round.'

Following Granddad's instructions, I rapped on walls, zoomed in on window frames and even nervously climbed up on an abandoned chair so he could take a closer look at cracks in the ceiling.

'I know it's concerning to see cracks, but they look fairly superficial to me. And every house this age will have some kind of woodworm in the beams. The surveyor will give you a second opinion, of course, but it's looking promising to me so far. It could be a very good investment. Do you want to show me what the upstairs looks like?'

The stairs creaked and groaned with every step I took, but fortunately they showed no sign of giving under my weight.

'Perhaps don't jump up and down on them,' said Granddad. 'I don't want to be responsible for my only granddaughter taking a tumble. What's inspired this sudden desire to buy with Charlie, anyway? I thought you were settled in that house share in Headingley?'

I found myself getting a little teary once again as I told him about Evil Stevil. Granddad shook his head in disgust.

'I was reading something on one of the online news sites the other day about unscrupulous landlords trying to exchange sex for rent. It's a trick as old as time. He's lucky that I'm not as spry as I used to be, otherwise I'd be round at the house showing him what I think of his behaviour. I'm happy to expose him on social media, if you like, though? Ted could get him cancelled in no time. He's got nearly 500 followers now, did you know?'

'Ted wields quite the power. But I'd rather let sleeping dogs lie. Besides, Leila's policeman friend Nim is onto him.'

'Good,' said Granddad. 'That's the least he deserves.'

I felt a strong sense of misgiving when I got upstairs and saw how the rooms were laid out. The two bedrooms were both a decent size with big windows which were currently rattling in the wind and letting in a fair amount of freezing air, but the views from them might almost compensate for that. However, the bathroom was another thing altogether. I could see past the dated avocado suite and the accumulated gunge of several decades, but I really didn't like the way the room was set out so the only way to access it was through the bedrooms.

'Now that's interesting,' said Granddad. 'A Jack and Jill bathroom. You'll have to make sure you have a system for letting each other know when you're using the facilities.'

'I suppose it's nothing a couple of locks wouldn't deal with, but it's not exactly very practical, is it?'

'Why don't you try tapping that wall where the hallway must be?' suggested Granddad.

I did as instructed and even I with my limited awareness of such things could recognise that it sounded hollow.

'As I suspected,' he said triumphantly. 'That's a simple wooden partition. A late addition, I think. That's easily remedied. I imagine it was originally another bedroom, and when they remodelled and put the bathroom in, they thought it would be a good idea to set it out like this. I reckon you'll be able to put a door back into the hallway, no problem, block up the other ones, and you'll have yourself a lovely big bathroom, the perfect place for you to unwind with a hot bath after a difficult day at school.'

'Now that sounds lovely. Tell me honestly, am I deluded to be even considering this property? It's the complete opposite of everything I imagined, but...'

Granddad smiled. 'At the end of the day, it's your money, love, but you might as well use it to pay off your own mortgage, rather than someone else's. And I can tell by the look on your face that you're falling for the place, despite the challenges it will undoubtedly present you both with. Trust your instinct and listen to your heart, not your head, for once. What's the worst that could happen? Now, I'm afraid I've got to go as the young sir is reminding me that it's long past his dinnertime. Speak to you soon.'

I waved goodbye, promising to pop round to visit him

and Ted in person after school next week, and then I gingerly made my way back down the stairs.

'Well?' asked Charlie, a hopeful expression on his face.

I answered by handing The Rules over to him.

'Read these first and then I'll give you my answer.'

Charlie rolled his eyes, but he took the paper without further complaint.

'Read them properly,' I admonished him, noticing the way his eyes were skimming over the page. 'Remember that I'm a dab hand at recognising when Year Nines are lying to me about reading the work.'

'Yes, Miss,' said Charlie, flashing that easy grin of his.

His grin got wider as he read on.

'Wow, you really have thought of every eventuality,' he said. 'And sub rules? I would never have considered such things. I see the sense in the financial guidelines, but some of these are starting to get into the realms of the ridiculous. Rule 16a, "toilet seat must be left down" – I'm a civilised human being, so that's not a problem. Besides, they say in Feng Shui that you should also close the toilet lid, otherwise you'll flush all your wealth away.'

'As neither of us have any wealth, I can't see that being a problem,' I said, slightly concerned by the reference to Feng Shui. I hadn't considered the possibility in The Rules of having to arrange furniture according to an ancient eastern principle.

Charlie's eyes sparkled in response, and I wondered if he was teasing me. He continued with the list.

'Rule 16b: "if there is only one bathroom and either

party intends to spend longer than half an hour in there, they must seek the permission of the other". I'm not sure I've ever spent longer than ten minutes in the bath. In fact, I'm more of a shower guy myself, but I'm happy to go along with it. Oh, and now we're really getting to the interesting part. "Relationship between house-sharing parties and others…" Let me read on.'

I felt my face grow flushed as he read the clinical way I'd set out how I saw our house-sharing arrangement working.

'Rule 18a: "prior warning must be given if an overnight guest is expected". That's almost as bad as being at my parents' place, although I trust you won't be quizzing any overnight guests about whether their intentions towards me are honourable? And rule 18c, this is very interesting. "No getting involved." Can you explain that to me? It's not quite as clearly expressed as the other guidelines.'

I examined his features carefully. Surely he knew exactly what I meant without me having to spell it out for him? Despite his seemingly innocent expression, I strongly suspected he was yet again trying to wind me up, but I had no choice but to take him at face value. My cheeks started to turn warm. Why was I getting embarrassed about discussing this? We were two adults, not children any more, and it was much better that everything was clear from the very beginning so there was no room for crossed wires.

'No getting involved. We remain friends, and friends only. With a joint mortgage at stake, we can't afford the complication of not keeping things platonic. Not that there's any chance of that kind of thing happening, of course.'

'Of course,' said Charlie, his voice completely neutral. 'Don't worry, I won't take the implied insult personally.'

'Charlie, you know I didn't mean it like that. What I meant was that you're like the brother I never had. I'm sure most women think you're really hot.'

We burst out laughing at the same time.

'Oh heck, I'm making it much worse, aren't I?' I said between embarrassed splutters.

Charlie put his arm around my shoulders and gave me a squeeze. 'You're quite something, Hutch. May I add an extra rule to the end? Let's call it Rule 50 subsection e. We mustn't take ourselves too seriously. As long as we can have a laugh with each other, everything else will work out for the best.'

'That makes sense to me.'

'Do we have a deal then?' Charlie held out his hand.

After a moment's hesitation, I put mine in his and we shook. 'We have a deal.'

What had I let myself in for?

Chapter Six

I returned to Leeds to spend the rest of the weekend alternating between marking schoolwork and nervously pacing up and down the living room of Leila's flat while I questioned my life choices. Charlie meanwhile went back to the estate agents, where hopefully they wouldn't be too disappointed that he'd failed to sell The Glades to me. He promised that he was going to spend all his time, between the other appointments he had booked, reaching out to new mortgage brokers with a view to getting us a meeting as soon as possible. I was glad that he was enthusiastic, and realistically I knew he'd probably have better contacts than me given his Saturday job, but it felt weird to be taking a back seat during this crucial stage. I'd be the first to acknowledge that I like to be in control, but I told myself it was a good exercise. We were buying a house together. It was only right that we divide the tasks up between us.

Fortunately, Charlie was true to his word. Late on Sunday evening he texted me to say that we had a meeting with a mortgage broker the very next day.

'I went for 4:30, hope that's okay?' he asked in the message. 'I figured you would have finished school by then, unless you have an after-school supervision to do, and it gives me a couple of hours before my evening ballet class.'

'You do ballet?' I messaged back, even though that wasn't exactly the most important detail of the text. It felt like an insight into adult Charlie's character, and I couldn't help feeling envious that he seemed to have a much more interesting life outside work than I did.

He replied with a gif of an elephant in a tutu. 'Yes. Boys do ballet too, you know.'

'That's not what I meant,' I tapped out, stung that he would even think I'd be judging him for being a man who enjoyed ballet. But, I reminded myself, we'd not spent enough time together as adults to really know each other's values. I firmly dismissed the slight churning sensation this thought produced in my stomach. Charlie had been a good kid, and if we had any differences of opinion on important issues, The Rules were there to protect us. 'I was wondering how you can afford to do evening classes when you're supposedly saving every penny for the mortgage?' I hit Send then instantly regretted it. I sounded like I was nagging him. What he chose to spend his money on was his own business. Just because I had ended up living a near-hermit life while pursuing my goal, it didn't mean that everyone else had to do the same.

'I clean the studio after class in return for the free session. Happy?' was his response, which made me feel even worse. Charlie didn't have to justify himself to me, and I didn't want him to think I was going to be a bossy and controlling house partner and make him change his mind, however keen he was to buy Oak Tree Cottage. But I couldn't really apologise further without making a bigger deal of the situation than it warranted, so I moved the conversation on by suggesting we have a phone call to get our stories straight.

'We want the mortgage broker to back us, and he or she is only going to do that if they believe we have a rock-solid relationship. Banks won't want to take a risk on us falling out three months down the line. I mean, of course we'll explain that we're friends, but perhaps we should gloss over the fact that we've been out of touch with each other for a little while?'

My phone rang thirty seconds later.

'Hello, Charlie,' I answered, without even checking the screen.

'Who's Charlie?' asked my mum, in that overly hopeful tone she normally put on when asking about my love life and whether I'd found myself a nice partner to settle down with yet. She was desperate for me to find someone new, mostly, I think, because she still felt guilty that she'd been the one to introduce me to my last boyfriend, Mark, who'd unfortunately turned out to be a manipulative and controlling bully behind the façade of nice guy that he presented to the rest of the world.

'It's a long story, Mum,' I replied with a sigh. I held a quick internal debate about whether I should tell her of the big plan, but reluctantly decided against it. My mum was the most logical, reasonable person in the world, and I wasn't sure I was quite ready to defend my decision against the thorough questioning which I knew would ensue. There were so many things that could go wrong before Charlie and I even got to the moving-in stage, and I wasn't sure she'd get the whole house partners thing. Time enough to fill her in once there was some actual progress. I decided to tell her an abbreviated version of the truth. 'Remember Charlie Humphries from primary school? We bumped into each other at the pub the other night and promised we'd catch up properly. I was knee deep in marking the Year Eleven mock exams so I didn't pay proper attention to who was on the phone.'

'If you say so, darling,' she responded, as always far too perceptive for her own good. 'And it's the weekend, surely the Year Elevens can wait a few days until they get their mocks back? If I were them, I'd rather not know the outcome straightaway. Let them enjoy a few days of blissful ignorance while you make the most of your weekend.'

'I'm not sure Mr Rhys would agree with your argument. He's set us the tightest deadline yet. A new Head of English started last term, and between you and me, I think they've got a bit of rivalry going on. It doesn't bode well for my workload for the rest of the year. I've got to keep up with it all otherwise there's no chance of me progressing in the department.'

'Make sure you take some time for yourself,' said Mum in a tone which suggested she was adding that aim to her list of tasks I should achieve. 'Anyway, aside from saying hello to my lovely daughter, the other reason I was ringing was to ask if you'd be able to join the rota I'm setting up to help your grandfather walk Ted.'

'Of course I'm happy to help. But why are you setting up a rota? He was okay when I talked to him yesterday.' I felt a jolt of anxiety. Granddad Arthur had always seemed indestructible to me, a man who epitomised the phrase that age is only a number. Ted was his pride and joy. There was no way he'd hand over the task of walking him to other people unless something was seriously wrong.

'I don't know if you follow him on his socials, but he's not always as "blessed" as he makes out,' she said. 'His neighbour rang the other day to let me know that she'd had to help him back into the house after he stumbled when he was picking the milk up from the step. He tried to make out he was okay, but she said he was clearly in pain.'

'Poor Granddad, that's a horrible thing to happen.' I could picture the situation all too clearly, knowing that he would have found the embarrassment more troubling than the physical discomfort. I wasn't surprised that he hadn't mentioned it on the phone, but I was disappointed that I'd not somehow been able to tell from the tone of his voice that something was up. I kicked myself for being too wrapped up in my own issues to pay proper attention to what was going on with him. 'Put me down for a regular Saturday walk, and I'll check with Leila to see if she can swap duties with me so I can do a midweek one as well.' However busy I was at school, I would find the time somehow to help out. Family came first, after all.

'Thank you, love, I knew I could rely on you. But when you show up, could you use some sort of excuse to explain why you want to take Ted out? I'm not sure your granddad is going to take too kindly to what he'll probably decide is interference, even though we've got his best interests at heart.'

'You know he'll catch on straightaway?' I said. 'He's not daft. And he'll probably be even more annoyed than if we come out and are upfront with him from the start.'

'Your father and I have discussed it, and we think this is the best way forward,' replied Mum in a tone of voice which told me that there was no arguing with her.

'If he asks me outright, I'm not going to lie to him,' I warned.

'You'll just have to make sure you're convincing so that he doesn't ask outright. I'm sure you'll come up with something.'

We chatted some more about the practicalities, and then ended the call. Had I asked too much of Granddad by seeking his advice on the house? I didn't want to put him under any pressure when he obviously had stuff of his own going on. Suddenly I didn't feel like speaking to Charlie tonight about our mortgage broker meeting. I'd worry about it tomorrow. I put my phone on silent and hid it away in my handbag so I couldn't see the screen, then I distracted myself from my concerns about Granddad and the house by continuing to plough my way through the marking.

Some time later, I heard Leila's key in the front door. She'd not come back home last night, texting me to say she wanted me to enjoy having some space to myself, although I think the fact that Nim was obviously back on the scene was her real motivation. I stretched my arms out and tried to ease the crick in my neck that had developed from spending too long hunched over my work.

'Tell me you're not still marking?' she asked as she staggered through the door, a heavy bag of shopping in each hand. I jumped up to help her.

'That's the lot of a history teacher,' I said. 'Loads of essays to read. Keeps me out of trouble, and, ultimately, will pay the mortgage.'

'You should have chosen PE, like me. The essays are much more infrequent.'

'Although you do have to stand outside in the horizontal rain attempting to stop the kids from injuring each other with hockey sticks and other dangerous implements.'

'Fair point. Now, put that marking away, and try to enjoy what's left of the weekend,' she said, uncannily echoing the words of my mum. 'I've treated us to a meal deal from the bargain shelf of the posh supermarket round the corner to celebrate that we are now housemates.'

'Temporary housemates,' I said quickly. 'I don't want to take advantage of your hospitality. Besides, things are looking up on the property front.'

'Temporary, permanent, whatever, it doesn't matter.' She shrugged casually. 'You know you're welcome for as long as you need. And while the food's cooking, you can choose whether you want to tell me about your meeting with Charlie first, or whether you'd like to hear how Nim's visit to Evil Stevil went.'

We made a good team stabbing holes in the plastic lids of the ready meals and shoving them into the oven. It reminded me of when we first met at university, although our fare then had been even more budget. As the smell of smoky bean chilli started to fill the flat, we sat down on the sofa with a glass of wine apiece.

'Tell me about Nim's visit,' I said, deciding it was best to get the bad bit over and done with. Hopefully it would be the last I had to hear of my former landlord.

Leila nodded. 'I hid round the corner and listened, in case Nim needed backup, you know.'

I suppressed a grin. I hardly imagined gym-obsessed Nim would have any problems with the seriously unfit Steve, but I knew Leila would have been an excellent second, should he have required it. She might be significantly smaller than Nim, but her years of experience refereeing all manner of ball sports meant that she was not a person to be messed with. If you could survive the Year Seven netball tournament, you could take on the world.

'You'll be pleased to know that Steve was quivering from the moment Nim showed him his identification. He tried denying what had happened, of course, but Nim soon put paid to that, and he made sure he spoke loud enough that all the neighbours will have heard the exchange. And to be on the safe side, he had a chat with your former housemates to check that they were okay. They were appalled by what happened and send you their love. Apparently the guys rounded on Steve pretty quickly, practically throwing him out of his own property, which, frankly, is the least he deserves. The conclusion was that Steve has decided to move into one of his other places for a while – a studio flat with no room for anyone he could try anything on with. And Nim let it be known that the police force will be keeping a close eye on him. Your housemates have time to find other places to live, and hopefully Steve is so freaked out by being confronted by Nim that he'll keep himself to himself in the future.'

I took a gulp of wine, disappointed in myself that hearing Steve's name was still proving to be anxiety-inducing. I was relieved that my housemates were okay. Although we'd barely seen each other when I lived there, due to our differing work hours, I still felt bad about abandoning them. I only hoped Steve decided to behave himself from now on.

'Please do say a big thank-you to Nim for me. It was very kind of him to get involved.'

Leila grinned widely. 'Oh, he's proven himself very determined to deserve that second chance I'm giving him, and he's in no doubt how pleased I am with him. Now, forget about all things horrible, and tell me about what's happening with Charlie. I take it from your happy but slightly nervous expression that he went for your joint ownership idea?'

I nodded. 'Not only did he agree to team up with me, we're actually going to try to put an offer in on a place called Oak Tree Cottage. I know things are moving pretty fast, but it feels like an opportunity I can't afford to miss out on.' I thrust my phone towards her. 'Here, have a look at the photos I took. It's a mess, I know, but it has a certain something.'

To give Leila credit, after her first shocked intake of breath at the state of the kitchen, she managed to make mostly encouraging noises.

'I guess when you know, you know. Best of luck to you both,' she said in a studiously neutral tone of voice when I got to the final picture and explained Charlie and I were meeting a mortgage broker tomorrow. 'It's a lot to take on together. But I'm sure you'll make it work.'

'We'll have to,' I said.

A busy Monday supervising the last mock exams and introducing the Year Eights to the horrors of Victorian medicine managed to distract me sufficiently to keep the nerves at bay during teaching hours. But when the bell rang to mark the end of school, I felt as sick as if I was one of the pupils lining up outside the exam hall. I'd not heard from Charlie since he'd confirmed the meeting yesterday evening, and I couldn't help fearing that he might have had a change of heart, especially as he'd not responded to my suggestion that we should agree on exactly how much we were or weren't going to say to the broker. Now that the prospect of getting my own place was so tantalisingly close, I couldn't bear for things to go wrong. I'd diligently submitted all my paperwork, bank statements, bills, in fact everything the mortgage broker could possibly need if they wanted to steal my identity and embezzle me. I knew they were legit because I'd done my due diligence when Charlie sent the details of the firm through, but as was my usual habit, I was thinking of everything that could go horribly wrong so as to be psychologically prepared in case it did.

Charlie drove the Land Rover up to the school gates to collect me, hooting the horn to attract my, and everyone else's, attention.

As I hurried to the vehicle, one of the bolder Year Sevens called out, 'Is that your boyfriend, Miss?' while the rest of his little friends collapsed in giggles.

I pretended not to have heard the question. However I answered, I knew a completely fictional version would spread around the school like wildfire.

'Good day at school? No change of heart, then?' asked Charlie as we accelerated away.

'It was fine. And no, for some reason this hare-brained scheme still seems like my best option. You?'

'I'm still most definitely in,' he said. 'There is one thing I should probably talk to you about before we go into the meeting, though…' His voice trailed off.

'That sounds ominous,' I said.

'The thing is, I was having a think about what you said in your text yesterday, you know, about what we should tell the mortgage broker so that we sound like a safe bet, and I may have slightly exaggerated the nature of our relationship.'

'By which you mean what, exactly?' I asked, experiencing a strong sense of foreboding.

'I may have implied that we're engaged.' He cleared his throat nervously, and made a great show of checking his mirrors before pulling out of the junction.

'And how exactly did you imply that we're engaged?' I said, already half anticipating the answer.

'Okay, so maybe "imply" isn't exactly the right word.'

'What is the right word?'

'It might be more accurate to say that I told him we were engaged.'

'Charlie, what on earth possessed you to do that?' I asked, frustration making my voice rise.

He glanced quickly across at me, before turning his attention back to the road. 'I wanted to be completely sure that we'd get the mortgage, and I guess I panicked. It seemed like a good idea at the time, the best way of making sure we get the loan.'

'For goodness' sake, Charlie, it's not like it's the 1920s and we're an unmarried couple turning up at a hotel and trying to get a room together. All I was asking for was that we emphasise that we have a steady friendship. Why didn't you think it through before you opened your mouth? The bloke's far more likely to turn us down because you're pretending that we're something we're most definitely not. This was not part of the plan.'

'I know, I know,' he said. 'It was a really bad idea, but it's too late to take it back. If I tell the truth now, we definitely won't get the mortgage.'

He had a point.

'I can't believe you've put us in this position,' I muttered. 'Now I'm even more nervous about the meeting than before. I'm rubbish at acting. There's no way I can convincingly play a fiancée. We're bound to give ourselves away.'

Charlie swung the car into an empty parking space, killed the engine, then turned to face me.

'You're going to be even more angry at me for this, but I reckon it will help us get through the meeting, and reduce the pressure on your acting abilities. People rarely look beyond the surface appearance.' He pulled something out of his pocket. 'Here, put this on. I had a rummage through Alexa's things in her old bedroom. It's only costume jewellery but I reckon it'll do the trick.'

'You're seriously suggesting that if I wear your twin sister's ring this mortgage broker bloke will happily sign a fortune over to us? Now I feel even more like I've travelled back a century. This whole situation is utterly ridiculous. Besides, maybe I'm the type of woman who'd only wear an engagement ring if her fiancé did too.'

'Fair enough. I'd wear it myself as a man-gagement ring, if it would fit. I only suggested it to make the charade easier. I'm really sorry, Freya. I was trying to do something to help us, but I realise instead I've made the situation so much more difficult.'

He looked so contrite that I almost found myself feeling sorry for him, even though I was still massively irritated by his lack of thought.

'Fine, I guess we'll have to try to style it out. It's not like you've left us much choice. But I am not happy about it. In future, all house-related decisions should be made jointly, as specified in The Rules.'

'Duly noted. I mean, calling a spontaneous choice a "decision" is slightly overstating it, but I'll do my best to curb my free-spirited tendencies from now on,' said Charlie, in such an overly solemn manner that I couldn't help but smile.

'Don't make me have to be the nagger in this partnership,' I warned him. 'You're going to have to show that you can be sensible too. Now hand that thing over and let's get on with it.'

I unceremoniously shoved the ring on my finger and got out of the car. 'Come on then, fiancé, if we're going to do this, we might as well do it properly.' I grabbed his hand and interlocked my fingers through his, trying to remember how to look relaxed in this position.

'What is it they say, "cold hands, warm heart"?' said Charlie.

'Very funny. Let's get this over and done with. And please try to concentrate on what you're saying when we're in there. If we don't keep our stories straight, this whole charade will be over in minutes.'

The mortgage broker, Mr Philip Andrews as he introduced himself, was a very solemn guy whose interrogatory style would not have been out of place in a police station. He seemed determined to examine every little detail of our application, as if it was his own money that he'd be lending us. Despite my lecture to Charlie, I had a horrible fear that I would be the one to let the side down, because while he seemed to be totally at ease during our grilling, I was finding it hard to form sentences.

'Your paperwork seems to be in order. And your combined income and joint deposit are just about healthy enough for the amount you're seeking to borrow,' said Philip. I felt some of the tension release from my forehead. 'Remind me, how long have you been together? Apologies, it seems like a very personal question, I know, but banks like to be reassured that there is stability where they are putting their money.' And lo, the stress headache returned with a vengeance.

'Um,' I squeaked, my mouth dry.

Charlie put his arm around my shoulders and squeezed. 'We've known each other since we were three,' he said smoothly. I managed to jerk out a nod in agreement, telling myself that it wasn't strictly a lie.

Philip finally smiled. 'That's great. I can't promise anything at this stage, but it all looks very hopeful and I can't envisage any problems in getting you approved. Give me a day or two, and I should be able to let you have the mortgage-in-principle paperwork to allow you to put an offer in.'

'So you think it's going to be a "yes" then? Seriously?' I asked.

'Off the record, yes,' he replied.

The sense of relief was overwhelming. This was the furthest stage in the buying process that I'd ever reached. I could tell from Charlie's stunned expression that he was equally astounded that our dreams were actually coming true.

We staggered out of the meeting, hand in hand once again, in case Philip happened to be glancing out of the window.

'We're doing it, we're really doing it,' Charlie said.

'No regrets?' I asked, slightly nervously.

'Everything's falling into place perfectly,' he replied with supreme confidence. 'What could possibly go wrong?'

Chapter Seven

And for a while it seemed like Charlie's confidence was well-placed. Our cheeky offer on Oak Tree Cottage was accepted with almost indecent haste, and our mortgage was approved, subject to a satisfactory survey. We both carried on with our separate lives while the slow grind of endless paperwork continued behind the scenes, occasionally texting increasingly ridiculous decoration ideas to each other, but otherwise living in blissful, naïve ignorance of the challenge we were soon to be faced with.

But when February half term came round and the results of the survey landed, I almost wished I was back at Evil Stevil's, so horrified I was by the long list of things that needed fixing with the house. I'd anticipated issues, but not as many as this. I called Charlie in a panic.

'Have you read the report?' I asked in lieu of a proper greeting.

'Hello to you too,' he replied. 'I'm having a lovely day, thanks very much for asking.'

'Sorry, hi, and all that. But I don't know how you can claim to be having a lovely day when this monstrosity of a document has landed in our inboxes. Have you seen how long it is? I thought these things were meant to be dispassionate but it reads like crime fiction. "Windows rotten beyond repair", "infestation of woodworm", "evidence of rodent occupation".' I shuddered at the very idea of rats scurrying around the floorboards, which were also apparently dodgy in the extreme.

'Did you see the bit about the chimney stack?' queried Charlie, unbelievably sounding like he was smiling when he asked the question.

'I think that might have been the point where I felt too sick to continue,' I said. 'It's too much, Charlie, it's really too much. I don't know if I can do this.' I felt like a failure saying the words out loud, but I'd never even put a shelf up, and from what Charlie had said, it didn't sound like he was particularly practical either. The thought of attempting DIY on this scale was terrifying. There was a lengthy pause on the other end of the line. Then Charlie cleared his throat.

'Look, I know it's a shock, but let's not jump to any hasty decisions. We should at least talk about it properly, and it's not ideal trying to do that over the phone. Can I come round to Leila's? Or you're welcome here too.'

I thought quickly. I didn't want to impose further on Leila's hospitality by inviting Charlie over, and it wouldn't be particularly easy for me to make it to Charlie's parents' remote farm on public transport. Besides, it would probably be better to have this conversation on neutral territory, without the distraction of family and friends around us adding their opinions. 'Tell you what, I'll book us a table at the Italian place down the road from school,' I suggested. 'We can talk over food. I'm sure we'll both think more clearly on a full stomach.'

Charlie sounded surprised. 'If you think you can get us a table, then fine.'

'It's a Monday night. How many people go out for dinner on a Monday?'

It turned out, quite a few. And as we were shown to our table in a dimly lit corner of the restaurant, I understood why.

'This was a mistake. I didn't realise it was Valentine's Day,' I muttered, mortified as the waiter motioned for me to sit down on a chair which was festooned with heart-shaped helium balloons. Charlie ducked his head to avoid colliding with the particularly nauseating Cupid decoration that was dangling from the ceiling. He waited to reply until we'd been handed the menus, which were on pink paper and reeked of some kind of synthetic floral scent.

'I don't know how you can have missed it. I would have thought you'd be overwhelmed with offers tonight,' he teased.

'All I cared about was that it's half term and I have

slightly more time to do my marking than usual. The rest passed me by in a blur. So that's why Leila was MIA. No wonder the restaurant said they could only fit us in for the early sitting. I hope I didn't spoil any of your plans?' I suddenly realised that I didn't even know if Charlie had a significant other. I'd assumed he didn't because otherwise, why would he be buying with me? But then again he might be seeing someone and just not be at the moving-in stage yet.

He brushed away my comment. 'Plans can wait. The house is the important thing. Or rather it will be, once I've had something to eat. I'm starving. Now by the looks of the pizza that couple over there has been served, the portions are massive. Do you want to go fifty-fifty on a veggie feast with me?'

'Just because we're surrounded by couples, it doesn't mean we need to start sharing food. I'll stick with my usual choice, the ravioli, thanks all the same. Anyway, stop trying to distract me. We need to talk about what's next.' I took out a printed copy of the survey, which I'd marked up with highlighter pen – there was a lot of neon red for danger – and put it down on the table with a thud. 'The thing is, Charlie, we neither of us know what we're doing. You're a social media manager and I'm a teacher. Our professions don't exactly give us any transferrable skills which we could use on a building site. And I don't know about you, but I barely have the time to function outside work, let alone adding construction into the mix. When it was a matter of ripping out a few cupboards and painting the walls, that was one thing. It would still have been a challenge, but an achievable one. But this, this is stress on a different scale. I mean—'

I broke off as the waiter sashayed over to take our order.

'Today is the day for *amore*, not for arguing,' he said softly.

'Oh we're not—' I started, but Charlie interrupted.

'You're absolutely right. We should be enjoying the atmosphere in this beautiful place. My fiancée is just feeling the stress about our wedding plans. Not long to go now,' he said, flashing me an infuriating smile.

I glared back at him.

'Congratulations, congratulations. I'm so glad that you came here to enjoy some time together before the big day. Let me fetch you some dough balls, on the house,' said the waiter.

'That would be lovely,' said Charlie, before I could say anything.

I seethed internally while the waiter took the rest of our order. As soon as he hurried off to the kitchen I confronted Charlie.

'First at the broker's, now at the restaurant. You really need to stop this stupid fake fiancée game, Charlie. Our life isn't one of Granddad's Mills and Boon books. And to swindle free dough balls from the restaurant as well, that's really underhand behaviour.'

'Relax, Freya, it was a joke. It was only meant to be a bit of fun. The waiter would be disappointed to learn that he's given the most romantic table in the restaurant to a pair who aren't even a couple, and as for the dough balls, if you'd read the menu properly, you'd realise that everyone is being given them as a freebie for Valentine's Day. But I'm sorry for messing around again and upsetting you. That wasn't my intention at all.'

The genuineness of his apology rather took the wind out of my sails.

'I suppose free dough balls are not to be sniffed at.'

'Exactly. I promise not to do it again. You will have sensible Charlie at your disposal from here on in. Now, shall we turn to the matter in hand? What is it about the survey that's worrying you?'

'It might be more accurate to ask what isn't worrying me. I couldn't even understand half the technical jargon within the report. I know we've both spent a fair bit of money pursuing things to this point, but it's not too late to change our minds. Perhaps it's best we do that now, before we get any further. I still think the principle of us buying together works, but I'm sure there's another place we could find which would be a better solution for both of us.'

'I thought you liked Oak Tree Cottage?' asked Charlie, as the dough balls arrived, complete with a pat of garlic butter in the shape of two interlocking hearts. I noticed he quickly destroyed the shape with his knife, perhaps worried it might set me off again.

'I do like it,' I said, picturing the tumbledown property and once again imagining what it could look like. Despite everything, there was something about the cottage that called to me, that said 'home'. I firmly corrected myself. It was a house with investment potential and it didn't have to become a home. 'But liking it isn't enough. We've got to be rational about this, much as the thought of having to back out frustrates me.'

'It's not all bad news. The walls aren't falling down. And the roof is mostly intact,' Charlie pointed out.

'Hmm, but even so… The amount of stuff that needs fixing means that we'd have to seek professional help. How are we going to make the budget stretch to cover all this?' I waved the survey report at him.

'Look, let's not be too hasty. The survey is a huge shock, but the mortgage company haven't backed out of the deal, which has to be a positive sign. Surveyors are always over-cautious because they have to cover their backs. Equally, the bank has to be careful about where it lends money, but as it's still happy to go ahead, then Oak Tree Cottage can't be a complete disaster zone.'

'Yes, but…'

'But what?'

I took a deep breath. 'But don't you think it would be better if we could find somewhere a little less challenging, a little less stressful for us both? Doing this amount of work would put both of us under massive pressure, when we've got day jobs that we need to be able to focus on too. On top of that, it would test the strongest relationship. And yes, we were the best of friends when we were eleven, but what do we really know about each other now, as adults? Sure, I know you were obsessed with the character Brains from *Thunderbirds* when you were six, but do I know how adult

Charlie takes his tea? No. I guess I'm questioning whether we're up to this both from a practical *and* an emotional sense.'

'I drink builder's tea, no sugar, simple.'

'Just because you drink builder's tea, it doesn't make you an actual builder,' I said lightly.

Charlie picked up the final dough ball with his fork and generously deposited it on my plate. 'So what you're really saying is that you don't know whether you can trust me to renovate this cottage with you?'

'When you put it like that, it sounds awful. But we have to be realistic. I'm trying to find a way of minimising the risk we're both going to be taking.'

Charlie nodded. 'I understand what you're saying. I could talk at you for ages about how you can depend on me and how I'm determined that we'll get through this together, but they're all just words. Ultimately, they're meaningless, and until we're in that situation, I can't prove them to be true. I'm not going to pile on the pressure about it. But can I ask, what's wrong with taking a leap of faith? You could buy a new-build property and then discover a load of fixes that need doing once you've moved in. You could buy a house with a boyfriend and find out once you're co-habiting that he's a lazy layabout. Yes, we're taking a risk, but aren't most of the best things in life a risk? And we have The Rules which you've so thoughtfully prepared. You've done a lot to mitigate the risk factor. Take a chance on us doing this successfully. Trust me.'

Before I could reply, the waiter brought our main meals over.

'Veggie feast for the gentleman, and ravioli for the lovely lady. Can I get either of you some extra parmesan?'

I nodded on autopilot. My mind was buzzing with Charlie's impassioned speech. He'd spoken sense, but was I brave enough to take that risk?

The waiter sprinkled a generous helping of parmesan onto each of our dishes, then hurried off to his next table, humming 'That's *amore*' under his breath.

'I can never have too much cheese,' said Charlie. 'Right, enough of the serious talk until after the meal. General chitchat, otherwise we're going to get indigestion.'

The food was good, but I would have enjoyed it more if the house situation wasn't hanging over us. We kept the conversation on a superficial level, both of us wary of straying back into territory that was yet to be settled, but it was nice to spend some time chatting and covering the basics. Gradually, the knot in my stomach seemed to be loosening, although whether that was from the food or Charlie's reassurances, I couldn't say.

Once we'd put our knives and forks down on our virtually clean plates at the end of the meal, Charlie gestured at the survey report once again.

'Look, I know I said I wouldn't put any pressure on you, and that still stands, but I think it's only fair to tell you that I took the liberty of DM-ing your granddad this afternoon and sending him a copy of the survey.' He held up his hand. 'Now before you tell me off for involving Arthur, I promise

I didn't do it as some kind of emotional blackmail. We've talked a lot of theoretical stuff about the building work, but as you've pointed out, neither of us are professionals. Whereas your granddad actually knows what he's talking about. I was interested to get his take on it.'

'I wasn't going to tell you off,' I said. 'Besides, it would be hypocritical of me to do that as I also sent a copy of the report to him.'

Charlie laughed.

'Granddad's got a lot on his plate at the moment. I thought he'd be interested to read it, a distraction from his own worries,' I added quickly.

'But the fact that you sent it to him must mean that you haven't completely ruled out going ahead with buying Oak Tree Cottage?' pressed Charlie.

'Well…'

'Only Arthur did message me back and ask if we wanted to visit and talk through the report with him in person,' he said. 'He sounded pretty excited about the project.'

'I don't want our problems stressing him out.'

'Absolutely not. It's only so we can make a final decision from an informed perspective, which I know is important to you,' replied Charlie.

'It should be important to you too,' I pointed out. 'Fine, you have a deal. Let's see what Granddad thinks.'

Chapter Eight

I knocked on the door of Granddad's house, then went straight in knowing that he'd have unlocked it as soon as he received my message saying we were on our way. Ted scurried towards us, a giant unicorn soft toy clamped between his jaws, and leaped around our feet, the whole of his small furry body waggling with joy. Charlie leaned down and scratched behind his ears, at which point Ted rolled on his back and stretched his legs out, exposing his tummy in an invitation for tickling. We were only too happy to oblige.

'Who's a good boy? Yes, you are, a very good boy,' said Charlie to Ted's obvious delight.

'Eh, calm down, lad, they're not here for the walking rota,' said Granddad, heaving himself out of his armchair in such a careful manner that it got me worrying about his mobility issues all over again.

'You're not meant to know about that,' I said with a smile, leaning down to kiss his soft cheek.

He tapped his forehead. 'I know everything that's going on. But don't tell your mother. She likes to think that she's got one over on me for a change, and I'd hate to take that achievement away from her. Charlie lad, nice to see you in person this time.'

We settled down in the armchairs either side of the fireplace, Ted snuggling up on my lap and falling asleep almost instantly. It must be nice being a dog, having nothing to worry about except what's for dinner, and how much of the sofa you can hog, I thought. Ted let out an almighty snore as if in response.

'You've come to consult my professional opinion. I used to charge good money for this, love, but as it's you...' Granddad grinned at me, then pulled on his glasses and peered down at his iPad which had a copy of the report on it. 'This document made for entertaining reading this afternoon. Certainly a lot to think about.'

'What's your verdict?' I asked. Ted half opened one eye and stared up at me, jolted back awake by the anxiety in my voice.

Granddad pursed his lips. 'It's not brilliant. But then again, I've seen much worse. Most of the issues the surveyor highlighted can be dealt with in a straightforward manner. Put it this way, I don't think the house is going to fall down around your ears, and with sensible planning, the repairs can be stretched out over a period of time, which will help you from a budgeting perspective. And I'm certain that the pair of you would be able to do a lot of the work yourself, with a little tutoring along the way. Windows can be replaced, woodworm treated. Rodents can be removed, and in a humane way. Fixing rotten floorboards and strengthening stairs can be done by sensible amateurs as long as they've got guidance.' I shot a glance at Charlie. Did we come into that category? He winked at me, amused that I was questioning how sensible he was.

'The electrical and plumbing issues are a different matter,' continued Granddad, 'as is the chimney stack and the loose tiles on the roof, even though there are apparently only a few of them. Last time we went up into the hills together, I distinctly remember the descent taking twice as long as it should have because you had to hold my hand and wanted to close your eyes for most of the way.'

'Granddad, that was quite a while ago,' I protested, embarrassed that he was bringing that story up in front of Charlie. The purpose of this visit was to get a builder's opinion on the house, not to highlight my weaknesses in front of my prospective house partner.

'Hmm, but even so, I'm not sure I want my beloved granddaughter clambering around on a roof, even if she claims she's no longer scared of heights.'

'Overall, you think it's a bad idea then?' I pressed him, sending a significant look at Charlie.

But Granddad's response surprised me.

'That's not what I said. I think it's possible to make this into a beautiful home, if you're prepared to invest in it. And I'm not just talking about the financial investment. There's all the time it will take, and don't underestimate the sheer physical energy you'll need. I was a builder my whole career, and look at the state of me now.' His eyes twinkled as he gestured at himself.

'Don't be ridiculous. You're still my super granddad,' I retorted.

His expression grew serious. 'But having said that, if anyone can do this, you can. You're a determined woman, Freya. You've never been one to shy away from hard work. It was hard work that got you your degree and your job as a teacher. And it'll be hard work that allows you to discover the potential in the house. If you put your mind to it, you'll do it.

'How about you, Charlie? Are you prepared to show the necessary commitment and determination?' I asked, although, being truthful, the question was directed as much at myself as at him.

'I am. I'm certain that between the two of us, we can do it. I'm not afraid to learn some new skills, and I'm sure you're the same. And who knows, once the house is fixed up, we might like it so much, we could end up living there.' He laughed as I frowned at his joke. 'Once the house is renovated, it will be a highly desirable property in a very sought-after area and we could definitely make enough profit to set both of us up as individuals in our own places. An opportunity like this doesn't come along very often, and I will do what it takes to make the most of it.'

Granddad handed me the iPad and I stared down at the survey report once more, then clicked onto the brochure for the house. I thought about all the work that would need to be done and the time it would take, time that was already in short supply because of the pressures of my job. But as I stared at the pictures of the tired old building, I felt a pang of longing. I thought about the house itself, and the visions I'd had when we visited of what it could look like. Much as I wanted to deny it, I did feel an emotional connection with the place, which was probably a bad idea given that its purpose wasn't becoming our home, but being an investment for both our futures. But regardless of that, the house had a lot to offer me: freedom, independence, the opportunity to achieve long-held dreams. I'd suggested we look elsewhere and find an easier option, but how realistic was that? House prices were already ridiculously high, and the market was horribly competitive. How likely was it that we'd be able to find another place in such a prime position that was within our price bracket? I didn't normally shy away from hard work. Maybe Charlie was right. Maybe I should take a chance on Oak Tree Cottage. But there were still important issues that we needed to iron out.

'Even if we were to do it, and take on a lot of the renovation ourselves, when would we find the time for it? You've got your business to run, you can't pretend that it would be easy juggling life as a sole trader along with this kind of project. And during term time, my life isn't really my own. If I'm not in lessons at school, I'm preparing for them, or marking homework.'

Charlie nodded. 'We'd both have to make sacrifices. My job is perhaps more flexible than yours in that I set my own hours and choose how many clients to take on. But at least you have school holidays. And before you say anything, yes, I'm sure you still have lots of stuff to do in them, but you could devote some of that time to working on the house, if you really wanted to.'

'Maybe if we were to take possession during the Easter holidays, then schedule the bigger tasks during the summer break,' I said slowly, thinking out loud. Charlie sat up straighter, his expression hopeful.

I mustered up my courage. Time to take that leap of faith. 'I really hope I'm not going to regret saying this, but I am up for buying Oak Tree Cottage if you are.'

Charlie punched the air with delight, his sudden movement making Ted let out a yelp of surprise.

'You won't regret it. You've made the right decision, I know it. Let's shake on it and push on with the paperwork.'

He reached out and took my hand in both of his, a move I'd seen politicians on the telly do, but unlike with them, there was no doubting the sincerity in Charlie's gesture.

Granddad reached over and put his hand on top of ours.

'Congratulations to you both,' he said. 'And without wishing to rain on your parade, get good insurance. Always sensible to make sure the practical side of things is sorted out.'

'Don't you worry, Granddad,' I said. 'Paperwork is my forte. I'll make sure we're covered for every eventuality. That just leaves one final thing to sort. Where are we going to stay while we do all the work?'

Charlie's face fell. 'I would have thought it's obvious. In Oak Tree Cottage, of course.'

I gaped at him. 'That's not a serious suggestion, right? It's barely habitable.'

'It's habitable enough,' he asserted. 'And as you yourself pointed out, time is precious. We'd be wasting valuable renovation opportunities if we were having to commute back and forth, not to mention how much money we'd have to throw away on rent if we found a short-term let nearby. Where did you think you'd stay?'

'Erm…' The trouble was, he had made two excellent points there. And my only viable alternative was staying on Leila's sofa, which was a big ask. She'd already been more than generous in putting up with me so far. I was going to have to reconcile myself to the fact that completing this project was going to push me far out of my comfort zone in more ways than one.

'Where's your sense of adventure, Freya? It'll be like camping. Great fun,' said Charlie confidently.

Great fun, or a total nightmare?

Chapter Nine

There was a certain irony in fixing our moving-in date for Friday the first of April. As we collected the bunch of keys from the estate agent, I wondered for about the fifty millionth time whether I was a complete fool to be doing this.

'Congratulations,' said the estate agent, dropping the keys into my grasp, before handing a bottle of bubbly over to Charlie and shaking his hand enthusiastically. The wide smile on the estate agent's face spoke of a man who was happy to be collecting commission on a place he'd probably never thought he'd be able to sell.

The keys felt heavy in my hands, the tarnished metal cold to my touch. These were keys that had been handled by several generations, worn smooth by the comings and goings of different families over the years. They even smelled old. I closed my fingers around them, savouring the moment. These were my keys, heavy and old-fashioned as they were, they were literal keys to my future. Or rather they were *our* keys, Charlie's and mine, keys to our separate futures. And between now and that hoped-for future, there was an awful lot of hard work to be done. I reckoned similar thoughts must be going through Charlie's head because his face had the slightly dazed expression that I was pretty sure mine had.

I worked a set of the keys off the loop and handed it over to him.

'Here you go. Yours and mine. We're really doing this.'

'We really are.' He grinned. Then suddenly he reached forward and picked me up, throwing me over his shoulder before spinning us round in a circle whilst whooping wildly.

'Put me down,' I said, half squealing and half laughing as I tapped his arm to reinforce my plea. 'I'm practically as tall as you are. Carting me around like this will do your back in, and we can't afford fifty per cent of the restoration team being injured before we even start work.'

Charlie did one final spin before he gently let me back down. I ruffled his hair in revenge on my way back to the ground.

'I can't believe that this is really happening. Hutch and Humph, the Terrible Twosome, actual joint home owners. How amazing does that sound?'

'Pretty damn good,' I agreed. 'After all the stress of getting to this point, I can't quite believe we're finally doing it. In fact, I'm not sure I'll really accept it until we put the key in the lock and let ourselves in. How do you feel about heading off to our house and getting settled in? I think the estate agent's neighbours are going to call the police to move us on if we continue making an exhibition of ourselves.'

'Lead on, partner,' said Charlie, clapping me in the middle of the back so enthusiastically that I staggered forward.

We made our way back to Charlie's long-suffering Land Rover, which thankfully was still parked up where we'd left it. I say thankfully because it was packed to the roof with our worldly belongings, the essentials that would keep us going during these first few crucial weeks in the house. Despite my misgivings about living in a building site, we were moving in with a large collection of second-hand tools, our clothes, a camping stove, kettle and pots, plus a couple of inflatable mattresses and sleeping bags to tide us over until the place became habitable enough for actual furniture. My parents had already promised to donate a sofa they no longer needed, as a very generous house-warming present, while Charlie said he'd got a few odds and ends of furniture stored in a barn at his parents' farm which we could take our pick from.

I'd made this journey in my imagination so many times over the last few months, but I couldn't quite believe we were actually doing it. As we rounded the corner into the village and bumped our way down the street, the watery late afternoon sun finally emerged from the clouds, sending soft rays down onto the wreck of a building which was ours, all ours. Well, ours and the bank's.

'Doesn't it look beautiful?' said Charlie. The pride of new ownership made both of us look past the flaws to see only the wonder of the warm stonework and the soft green of the mossy slate roof. He stopped the engine and we got out, silent as we experienced this special moment. Somewhere in the distance a blackbird was singing to its mate, but aside from that and the gentle creaking of the branches of the oak tree, everything was quiet. It felt like a delicious balm to the soul after all my years of renting in the city. I was finally at a place I could call my own. I reached out and pressed my palm against the stonework, disturbing a couple of spiders who scurried out of the gaps in the render.

'Shall we?' said Charlie, gesturing to the front door. 'I know being country folk we should traditionally use the back door, but it feels like for this first entrance we should go through the front, and cross the threshold in a proper way.'

We picked our way up the tumbledown steps and pulled out our keys. For a couple of moments we dithered over who should have the honour of ceremonially unlocking the door, each of us too polite to say that we were desperate to be the one to do it.

'Let's Rock, Paper, Scissors for it,' I suggested after an awkward few rounds of 'No, after you, I insist.'

'Bring it,' said Charlie.

'Three, two, one, go,' I said, racking my brains to see if I could remember from childhood which way Charlie normally went. I spread my hand out flat to signify paper, while he bunched his fingers into a fist and moved his thumb up and down.

'I win, paper beats rock,' I said triumphantly, wrapping my hand over his.

He continued moving his thumb, tickling the centre of my palm until I removed it.

'Wrong, that wasn't a rock, it was a flame-thrower, which definitely beats paper.' He made a swooshing sound and then mimed my paper going up in smoke.

'You're so infuriating, Charlie Humphries. Since when was a flame-thrower part of the weaponry in Rock, Paper, Scissors?'

'Sticking to three items is boring,' said Charlie. 'I distinctly remember you inventing a hand grenade gesture when we were in Year Five. I sulked for days.'

'And this is your long-held resentment coming to the fore? Fine, if you're that desperate, you open the door,' I said, elaborately gesturing for him to go ahead, fighting to keep the stern expression on my face.

Charlie grinned at me, then stepped forward and ran his hand over the ancient wood of the front door, as if asking its permission for entry. Then he turned back to face me.

'Hand me your keys. I'll turn the lock but do it with your key. That way we're both involved,' he said, suddenly serious.

I passed it across and then Charlie brushed the cobwebs away from the metalwork. He examined the set of keys and chose the biggest one, pushing it into the lock.

'Here we go,' he said. He started trying to turn the key.

'It's a bit stiff. We might need that WD40 your granddad gave us.' He scrunched his face up as he twisted harder.

'Be careful, you don't want to break the key,' I said.

'Or do myself some damage,' he replied, letting go for a moment and stretching his fingers, before trying again with growing frustration. I leaned against the wall watching the spectacle.

'We could do with your flame-thrower now to heat up the lock and make it easier to turn,' I couldn't resist teasing him.

'Perhaps you should have a go,' he said slightly huffily, taking a step back and folding his arms, no doubt anticipating my imminent failure.

'Without wanting to sound smug, one of my special talents is opening jam jars,' I said, confident that I would be able to open the door without any problems. Of course, I spoke too soon, as I realised that Charlie hadn't been pretending. The lock was so stiff I feared the whole mechanism must have rusted into position about a century ago. Nevertheless, I persisted. It seemed symbolically important that we get past this hurdle. If we couldn't even open the front door, it didn't bode well for how the rest of the restorations would go.

'Had enough?' asked Charlie. 'You're going to give yourself a friction burn if you're not careful. Why don't we add the front door to our list, and we can sort it out on another occasion? We can always get into the house through the back door, which at least we know actually works.'

'No, it has to be this way,' I said, my determination

growing. I took hold of the key and twisted hard again, ignoring the heat in my flesh which warned me I was about to tear my skin open.

'Then let me help,' said Charlie. He placed his hand over mine and we fought the key together. There was an ominous crunching sound from within the lock, and then finally I felt the key start to move.

'We've done it,' I said. 'It's open. I wonder when this door was last unlocked.'

'And who by,' said Charlie. 'Maybe once the house gets to know us it will reveal some of the secrets of its former occupants. Shall we push open the door? I think it'll be another task for two.'

We stood facing each other, a shoulder each against the wood, and shoved hard. The door gave a shuddering creak worthy of a butler making a dramatic entrance in a murder mystery film, but it finally groaned open wide enough for us to shuffle inside sideways.

'Home sweet home,' said Charlie as we stood in the grimy dark of the living room. The nervous tone of his voice did not reflect the happiness of his words.

It wasn't a particularly warm day, but the air in the house was even cooler than it was outside. I shivered, both from the cold and the sudden chilling realisation of the scale of the task we had taken on. Ever since the first viewing I'd known renovating this house was going to be a huge challenge, something the survey report had reinforced in stark clarity. But somehow, over the last few weeks of trudging through the painful buying process, my mind had dulled its memories of the reality of the place, probably a form of self-protection. Now my senses were in overdrive as the sight and, more importantly, the smell of the house reminded me how much work there was to do. I thought I could hear the scrabbling of creatures running underneath the floorboards, a sound that sent a shiver down my spine. It was overwhelming, and if it hadn't been for the door being so hard to get open in the first place, I think I would have run straight back out of it and kept on running in the opposite direction. I sniffed, hoping Charlie would put it down as a reaction to the dank smell in the room, rather than recognising it for what it really was, a teary response of terror and regret.

Fortunately, Charlie pulled himself together more quickly than me and adopted the role of Mr Positive.

'First things first. We haven't decided who's getting which bedroom. Do you want to Rock, Paper, Scissors for it?'

'I don't mind, you choose,' I said dully. I wasn't sure I even wanted to risk climbing up the stairs at this point.

'Tell you what, you can have the room at the front as it's slightly bigger, and I'll take the one at the back. It seems only fair that I take the smaller room as we're going to convert the outbuilding into an office for me.'

'Sure,' I said.

'Come on, Freya, penny for 'em,' said Charlie, putting his arm around my shoulders and squeezing.

I allowed myself a few moments to take comfort from

the warmth of his body next to mine, then I pulled myself together and stepped away.

'Sorry, Charlie. It's been a long day in the coming, and it all felt a bit much. But if we could open that menace of a front door, we can manage anything between us. Right?' I was still desperately looking for reassurance.

'Absolutely,' said Charlie, his voice artificially hearty. 'I think we should toast our future. Let me grab the bottle of bubbly the estate agent gave us and we can start as we mean to go on.'

Of course it turned out that neither of us could remember if or where we'd packed the mugs, let alone champagne glasses. But we didn't let that stand in our way. I did the honours, carefully twisting the bottle as I eased the cork out so I didn't spill a drop. Not that spilled champagne would make much of a difference to the heavily stained carpet of the living room.

'Here's to our fixer upper,' I said.

'Cheers,' replied Charlie, then we mimed clinking glasses before taking it in turns to have a glug straight from the bottle. The bubbles tickled the back of my throat, setting off a laugh which was half giggling, half choking.

Charlie joined in and then the pair of us were laughing hysterically without really knowing why.

'Are we completely deluded?' I asked, as I clutched my sides and took another generous gulp from the bottle.

'Without a doubt,' replied Charlie. 'We are massively in over our heads. I mean, we couldn't even open the bloody door without a battle. But doesn't it feel good?'

Now my initial horror had been softened by the anaesthetising fuzziness of booze, I had to admit Charlie was right. I was no longer throwing hundreds of pounds away to help pay off somebody else's mortgage. I was investing in my own future. Whatever challenges were ahead of us, we would face them. And if we had to endure some hardship along the way, then it would make the final outcome that bit sweeter.

I took a final swig from the bottle then passed it across to Charlie to finish off.

'Shall we unpack? Perhaps we should see if we can get the gate open. It might be easier to lug our stuff in through the back door. At least that opens wider than the front one.'

'Good plan,' said Charlie.

'I'll dump this in the kitchen and start a recycling pile,' I said, picking up the bottle again.

Charlie reached out and grabbed the bottle from my hand. 'No, let's save it for posterity. We can clean it up and put it above the fireplace when we've restored it. A memento of our first day in Oak Tree Cottage.'

'I didn't have you down as the sentimental sort, Charlie.'

'Let's blame the fizz. Despite the tough guy appearance, I'm a softie at heart. Besides, it's not every day that I move into my very own house.'

I laughed. 'Tough guy appearance? You're as tough as a teddy bear. And that's why I like you,' I added lightly, when Charlie pretended to look hurt. 'And who gets custody of the bottle when we sell up?'

'We'll worry about that when the time comes,' he

replied. 'Right, let's take a look at this gate before it starts to get dark. Teddy bear or tough guy, the work still has to get done.'

Fortunately the gate gave up with less of a fight than the front door. We propped it open, then Charlie drove his car onto the patch of waste land that we were optimistically referring to as the driveway and we started unpacking.

'Remind me why we turned down the kind offer of both sets of parents to help us move in?' said Charlie, panting as he lugged another box of tools into the house.

'I have absolutely no idea,' I said, equally breathless as I attempted to balance five bags of various homeware essentials on my shoulders. 'Didn't we think it would be better if we did it ourselves, put our own stamp on the place and demonstrate that we're independent and capable individuals? Because if that was the logic behind our decision, it was completely stupid and we need to remember that in the future. Does your car have some kind of Mary Poppins function? We must have done about fifty trips apiece and it still looks as full as it did when we started.'

'Nearly done,' said Charlie, putting on the kind of overly positive voice I would normally use when persuading the Year Sevens to complete their end-of-term projects.

'At least the weather is playing ball,' I said, then immediately regretted saying the words out loud. 'Sorry, I've just condemned us to a massive thunderstorm or something, haven't I?'

Charlie tramped past with the box containing the camping stove and kettle. He glanced up at the now very dark sky.

'I think we'll be okay for a few hours. But perhaps we should call it a day for the time being and have something to eat? We've got the sleeping bags and cooking stuff inside. The rest can wait until the morning.'

'Good call,' I agreed, glad that I wasn't the only one feeling incredibly hungry.

We tramped into the kitchen, which was now so gloomy I could barely see my hands in front of my face.

'Dare we?' I said, my finger hovering over the light switch.

'What's the worst that could happen?' said Charlie.

'I'd rather not think about that.' I closed my eyes and pressed down, bracing myself for the huge jolt of an electric shock which must inevitably follow. But aside from a slight fizzing sound from the switch, which was rather unnerving, I remained unharmed. 'Is the light on?' I asked, not daring to look.

'Let there be light, and lo there is,' replied Charlie.

I opened my eyes and saw him standing in front of me holding a large battery-operated camping lamp. I looked up at the ceiling light hopefully, but the bulb remained dark.

'Oh. No power in the kitchen then.'

'Who needs electricity when we've got a super lamp like this? My sister sent it to me as a housewarming present. Ever the practical lawyer, that's Alexa for you. She was probably worried you'd sue me if you got electrocuted.'

'If I got electrocuted, I'd be dead, and therefore in no position to be suing anybody,' I replied pedantically, irritated by his easy acceptance that we were going to have to spend our first night in this place without proper lighting. I'd forgotten how very dark the countryside could be, making every noise around us sound that little bit louder and more disconcerting. I told myself everything would look a lot better in the morning, but for now I would happily have given almost anything for a functioning 100-watt lightbulb.

'Let's get this camping stove working,' said Charlie, tactfully ignoring my mini hissy fit. 'We'll boil a kettle, get a cup of tea each and then decide what we can prepare for dinner.'

'I'll work the stove, you can turn the tap on. See if you have better luck than I did with the light.'

'No problemo.' Charlie whistled cheerily as he waltzed over to the sink. The tap let out a squeal of its own in response, then a groan followed by an eerie silence.

'It's only air in the pipes,' he said, although the tone of his voice did not match the confidence of his diagnosis. 'Give it a minute and it'll be flowing through easy as anything.'

The tap let out another grinding noise which was then answered by a shuddering which seemed to emanate from the very walls of the kitchen.

'What on earth is going on?' This time Charlie's voice had definitely reached panic level, and was at a pitch that instantly transported me back to our schooldays. Now I got to play the irritatingly calm one. I reached across and turned the tap off. After a short while the walls stopped vibrating.

'I think that's another one to re-examine in the morning when apparently all things will be brighter. Thank goodness Granddad suggested packing those water containers. I'll go and fetch one, and perhaps you can check to see if we can get a food delivery out here. I think this is the kind of evening that calls for emergency pizza.'

It turned out ordering a takeaway wasn't a problem at all, but directing the delivery driver to the house was a whole other issue as he struggled to find the address on his system. He finally arrived at the front door half an hour later than promised with two boxes of cold pizza.

'If you could tip them sideways, we should be able to get them through the gap,' I said as he blatantly displayed his horror at the state of the place.

'Do you actually live here?' he asked.

'Oh yes,' I replied.

'Good luck,' he said.

Chapter Ten

I woke the next morning with two distinct sensations, both worrying in their own way. The first was that I really, really needed the toilet. The second was that something was tickling the side of my neck. I told myself to think of it as tickling, rather than what it probably was, an insect crawling along and using me as its personal playground. I brushed at my skin and saw a spider with very long, very hairy legs tumble down and start scuttling across the floor. Shuddering, I tried to look on the positive side. At least I'd stopped it before it had headed anywhere near my mouth. If I'd woken up to a spider tap-dancing on my lips, I'd have moved into the staffroom at school, signing my half of the house over to Charlie without a second thought.

I rolled over and swallowed a groan as my aching muscles protested. Stretching out, I tried in vain to ease the stiffness in my limbs. Although I'd jokingly complained about Leila's sofa bed giving me a crick in the neck, it was nothing compared to the discomfort of a night in a sleeping bag on the floor. Charlie and I had both invested in air beds, but unfortunately the pump to inflate them was an electric one, and after trying the light in the kitchen, neither of us had felt like daring to plug anything into a socket. The only real function the air bed mattress *sans* air had performed was providing a clean layer between my sleeping bag and the mess that called itself the carpet. I dreaded to think what other creepy crawlies were nesting in there. My only comfort was that there were two of us to deal with whatever other fauna decided to become more closely acquainted with us. Without really discussing it, we'd ended up sleeping in the living room rather than retiring to our separate bedrooms. After half a bottle of bubbly apiece and the emotions of the day, we'd tacitly agreed not to try venturing upstairs until daylight. The first night in a new place was always strange, but having Charlie in the room had made me feel slightly less weird, even if he had dropped off irritatingly quickly and then turned out to make annoying little sighing noises in his sleep. Only dogs have enough cute factor to get away with being noisy sleepers.

I propped myself up on my elbow, the floorboards beneath the thin layer of carpet giving my hip an unwanted firm massage, and peered blearily across the room. Charlie was still fast asleep, blissfully unaware of the disaster scene which was now lit up by the shards of sunlight coming in through the windows. I didn't even know where we could begin with getting this place properly habitable.

But the pressure on my bladder forced my thoughts to a more urgent focus. Given that I did not want to christen our garden by peeing on the weeds, I was going to have to try out the bathroom. And judging by what had happened, or rather, not happened, when we'd attempted to turn on the kitchen tap last night, it was not going to be a pleasant experience. I pulled my phone out from where I'd left it in my shoe and quickly Googled 'how to flush a toilet without running water'. Once again I thanked Granddad Arthur for insisting we brought water supplies with us. According to my rudimentary research, a bucket of water poured down the bowl would help me flush on this occasion. But the internet's suggestion about how to deal with more solid waste, which involved lining the toilet bowl with a bag, did not bear thinking about. There was a reason why I'd chosen to become a teacher rather than an outdoor adventurer. If our entire budget literally went down the drains to resolve this plumbing problem, it would be a price worth paying.

I filled a bucket from one of the water containers, and tried to make my way upstairs as quietly as possible so I didn't disturb Charlie. I told myself it was because he probably needed the sleep, although if I was being truly honest it was more because I felt that this was a test that I needed to get through by myself. If I couldn't do this, I was hardly going to thrive over the next few months while we attempted to transform the place.

The stairs sounded horribly loud in the peace of the

morning, but fortunately no tousle-headed Charlie emerged from the living room to see what was going on. I dashed through the room which was going to be mine and made it to the bathroom, my increasing urgency making me almost oblivious to the festering smell in there. I hovered above the porcelain bowl, not wanting to risk sitting on the seat until it had been thoroughly scrubbed. I already had a strong feeling that this house renovation was going to do wonders for my muscle tone. Once I was done, I experimentally tried the handle in case by some miracle a flush occurred, but instead the thing fell off in my hand, which I should have expected. Thankfully the bucket of water did the trick, and once I'd reattached the flush handle and cleaned my hands with my trusty bottle of sanitiser, I felt almost human again.

Now I was upstairs, I decided I might as well take the time to have a proper look around my room. I couldn't sleep in the living room every night. It was at the front of the house, and took up the whole width of the building, with a boarded-up fireplace at one end, and two large windows looking out across the valley. The floorboards were bare, and the zany geometric wallpaper was peeling off the walls, but the room was beautifully light despite the mucky windows, and I could already picture myself curling up in an armchair by the fireplace, reading a book or, more realistically, marking essays on the Tudors and Stuarts. I would paint the walls in a pale colour, perhaps a warm cream with a hint of yellow, or maybe the softest of greys, something peaceful and serene, the exact opposite of the intense pattern that currently dominated the space.

I took hold of a corner of the wallpaper and gave it an experimental tug. It pulled away from the wall in a pleasingly smooth way, giving me a burst of satisfaction akin to popping bubble wrap. In a matter of seconds, I'd pulled the whole strip off, revealing the discoloured plaster behind it. Fired up with enthusiasm, I picked at the next piece. It wasn't long before I had quite a pile of paper in the middle of the floor. Not all the strips were as easy as the first one, but if the decor of every room was going to be this speedy to get rid of, then perhaps I could reassess the careful timetable of work I'd planned out before we moved in.

Inevitably, that thought tempted fate, and the next strip of wallpaper I tried to remove took with it great chunks of the plaster, some of which ended up in my hair, while my face was sprayed with a fine coating of dust. I choked as particles made their way into my nose, clogging my lungs and setting me off wheezing. I cursed myself for my over enthusiasm. Giving myself an asthma attack was not exactly a great way to get started, and of course, my inhaler was still in Charlie's car, probably hidden somewhere at the very bottom of the bags of stuff we couldn't be bothered to unpack last night.

Snatching uncomfortable breaths, I slowly made my way back to the top of the stairs, then nearly fell down them in surprise when I heard a sound I would never have expected to hear. A moment later, Charlie emerged from the door of his room, drying his hands on a towel.

Not having enough breath to ask the question I wanted

to, I gestured at the towel, then in the direction of the bathroom, from which I could still hear the final splashes of the toilet flushing.

'I found the stopcock,' said Charlie, reading my mind. 'I can't believe we didn't think of it last night. Why would the water still be turned on when the house hasn't been occupied for years? We'll have a look at the fusebox in a bit in case there's a similarly easy solution there.'

I started laughing, but thanks to the unwelcome reappearance of my asthma, it sounded more like I was taking my dying breaths.

Charlie dropped the towel and rushed forward, wrapping his arm around my waist to support me where I stood.

'Hey, Freya, are you okay? Let's try and get you some air.'

He half carried me back into my bedroom, then propped me up by the fireplace while he wrestled with the window.

'Two seconds, and this will be open, and the lovely country breeze will help clear your lungs,' he said, throwing worried looks in my direction as he tried to figure out how to pull open the sash.

'By which you mean the wonderful scent of cow manure,' I tried to joke, but the amount of effort each word took really spoiled the delivery.

'Perhaps save the stand-up for when you're not gasping for breath,' said Charlie. I saw him flinch and quickly shake his hand before he attacked the window with renewed vigour. In the end, the window was no match for his determination. The entire thing gave way, glass and frame detaching from their position in the wall and falling down to the ground with a horrifying smashing sound.

But I didn't have time to contemplate the destruction, because Charlie was back at my side, scooping me up and depositing me by the side of the gaping hole.

'Do you have an inhaler or should I call for help?' he asked, a note of panic in his voice.

I shook my head, and managed to convey where my inhaler was through a mix of wheezed words and mime.

'Got it. You rest here, and take it easy while I fetch it.' He ran to the doorway, then turned back to face me. 'Try not to lean too heavily on the stonework. Now the window's not holding everything in place, it might be a bit unstable.'

'I thought you were trying to make me feel better,' I gasped.

'Hold onto that thought, I'll be back in two minutes,' said Charlie.

He thundered down the stairs, apparently unconcerned that they too could collapse under him. I tried to do as advised and take gulps of fresh air, but it was hard to get enough oxygen in when it felt like an elephant was sitting on my chest. The sight of the destroyed window down on the ground didn't exactly help me to feel any better. I was literally allergic to this place.

Thankfully Charlie was as good as his word and reappeared in record time with the inhaler triumphantly held out before him.

I took a couple of doses to be on the safe side, and

gradually felt the pressure on my lungs start to ease. I slumped down onto the floor, not caring how dirty it was, and tried to summon up my energy.

'Sorry about that,' I said, feeling somehow exposed that Charlie had witnessed me in a moment of fragility. It was illogical, I know, but I didn't want him to think that I was going to be the weak member of our house partnership. I hated being vulnerable in front of other people, and I didn't know the adult version of him well enough yet to know how it would affect the way he saw me.

Charlie unfortunately was far too perceptive for his own good.

'None of that, Freya,' he said. 'Nothing to apologise for. Paula Radcliffe has asthma, and it didn't stop her running marathons. You're not going to get away with avoiding restoration work because of a bit of wheeziness.' He smiled at me, so I could be in no doubt that I was being teased.

'Damn, that's my plan foiled,' I managed to retort. 'Thanks, Charlie. Don't know what I'd have done if you hadn't managed to find my inhaler.'

He responded with a thumbs-up, or rather he tried to, but winced as he attempted to make the gesture.

'What's the matter?' I asked.

'Just worried about how you're going to respond when you discover the mess I made while rooting through your stuff to find your inhaler. You have quite an interesting collection of possessions.'

I noticed him trying to move his hand out of my eyeline.

'Nice attempt to distract me. Now show me,' I said, in the voice normally reserved for cheeky Year Nines.

He reluctantly uncurled his fingers to reveal a very large, very painful-looking splinter stuck deep in his palm.

'It's nothing to worry about,' he said.

'That doesn't look like nothing.'

I traced my finger along his skin, trying to feel where the splinter ended. It must be at least half an inch long, I realised, and razor sharp. He shivered.

'Perhaps I should go and knock on one of the neighbours' doors and see if they can give me some tweezers to get this out. Maybe they'll let us use them in their house as well. This isn't exactly a clean environment to be doing minor surgery in.'

'Not a brilliant way of introducing ourselves to the neighbourhood,' said Charlie. I could see my earlier embarrassment at my moment of weakness mirrored on his face now. 'Don't fuss, Freya. It'll fall out of its own accord. I'm not going to let it stop me doing anything.'

I frowned. 'I don't think it works that way. Let me try and see if I can pull it out. I'll be as gentle as I can, I promise.'

'You better be,' said Charlie, only half joking. Then his voice grew more serious. 'It's okay, I trust you.'

My fingers were wobbling slightly as I tried to grasp the end of the splinter, nervous that I might be about to inflict more pain on him. I felt responsible for the injury. If he hadn't been trying to open the window to help me breathe more easily, he wouldn't have been hurt in the first place.

'I could really do with my glasses to see this better,' I said, my frustration growing as I failed to get a proper grip on the splinter.

I tried to get up, but Charlie urged me to stay seated. 'You're still getting your breath back from that asthma attack. Don't worry, my hand's in no imminent danger of falling off.'

But I could tell from the tightness in his voice that the shard of wood was troubling him, so I ignored him and hurried off to collect another container of water from downstairs. The taps might be working again, but I wasn't going to trust that the water coming from them was clean, especially not for such a delicate operation. I poured water into a saucepan from our stash of camping equipment and added a bit of hand sanitiser for good measure. Then I put my glasses on and hurried back upstairs.

'Soak your hand in this for a few minutes and then I'll try again.'

He gave a harsh intake of breath as the sanitiser and water did their thing.

'Sorry, I know it stings, but at least we know it's clean now. Can't have you picking up an infection from the ancient woodwork.'

'I suppose if I did, I could sell my story to the papers and it would boost our renovation budget,' said Charlie, ever the optimist.

We sat side by side, our backs against the now bare wall.

'You've made some good progress in here already,' said Charlie, nodding towards the pile of wallpaper in the centre of the room. 'What shall we put up in its place? Once we've checked for damp and replastered first, of course.'

'A functioning window might be a good place to start,' I said trying to keep my tone as positive as possible, even though I was already calculating what the unexpected damage might do to our budget. Although we'd known we'd have to replace the windows at some point, I hadn't anticipated it would be quite so soon.

'We'll find a way of boarding it up until we can afford a replacement,' said Charlie. 'It's no big deal.'

If only that was true.

'I suppose at least now we have some running water, we can move the plumber back down the priority list,' I said.

'Judging by efficiency of The Rules, that'll be a colour-coded list in an Excel spreadsheet, I'd imagine.'

'Never underestimate the power of an Excel spreadsheet, Charlie,' I said, unable to resist taking the bait. 'I like being organised and in control of my situation. There's nothing more satisfying than ticking something off a to-do list.'

'I can think of plenty more satisfying things,' said Charlie, mischief in his expression.

I cleared my throat. 'How's that hand doing? I think it's probably soaked for long enough now. Ready for me to have another go?'

He flexed his fingers, shaking the excess water off, and then looked away from me. 'Count me down to it, so I know to brace myself for the pain.'

'Three, two...' I pulled the splinter out before I reached

one, figuring he'd be more relaxed that way, trying to do it as swiftly and gently as possible.

'Ooooo-uch,' wailed Charlie, rolling over onto his side and clutching his hand to him.

'Oh my goodness, I'm so sorry. Are you okay?' I said kneeling beside him and patting his shoulder, feeling horribly guilty that I'd removed the splinter when he wasn't ready for it.

'My hand, my hand,' he groaned, in such a melodramatic manner that I could be in no doubt that he was faking the whole display.

'You'll definitely be the leading man of the local amdram group, you great big wuss,' I said, relieved that his play acting had dispelled the unexpected tension I had been feeling. I playfully slapped his side as he rolled back towards me and grinned widely. 'Either that, or you'll be the star signing of the local football club, trying to distract the ref from your dirty tactics by pretending to be mortally wounded. I think we're even on the house-induced injury front. Perhaps now we've had our quota of drama for the day, and hopefully for the week, we can work out what we're going to do about breakfast.'

'Fine, if you're not going to kiss it better, I guess we can get the kettle on,' said Charlie, leaping up and putting his injured hand out to help me up too.

I rolled my eyes, then got up under my own steam. I was rapidly realising that sharing a house with Charlie was definitely going to keep me on my toes.

Chapter Eleven

C harlie didn't tell me we were drinking water from the tap until I was on my second sip of coffee. I hastily put the mug down and experimentally smacked my lips as I tried to work out if it tasted any different to normal.

'We'll be fine, Hutch. The water was boiled. That will have killed off any nasty bugs,' he said confidently.

'I hope so. I had planned to spend the Easter holidays getting started on the renovation work, not curled up nursing a dodgy stomach.'

We were sitting on the fold-out chairs in the kitchen, the camping stove set up before us, a couple of veggie sausages apiece starting to sizzle in the frying pan.

'You'll be fine. And if you do get the runs, at least the toilet is flushing now.'

I pulled a face. 'Delightful, thanks for that, Charlie. I'd really rather not think about that eventuality. How's your work schedule looking anyway?'

'I have a few bits I need to do for some clients, but I've tried to keep the next couple of weeks while you're on school holidays as free as possible so we can make a joint start on things. I was going to suggest we began by clearing as much of the decor as possible, but after what happened with the wallpaper in your room, I'm not sure that's such a good idea.'

'We'll dig out some masks, and I'll be fine,' I said. 'The problem earlier was that I got a proper faceful of dust. My lungs will acclimatise to the new environment before long. I think we should wear masks anyway. I don't think it would do either of us any good to inhale too much of the accumulated dirt of several decades.' I glanced around the kitchen and sighed. 'Everywhere I look, I spot something else we're going to have to sort out. Perhaps it'll look less daunting once we've eaten.'

'Speaking of which, I think these are done,' said Charlie, leaning forward and turning the camping stove off. 'Red or brown sauce in your sausage sandwich?'

'Charlie Humphries, what a question to ask. Red, obviously. It's sacrilegious to suggest anything else.'

As I prepared the sandwiches, Charlie rummaged in our box of food stuff, which we'd placed on a counter top, hoping it would deter any of the house's four-legged residents from exploring it.

'And it's a question I'm going to regret asking, as it would appear that I failed to pack either. Or the rats have run off with the ketchup already. Oh well, at least the sausages are hot. Cheers.'

He knocked his sandwich against mine like we were clinking glasses, then we settled into enjoying our meal.

'The food of champions,' said Charlie some time later.

'Agreed. And as you cooked, I'll do the washing up.'

'How very civilised of us. Perfect house partners.'

Unfortunately the good-humoured sense of togetherness slightly wore off during the course of the day. We'd jointly decided – after some heavy persuasion on my part – that the first room we would tackle would be the bathroom. We weren't going to be replacing the fixtures and fittings instantly or knocking through a new doorway into the upstairs hallway straightaway, but we could at least make the place clean and functional so it was a bit more civilised using the facilities. But what Charlie had in enthusiasm, he was sadly lacking in good sense, darting between one area of the room and another as he tried to simultaneously tackle multiple tasks, continuously adding stuff to his workload as he spotted it, yet never quite finishing off anything. I preferred a more logical approach, dealing with one thing at a time, working away at scrubbing the bath until it was pristine, and then focusing on the shower. Each of us thought our own method was the best, and after several hours of back-aching work with very little to show for it in results, our tempers were beginning to fray as our contrasting approaches wound each other up.

'Charlie, for the thousandth time, will you move the pile of debris away from the middle of the floor? Every time you decide to dash between the toilet and the sink, you kick it out of place and then I have to sweep it up again.'

'Where do you suggest I put it then?' said Charlie. 'Because when it was by the door into your room, you said it was stopping you leaving, and when I put it by the door to my room, you said it was in the way there too.'

'How about you don't put it in the middle of everything? Why do I have to be the sensible one making all the decisions? I have enough of telling people what to do at work. I don't want to have to do it in my free time too.' I knew I sounded petulant but I was tired, overwhelmed and experiencing some serious regrets. Why had I deluded myself into thinking that this house transformation was possible? And why was I allowing myself to feel this way on our first day of working at it?

'Forgive me, I thought you were enjoying bossing me around,' retorted Charlie, sounding as exasperated as I felt. 'You're certainly treating me like one of your naughty schoolboys.'

'If you insist on acting like one of them, then that's what you should expect.'

We stared at each other, furious and frustrated, neither of us wanting to be the one to back down first.

A sudden clattering noise from downstairs broke the impasse.

'Tell me that's not another window falling out,' I said.

'The one in your bedroom did have some help from me,' said Charlie sheepishly. 'I don't think things are quite at the stage that the rest are going to spontaneously take the plunge.'

There was another rattling sound followed by a bang.

'Well, whatever it is, it's not good. Something is breaking or we have an intruder,' I said.

'There's not much worth stealing,' said Charlie, although I noticed he'd lowered his voice and was now holding his broom in front of him as if it was a weapon.

'Only our worldly possessions, which are still handily all in boxes downstairs and in your car. All the easier for Burglar Bill to march straight out with.'

'I guess we'd better take a look,' said Charlie.

I nodded, not quite trusting myself to speak. I was having serious flashbacks to the night when Steve broke into my bedroom. I knew this scenario was completely different – it wasn't night, I wasn't alone – but that didn't stop my heart thudding with anxiety.

We went downstairs, taking an age on each step as we tried to be so quiet that the intruder wouldn't know we were coming. I wanted nothing more than to hide and hope the problem went away, but I didn't want to let fear get the better of me so I walked by Charlie's side, determined to demonstrate that we were equals in everything house-related, even in tackling burglars.

'Do you think we should ring the police?' Charlie whispered, his breath warm against my ear as he stood close so his voice didn't travel further than it needed to.

Before I could answer, there was a scrabbling of paws, and a furry whirlwind scurried to the bottom of the stairs, spun round three times, and then disappeared back out of sight. I experienced an overwhelming sense of relief.

I let go of Charlie's arm. 'I think we'll be okay,' I said. I fairly skipped down the last couple of steps, and beckoned to Charlie to follow me.

'Hello, Granddad,' I said as we emerged into the kitchen. 'Be careful where you're stepping, the floor is rather uneven.'

Ted zipped into view once again, this time carrying something in his mouth.

'Oh heck, please don't let that be a dead rat,' I said, as Charlie hurried to intercept him. Ted let him get within grabbing distance, then put on a burst of speed, his back legs lowering closer to the floor as he whizzed out of reach. If he was human, he would definitely be laughing.

'Drop it, Teddy boy,' said Granddad in a tone which was completely lacking in authority. He tried to grab Ted as he sped past, but wobbled. For a horrifying moment I thought he was going to fall forward onto his face. I ran towards him and took his arm.

'Eh, don't panic, love, I'm perfectly steady on my pins,' he said, although I noticed that he didn't let go of me.

Ted, sensing that the attention had moved away from him, consented to being caught, although he still gave Charlie a challenge by keeping his jaw clamped tight. Eventually Charlie managed to prise it open and removed a half-chewed duster.

'Not a rat, thankfully. I think Ted was offering to help us.'

'He would probably do a better job,' I said.

Ted gave a happy shake in response, sending bits of fur and slobber flying in all directions.

'Thanks, matey,' said Charlie, wiping stray saliva from his already filthy jeans. He reached down and scratched Ted's head affectionately. 'Lovely to have you giving the house a properly lived-in feel. Now then, Arthur, can we offer you a cup of tea? I was about to put the kettle on. Cleaning the bathroom is thirsty work.'

'Interesting use of the word "cleaning" there, Charlie,' I couldn't resist interjecting, my frustration at his lack of efficiency bubbling to the surface once again. Charlie feigned ignorance.

I helped Granddad ease himself down into one of the folding chairs. It was a bit lower to the ground than I would have liked and I was worried about how we would get him up out of it, but we didn't have any choice.

'That would be grand. Thanks, Charlie boy. How are the two of you getting on? No regrets?' asked Granddad, cutting to the chase in his customary manner.

'Many, and varied,' I said. 'So far we've been more successful at making a mess than clearing it up.'

Granddad nodded. 'I noticed the smashed glass out front. I'm afraid my house-warming present has been a little too late.'

'You didn't have to get us a present, Arthur. All the advice and support you gave us when the survey came through was a present enough,' said Charlie, snatching the words right out of my mouth.

'Nevertheless, it wouldn't be right not to mark this momentous occasion with something special. I decided to go for something practical. You may have heard it being delivered a short while ago.'

Granddad gestured for us to go through to the living room.

'Take a look out of the front window.'

I led the way, Ted dashing back and forth between me, Charlie and Granddad, unsure who was the most exciting prospect.

I rubbed the grimy glass with the sleeve of my sweatshirt, and gingerly knelt on the deep windowsill so I could get a proper look. Charlie went to the other window, but stood a little back from it, thankfully more cautious after the drama with the upstairs one this morning.

'Granddad, that's the best present anyone could have given us,' I called back into the kitchen. If anyone had told me a year ago that I'd be thrilled to be presented with a hired skip, I would have laughed at them, but today the cavernous yellow thing was definitely a joy to behold.

'It belongs to the granddaughter of a former colleague. She runs the family building business now, and I've hired it for the duration of your renovation project. When it's full, give her a call, and she'll replace it with a fresh one.'

'I fear that's going to be a regular occurrence,' said Charlie. 'Right, let's get that tea sorted. I could do with a rest.'

It was good to sit in the kitchen with Granddad, enjoying a hot drink even though I felt guilty having a break as we'd barely got started. We talked over my list of jobs and I took notes as Granddad described a less-risky method of stripping the wallpaper. Charlie meanwhile entertained Ted by throwing the duster for him to fetch. The little dog snuffled around the nooks and crevices of the room, dragging bits of rubbish out from the dark corners along with the duster. He failed to discover any creatures living or dead, but that didn't mean they weren't lurking there. Granddad seemed in no hurry to return home, even though he couldn't be comfortable sitting on the low camping chair in the draughty house.

Eventually, though, he checked the time on his phone and sighed. 'I should probably be ordering a taxi and getting going.'

'Didn't you drive, Granddad? I thought you'd parked round the corner to leave room for the skip lorry to drop its load off.'

'I decided it would be easier to get a cab for that very purpose,' he said, although there was something shifty in his expression which made me wonder if that was the true reason. I made a note to try to ask Mum about it. I'd have to make my question subtle – no point in worrying her pointlessly – but Granddad loved driving, and if he was choosing to rely on taxis instead, there must be a good reason behind it.

He made a point of moving the conversation on. 'Have you got your internet installed yet? I've been collecting some useful renovation channels on YouTube. I thought they could be good for you to follow for step-by-step instructions when I'm not able to pop round to help.'

'That's very good of you, Arthur,' said Charlie. 'We're

still relying on our mobile phones at the moment, but getting the internet working is high up on my priority list.'

'Once we've got the bathroom functioning,' I said. 'We're both going to become miserable pretty quickly if we can't get rid of the grime at the end of the day.'

'I reckon another hour of work, and the bathroom will be cleared up enough for us to be able to take a shower. The water won't be hot, but it'll be better than nothing.'

I mentally added another couple of hours to Charlie's estimation.

A car horn hooted outside.

'That sounds like my driver,' said Granddad. 'Come on, Ted, lad, time for us to take our leave.'

He made as if to stand, but as I'd feared, the low chair proved too difficult for him. The loose canvas of the arms didn't help either, as there was nothing for him to push against to lever himself up.

'Do you need a hand, Granddad?' I asked tentatively, knowing that he'd hate admitting that the answer was yes.

'I've got so comfortable I'm finding it difficult to prise myself away from you both,' said Granddad, forced jollity in his tone.

Charlie stepped forward. 'May I, sir?' he asked, his tone polite and respectful, making sure that Granddad could retain the dignity he so feared losing.

'Perhaps just this once, thank you, Charlie,' said Granddad, a sigh of defeat in his voice.

Charlie helped lever him up, waiting until he was sure that Granddad was steady, then he stepped quietly back and carried on with tasks around the kitchen, allowing us all to pretend that everything was fine, when it really wasn't.

I looped my arm through Granddad's and walked slowly with him to the front of the house where the taxi was waiting. Beneath his smart jacket, his arm felt a lot smaller than it used to, and I was upset to realise how stooped he was when he was walking. I cursed myself for being so wrapped up in my own selfish needs that I hadn't noticed how much frailer he had grown. Ted scampered at our feet, rushing between interesting smells. But despite his eagerness to move quickly, I noticed that he was slowing his pace when he neared Granddad, sensing that he shouldn't get under his feet.

I waved Granddad and Ted off, and walked slowly around to the back of the house again, trailing my fingers through the weeds.

'Penny for 'em,' said Charlie.

I looked up and saw him leaning against the back door, his arms folded as he watched me closely.

'He seems to have got so old all of a sudden,' I said. 'I mean, objectively he is old. But he's never seemed that way until now.'

Charlie nodded. 'We'll keep an eye on him. I know you're doing the dog walk rota, but I'm sure there's more we can do to support him.'

I tried to pull myself together. 'Thanks, Charlie, that's very sweet of you. But you shouldn't be worrying about it. He's not your responsibility.'

He frowned. 'I don't think Arthur would like being referred to as a "responsibility".'

'You know what I mean,' I snapped. I knew I was being unreasonable, that he was only trying to help, but my worry about Granddad was making me lash out. Charlie just happened to be the person on the receiving end.

'You don't have to carry everything on your shoulders, you know, Freya,' said Charlie quietly, refusing to rise to the bait. 'From The Rules to your "to-do" lists, I know you like to be in control. But there are some things that can't be controlled. And with those, you just have to do your best to react in whatever way seems most feasible at the time.'

'Yeah, yeah, I know. "Give me the wisdom to know the difference between those things I can change and those I can't," yadda yadda. It's all well and good in theory, but it's a lot harder in practice.'

I stomped back upstairs to the bathroom to continue taking my frustration out on the fixtures and fittings by scrubbing them to within an inch of their life. Since when had Charlie become a master of Zen?

Eventually I sat back on my heels and surveyed my handiwork. The avocado of the suite was now shining in its full glory, and although the flooring desperately needed replacing, it was now at least free of debris. I was confident that neither of us would be risking our health by washing in here. I only hoped the division of labour for the rest of our renovation wasn't going to continue like this.

But when I got downstairs, I realised what Charlie had spent the last couple of hours doing instead of helping in the bathroom. My air bed had been set up in the living room, and this time it had actual air in it. My sleeping bag and pillow were laid on top, and after a hard day of both physical labour and emotional strain, the makeshift bed looked extremely inviting.

There was no sign, however, of Charlie. I wandered into the dining room, holding my breath in preparation for its pungent smell, but the windows had been opened and the fresh air filtering into the room was definitely making a difference. Finally, I ventured outside and discovered Charlie inspecting the outbuilding.

'There you are. You might like to know that the bathroom is no longer a health hazard,' I said.

'Nice one. I thought as you had such a good system going, I'd be better off leaving you to it. But I haven't been idle in the meantime, I promise.'

'Yes, thanks for sorting out my bed. How did you manage it? Does that mean the electricity is working?'

'I took a look at the fusebox, but a look was all I dared. It's like when I kick the tyres of my car to pretend I'm knowledgeable about vehicles. I'm afraid I don't have the first clue about what I'm doing, and electrics, along with car engines, are things best left to the professionals.'

'So the air bed?'

'As I've been told by my sister many times, I'm full of hot air. While you were doing battle with the bathroom, I was blowing the thing up like a balloon. You're welcome.'

He pretended to bow.

'Blimey, Charlie, you really must be full of hot air to

have managed that. I appreciate it. Did you manage to do your own?'

'My sleeping arrangements are all sorted,' he said, neatly swerving the question. 'I felt guilty that I was responsible for the unwanted air conditioning that your room now has, so I thought it was best to sort out the living room for you.'

'Speaking of unwanted air conditioning, what are we going to do about the hole in the wall? Never mind the draught, I would have thought it would invalidate our insurance.'

'I highly doubt any burglar is going to be committed enough to clamber up the side of the building and try to get in through your bedroom window.'

'Stranger things have happened. But seriously, we need to find a way of blocking it up until we can get new windows fitted.'

Charlie nodded. 'Let's see what we can come up with.'

What we came up with was a makeshift shutter made up of several flattened cardboard boxes held in place by a vast quantity of gaffer tape.

I sat back on my haunches and surveyed the result.

'I'm not sure it really adds to the aesthetic of the room, but I guess it'll do the trick for the time being. Let's hope it doesn't rain any time soon.'

Chapter Twelve

I was dragged from deep sleep at an unreasonably early hour by the sound of someone thudding on the front door. I buried my face in my pillow, trying to tell myself the noise was another one of the orchestra of sounds which the house seemed to be permanently producing, as the beams creaked and the walls sighed in tune with the wind outside. Every muscle in my body felt stiff after yesterday's hard work, and that had only been the start of it. It was too much to contemplate. Just five more minutes in bed, and then I'd face the day, I told myself. But the rhythmic banging persisted and as there was no responding clatter of Charlie coming down the stairs to answer the door, I groaned and got up to do it myself.

After running my fingers through my hair to try to look vaguely respectable, I managed to heave the front door open a couple of inches. Perversely it seemed to be getting stiffer rather than easing with use, which seemed to be typical of Oak Tree Cottage's eccentricity. I stuck my head through the gap and hoped that I didn't appear rude by not being able to emerge fully.

'Good morning, good morning, welcome to the village,' said a smiling woman on the doorstep. She held her hand out. 'I'm Sheila, one of your new neighbours. Well, almost neighbours. We're down the road, but I reckon that still counts, as Oak Tree Cottage is rather out on a limb.'

'Hi, Sheila, lovely to meet you. I'm Freya.' I managed to yank the door open a little further so that I could get my arm through the gap and shake her hand. I was touched that she'd made the effort to visit. In all my years of renting in the city, I'd never really graduated beyond being on nodding terms with the neighbours. I found myself feeling unaccountably nervous, wanting to make a good first impression.

'And I'm Charlie,' said the man himself as he appeared behind me, irritatingly looking far more rested than I felt. But then again, I had done the lion's share of the bathroom clearing yesterday. He reached over my shoulder so he could shake Sheila's hand too.

She beamed in delight. 'How lovely, a nice young couple moving into the village.'

'We're not...' I started to say, then fell silent as Charlie nudged the back of my foot.

'Do you happen to know mortgage broker Philip Andrews?' he asked.

Sheila looked confused. 'I don't think so.'

I felt Charlie's shoulders relax. 'He was full of praise for this village when he was helping us,' he said, smoothly covering the real reason for his question. 'Freya and I are actually old friends who decided to do the place up together.'

'What an exciting project to undertake,' said Sheila. 'We're all so pleased that someone is finally going to show some love to the cottage. Now I'm sure you must have plenty to keep you occupied, but as well as introducing myself, I wanted to invite you both along to the village Easter egg hunt today. It's a little early, of course, but the children get so excited about it that we thought we'd do it at the beginning of the school holidays so they didn't have to wait.'

'We do have rather a lot to do,' I said as Charlie simultaneously answered, 'We'd love to come along.'

Sheila looked pleased. 'Excellent. Or should I say, *egg*-cellent. Right, it kicks off at eleven a.m., here's a leaflet with all the information on, and we'll see you there. Everyone is so excited to meet you.'

'We're *egg*-cited too,' said Charlie, which earned him an elbow in the ribs.

Sheila chuckled with delight. 'We'll have you on the village hall committee in no time; just what this area needs, some new blood. See you later,' she trilled. We waved through the gap in the door as she sashayed off, and then we managed to shut it once again by some joint brute force.

'Without wishing to sound horribly anti-social, why did you agree to us going to the Easter egg hunt?' I asked. 'I'm sure it'll be lovely, but it sounds like it's really aimed at the village children, plus we have so much to do. We can't afford to waste a second. It will completely disrupt the schedule of work for today.'

'Is that so very bad?' said Charlie. 'Relax, be spontaneous for once.'

'I used up my quota of spontaneity when I was persuaded to buy this wreck,' I retorted. 'Please don't force me into having to be the boring one, but we really need to keep our focus. Sheila was very kind to invite us to join in, but we've both got enough on our plate trying to juggle our jobs and tackling this place. The Easter holidays will be over before we know it and once I'm back at school, there'll only be so much restoration work I'll have time to do.'

Charlie shrugged. 'It might be fun. It will help us become part of the local community.'

'I hate to say it, but we're not here to become part of the local community. It's not fair to them if we get involved in village life when we know we're not staying here long term.'

'Don't you think you might be overthinking it somewhat?' said Charlie. 'It's only an Easter egg hunt.'

'An Easter egg hunt today, village hall committee tomorrow, you heard what Sheila said.'

I knew I sounded cold and uncaring, but one of us had to be sensible and think of the bigger picture. Charlie seemed to be getting carried away at playing house.

'How about we compromise? Let's see how much we get done before eleven, and then make a decision,' said Charlie.

'Fine,' I said. 'But don't blame me if we get to Christmas and we're still living in a building site.'

Inevitably eleven o'clock came round and I found myself walking along the main street to the village green accompanied by Charlie, who'd decided it would be fun to dress up as the Easter bunny in a bright pink onesie with a pair of cardboard ears. There was no chance of keeping a low profile while he was around. Under protest, I'd allowed him to draw some whiskers on my face with eyeliner. While he somehow managed to pull off his look with aplomb, I was pretty convinced that I looked ridiculous. I took a deep breath and told myself to try and loosen up. If Charlie could look so relaxed walking around in public in a fluffy onesie, then I could cope with saying hello to a few of the neighbours while sporting a very bad attempt at face paint.

'I'm so glad you could come along. Let me introduce you to everyone,' said Sheila, swooping down on us as soon as we arrived at the village green. The whole area was decked out in pastel-coloured bunting and, despite the chilly weather, a large crowd was gathering. There were a couple of stalls selling hot drinks and a barbeque with a cloud of black smoke above it. Children were running around playing chase as a harassed-looking person dressed as an Easter chick tried to call them to order through a megaphone. For one horrible moment, I thought Sheila was going to seize it so she could follow through on her promise to introduce us to literally everyone. Fortunately she decided to take a more personal approach, parading us around the crowd like a proud parent. Charlie was in his element, laughing and joking, while I desperately tried to keep track of everyone's names. We received a very warm welcome, although it was worrying how many of them pulled shocked faces when we said we'd bought Oak Tree Cottage. At some point during the introductions, we got separated, and I was left alone to field questions about our plans. I knew people were trying to be helpful by telling me all about their decorating experiences, but I wished they had a few more positive tales to relay rather than the horror stories they treated me to. I did not feel confident enough in my decision to be constantly defending it to strangers. Eventually I managed to sneak away to a quiet area behind the food stands and rang Leila.

'Hello, stranger, missing me already?' she answered cheerily. I pictured her lounging around in her neat little flat with its central heating and functioning electricity and wished for the fifty millionth time that I'd stood my ground about staying elsewhere while we did the renovations.

'Of course. And I'm harbouring some serious nostalgia for your luxuriously comfortable sofa bed.'

'My flat is always there waiting for you if you need a retreat.'

'Be careful, I might take you up on that offer.'

'Already? I thought you'd be in the blissful honeymoon phase of house ownership?'

'That wore off as quickly as the effect of the champagne

the estate agent gave us. There is nothing blissful about Oak Tree Cottage, and if Charlie has anything to do with it, it's going to stay that way.' I quickly explained about the village Easter egg hunt and the well-intentioned but ultimately unhelpful comments from my new neighbours. 'I feel like I've got on a rollercoaster and I don't know how long the ride is going to last, and whether it's actually safe.'

'My advice to you is to try to enjoy the journey, and not beat yourself up if you're not spending every minute of every day working on the house. You'll get it done eventually. There's no point in giving yourself a breakdown in the process.'

'You know me too well. I just can't help worrying when I think of how big a challenge we've taken on. And I don't want to end up bossing Charlie around, but he seems way more chilled out about the whole thing than I can manage. I'm finding it rather frustrating, if I'm being honest.'

'Your work ethic is always something I've admired, hon, but consider this your permission slip to cut yourself a little slack. Let Charlie pull his weight in his own way. That's what you've got The Rules for, right? You might have different approaches, but you have the same goal, and I have faith that you'll achieve it. Now why don't you go and find yourself a coffee, and enjoy being part of village life?'

With Leila's pep talk ringing in my ears, I picked up a couple of drinks and tracked down Charlie. At least the luminous onesie made him easy to find.

'Freya, there you are,' he bounced over, full of enthusiasm. 'Shame you missed the fun but don't worry,

I've saved you an Easter egg. They got enough for the adults as well as the children. By the way, I thought you'd be pleased to know I've volunteered to help out with the village hall social media accounts in exchange for some help from Sheila's husband Frank, who's apparently a dab hand at tiling.'

'Oh, thank you,' I said, recalling Leila's advice. 'Chocolate and a friendly craftsman. You were right, it was worth coming along after all.'

Charlie waggled his bunny ears. 'Ye of little faith. Trust me, there's always method in my madness.'

Chapter Thirteen

The remaining days of the Easter holidays were spent on solid labour, to the point where I was actually looking forward to going back to work at school because, in comparison, it would seem like a break. The first skip was full of detritus within three days, and we were well on our way to filling its replacement, Charlie having rung Granddad's contact and managed to persuade them to come out more quickly than they normally would. But no matter how many things I tore down and threw out, it seemed that there were still countless more in their place, and my to-do list was growing terrifying long with tasks I would never have thought existed when I first drew it up.

As term time grew closer, I had to balance renovation with preparing lessons, and my forehead started to develop a permanent dent from the head torch I wore to carry out my work in the evening, much to Charlie's amusement.

We'd agreed to leave the electrics to the professionals, but it turned out that the professionals in this area were in such demand that they had a waiting list, and it would be three weeks before they'd be able to come out to provide a quote, even though Charlie's village hall contacts had tried to pull some strings for us. The spring evenings were gradually growing lighter, at least, but I would greatly have preferred not having to live as if I was in an historical re-enactment. I was nervous of using candles in case we set the place on fire, and even the most powerful battery lamps still made my eyes ache by the end of the night.

And although we'd managed to work out how to turn the water on, it was still running cold, despite our best efforts. I'd mastered the art of the two-minute shower, but I was yet to manage it without yelping in pain at the sheer cold. The first night Charlie had come charging upstairs, thinking something had fallen on me. Thankfully I'd managed to convey the real reason for the noise before he'd thundered into the room in full-on saviour mode. He teased me about it for all of an hour until he tried the shower himself, after which he fell suspiciously quiet on the topic.

Unfortunately, Charlie was so good at not making a noise in the freezing shower that one day I barged in while he was mid-wash.

'Oh heck, sorry, Charlie,' I said, quickly covering my eyes, but not quickly enough to wipe the image of his chest glistening with water, plus the rest of his unexpectedly attractive physique, which was already imprinted on my brain. I swallowed, my mouth suddenly dry.

'Did you want something?' asked Charlie. 'Can you chuck a towel over?'

I groped around, my hand still covering my eyes, until I found one and threw it in what I hoped was the right direction. There was a pause, then the shower stopped.

'You can open your eyes, I'm decent now,' he said. 'What were you after?'

'Erm, I...' I stammered, trying to reboot my mind back into sensible mode, and keeping my eyes firmly shut. Why were my thoughts running in such an unexpected direction? It was disconcerting to be seeing my old friend in *that* way.

'Freya? Are you going down with something? You're looking awfully pink,' said Charlie, a note of amusement in his voice. I knew he was teasing me, but I hoped his powers of perception hadn't been up to detecting my increased heart rate.

'I'm fine,' I squeaked. But sorting out the Jack and Jill bathroom arrangement had definitely risen up my priority list. Either that or fixing locks to both of the doors. I backed out of the room, feeling my way out with one hand while the other stayed safely in position over my eyes, Charlie's low rumble of laughter ringing in my ears.

But the bathroom situation soon reared its head again. It was two days until the new term was due to start, and I was tired, filthy and aching all over after being up since dawn pulling up the carpet in the kitchen. It was a particularly stubborn beast, held in place by rows of grippers with lethal spikes, and a fair amount of glue besides. In other words, the reality of dealing with it bore no resemblance to the YouTube tutorial which I'd carefully studied. The smiley American lady, who incidentally remained unnaturally pristine throughout her DIY tasks, with not a single one of her manicured nails broken or chipped, had pulled the demo carpet up with ease, reassuring viewers with a cheery double thumbs-up followed by 'This literally works every time, I promise.' The fact that she hadn't even broken a sweat had filled me with confidence, which turned out to be seriously misguided, leaving me wondering where I'd gone wrong. But then again, the smiley American would probably have been a whole lot less smiley if she'd encountered the stubborn decor of Oak Tree Cottage. Every time I thought I was starting to get somewhere, I'd discover another gluey patch and have to set to with the chisel.

Charlie meanwhile had been focusing on the walls, scraping away layer upon layer of wallpaper in an attempt to get back to the original plaster. His technique was far removed from the step-by-step guide I'd found online and sent him, but even with his haphazard non-system, he'd managed to get rid of so much gunk from the walls I swear we'd gained several more inches of space. He was doing his usual trick of darting here, there and everywhere around the room, deciding that another section of wall looked much easier than the one he was working on, then just as quickly changing his mind, but I wasn't going to complain. He seemed to be making better progress than I was with the wretched carpet, even if I was being much more methodical and precise in my approach.

I leaned back on my haunches and surveyed the mess surrounding us, still marvelling at how we were managing to make things look so much worse than they had been.

'I hate to admit it, but I think the carpet has defeated me for the day. What I want more than anything in the whole wide world is to sink into a hot bath,' I said, kneading the small of my back in a futile bid to stop it throbbing.

'I didn't like to say, but…' said Charlie, letting his words tail off and pinching his nose as if he could smell something horrible.

'Thanks a lot. You're pretty pungent yourself.'

'The scent of a real man,' said Charlie, flexing his muscles like a bodybuilder in a contest. The effect was somewhat spoilt by the fact that he was wearing a white boiler suit that made him look like a Bond villain's hopeless lackey, and he had a giant cobweb in his hair.

I tossed a tatty chunk of carpet in his direction, which he deftly caught in one hand and bowled right back at me, catching me squarely on the shoulder. A cloud of dust sprayed over my dungarees, adding to the patina of grime already covering the denim.

I pretended to cough, even though my nose and mouth were safely protected by the industrial-strength mask I was sporting.

Charlie's gleeful expression immediately turned to one of remorse.

'Sorry, Freya, that was thoughtless of me. Do you need

your inhaler?' He was already moving across the room towards it.

'Fear not, nothing dodgy is going to get through this thing.' I unhooked the mask and took the welcome opportunity to scratch my nose.

Charlie started laughing.

'What? Do I have something on my face?' I said, patting my skin and wondering what was tickling him.

'Just a very clear tide mark between where your skin has been covered by the mask and where it hasn't. As I haven't been wearing a mask, I'm sure my entire face is filthy.'

'Now I want a hot bath even more. Even the showers in the changing rooms at school would seem like a welcome prospect at the moment.'

Charlie checked his watch. 'It's going to be getting dark before too much longer, so I think we can legitimately call it a day. Tell you what, why don't we boil some water on the camping stove so we can have that hot bath of your dreams?'

I raised an eyebrow, the image of Charlie in the shower making a reappearance in my mind's eye.

'Separately, of course,' he added hastily. 'Not sure we should risk two of us in a full bath. It would probably go through the floor.' There was a wicked sparkle in his eyes. I knew I was being teased, but I still felt I had to say something, in case he could somehow read the inappropriate thought I'd just had.

'And shared baths are most definitely not in The Rules.'

'Of course. The Rules must be obeyed.' He clicked his heels together and sketched a mock salute in my direction.

I rolled my eyes. 'Once we have walls that aren't covered in hideous decorations, I'm going to frame a copy of The Rules and hang them up.'

Charlie grinned. 'I'll look forward to it. Doesn't mean I'll promise to follow them.' He held his hand up to stop the interruption he knew I was about to make. 'Only joking. Now, do you want to help me fill some buckets?'

'Without wishing to be the party pooper, let's not bother. I'm not sure I've got enough energy. We both know that it would take most of the night to boil enough water to get anything approximating a warm bath, and I have no idea how we'd balance buckets over the fire. I should have paid more attention at Girl Guides. No, I've resigned myself to another cold shower. It's meant to be good for the circulation after all. Don't the Scandinavians swear by cold water immersion?'

'They do, but they also bookend it by getting up a sweat in a sauna. Now you've mentioned the idea of a hot bath, it's all I can think about. Do you think Leila would let us use her bathroom for a wallow?' asked Charlie.

'Well, she did mention I had an open invitation to drop round whenever I like. And I'm sure she'd extend the invitation to you too. But it's a bit much to turn up on a Saturday evening and suddenly demand to use up all her hot water. What are you doing?'

Charlie had picked up my mobile and looked like he was about to tap out a message.

'Oi, nosy parker, let go of my phone. If you imagine I'm telling you the passcode, think again, mister,' I said, sending the clump of carpet spinning back towards him again.

He managed to catch it without even looking up, surprising himself.

'Hey, did you see that? I bet if we tried fifty times over I'd never be able to manage that again. We should start a double act.'

'Stop trying to distract me. Give me my phone back.'

'Make me,' he said, his grin growing wider than ever. 'I reckon I could guess your passcode. Never mind texting Leila about using her bath, how about your lovely boss Mr Rhys? I bet he has bathrooms galore. I'm sure he'd be delighted to share his facilities with his best member of staff.'

Typical Charlie, always a compliment hidden amongst the teasing. But I wasn't prepared to risk him actually following through on his threat, even though I was ninety-nine per cent sure that this was another one of his jokes. I hurried across the room and grabbed him round the waist while he held the phone up high.

'At least put some effort in, Hutch,' he said, holding it out of my reach with some considerable effort. 'Do you think Mr Rhys will lend me a dressing gown? What style do you think he goes for? Maybe a Hugh Hefner silk look?'

I pretended to vomit, which of course made him laugh even more, loving getting a rise out of me. I decided I might as well play along seeing as he was determined that we were going to regress to primary school levels of behaviour.

'You asked for it.' I let go of his waist and then started tickling him beneath his right armpit, remembering how it used to send eleven-year-old Charlie into paroxysms. It turned out grown-up Charlie was equally vulnerable to attack there. He tried to squirm out of the way, but I was determined to be as relentless as he had been in teasing me. Eventually he managed to wriggle out of my grip, both of us crying with laughter. It felt good to be letting loose after days of hard labour and worry.

'Okay, okay, I surrender,' said Charlie eventually. 'Have the phone back. Mr Rhys is a definite no-no, I accept that now. But how about you swallow your pride and message Leila? She wouldn't have given an open invitation if she didn't mean it.'

'I still think it's a bit unfair on her. She'll probably have Nim over. The last thing she'll want is us two getting in the way and tramping filthy footprints all over her immaculate flat.'

'Stop making excuses. She's your friend, and she'll be delighted to help. Stop thinking you're not worthy of being helped out by a mate. Grab some clean clothes. Like the ancient Romans, we're going to the bathhouse, aka Leila's flat.'

Charlie scrunched up the clump of carpet I'd used as my original weapon and shoved it in the bin pile, then beckoned me to follow him.

'You're not being serious?' I asked, as he took his car keys off the plyboard worksurface.

'I never joke about hot baths. You can text her on the

way. Besides, I'm doing this for purely selfish reasons. I'm hoping once you've finished in the bath, she'll let me jump in too. Once it's full of fresh hot water, obviously. I dread to think how scuzzy the water will be once you've finished with it.'

'Fine, I give up. If you absolutely insist. But I still think we're being a bit unfair inviting ourselves around like this.'

'Stop being a martyr to the renovation. We're in this for the long haul. I don't see why we can't treat ourselves every now and then.'

I nodded, already imagining the wonderful sensation of sinking into hot, floral-scented bubbles. I sent Leila a brief begging message to which she thankfully replied with a yes in capital letters and lots of exclamation marks, then grabbed a clean set of underwear, some jeans and a top, none of which were the kind of thing I'd wear for house transformation, and joined Charlie on the driveway where he was coaxing the Land Rover to life.

Even sitting in the ancient vehicle with the noisy heater on seemed like the greatest luxury compared to how we'd been roughing it over the last few days. As we whizzed towards Leila's I looked longingly at the other houses, houses that weren't falling to pieces like ours. I realised that since we'd moved in I'd not set foot beyond the boundaries of the village, which perhaps was why I'd been starting to forget that a world existed beyond the tumbledown walls of Oak Tree Cottage.

'We'll get there eventually,' said Charlie, somehow

knowing exactly what was going through my mind. 'We can't expect to do a complete transformation in the two weeks of the Easter holidays.'

'I know that. But I fear I may have underestimated the scale of the challenge, despite my colour-coded list of tasks. I'm already worrying about how I'm going to cope when I go back to school. It's all well and good joking about managing with cold showers and cooking on a camping stove, but it's going to be a lot harder when I'm trying to juggle all that with marking, lesson prep and the renovations, plus it'll be exam term, and the pressure is always even bigger then.'

'If it makes you feel any better, I'm worried about keeping my business going while we're doing all this building work. And I won't have a lovely warm school building to escape to.'

I glanced across at Charlie. 'That doesn't make me feel better. In fact, it makes me feel a whole lot worse. I've been too busy focusing on myself, without considering the impact on you. Sorry, I'm a rubbish house partner.'

'No, you misunderstand me. I didn't say it because I was looking for sympathy. And you're anything but a rubbish house partner. You're the perfect house partner because you have a friend who's prepared to let us descend on her and use all her hot water.' He glanced away from the road for the briefest of seconds to send another of his annoying grins in my direction. 'But seriously, we're in this together, and the only way we're going to get through this is together.

We're both going to have wobbly moments. The important thing is that we keep on talking about them, that way we can get each other through them. And if that's not in The Rules, then it should be added immediately.'

'That and the need for a hot bath at least once a week.'

'That sounds like a subsection I could definitely go along with. Right, you'll have to direct me from here.'

I navigated Charlie through the final few streets and then we pulled up in front of Leila's flat. She was waiting for us by the front door with a pair of very large bath towels.

'Blimey, have you travelled straight from a war zone?' she said. 'There's the artfully rumpled look, and then there's looking in a proper state, and I'm afraid you two are most definitely the latter. If the neighbours see you, they're going to think I'm taking in a pair of rough sleepers.'

'Thanks, Leila, lovely to see you too. And rough sleepers is a pretty accurate description of us. Right, Charlie, are we going to Rock, Paper, Scissors for who gets first dibs on the bath?'

'Ladies first,' said Charlie.

'In this instance, I will forgo my feminist principles and accept that offer without argument. And I'm afraid I'm not going to hurry, so maybe if Leila puts some newspaper down on the sofa, you can sit on it and wait for me.'

'You could always share the bath,' said Leila.

'Don't you start too,' I said as I hurried past her.

'Interesting,' she said, looking from me to Charlie with a

curious expression on her face. I hesitated by the bathroom door, knowing that I was probably abandoning Charlie to an interrogation Leila-style. But the siren call of the hot water was too strong. If Charlie could navigate the treacherous environment of social media for a living, then he'd be able to withstand Leila. Probably.

I must have put half a bottle of bubble bath in, and I barely turned on the cold tap, while the hot water thundered out like a thing of beauty. I had a quick pre-wash in the shower, a sensible decision given the colour of the water which went down the drain, and then I closed my eyes and sank into the bubbles so only my nostrils were above the water line.

No less than an hour later, I emerged from the bathroom, circulation restored and skin glowing, feeling like an actual human being for the first time in nearly two weeks.

Charlie did a double-take. 'Hello, and who are you? I don't suppose you happen to have seen my housemate, Freya? She's about yay high, pretty grimy and is a dab hand at chucking stuff in a skip.'

'Back off, Charlie, you're not coming anywhere near me while you're still covered in gunk. Off you go, enjoy your bath. If there's any hot water left…'

He pretended to lunge towards me, reaching out his grubby hands, before he made a swift U-turn and disappeared into the bathroom, still laughing.

'You two seem to be getting on very well,' said Leila, her tone loaded.

'What do you mean by that? Do you mind if I put the kettle on, by the way? I want to enjoy the luxury of being able to plug something in and watch it miraculously heat up water, rather than having to light a match and do battle with a camping stove.'

'Be my guest. And I don't mean anything. Just making a passing comment that you seem to be very friendly with each other. If it was anyone other than Charlie, I would almost say you were flirting.'

'We are most definitely not flirting. We're sharing a house. It helps that we've picked up our friendship from where we left off. He may be utterly infuriating at times, but he's practically a brother to me.'

'Remind me of how that goes in that Jane Austen book. *Emma*, is it?' Leila had a worryingly gleeful expression on her face which I refused to rise to. When I remained stubbornly silent she shrugged. 'Well, I'm glad things are going well. Neither at the killing nor the kissing stage. Yet. I'm proud of you. And how is Oak Tree Cottage?'

'Full of character. By which I mean reducing my life expectancy by about a year with every additional problem we find. But we'll get there eventually. Or so I keep telling myself. And of course, Charlie and I aren't going to kill each other. Or kiss, for that matter.' I knew Leila had only said it to provoke me, but I still felt the need to correct her very misguided assumption. Just because she was all loved up with Nim now, it didn't mean the rest of the world had to conform to her rosy-tinted life-is-one-big-romance point of view.

'Who's getting a kiss?' said Charlie, emerging from the bathroom a whole lot quicker than I'd expected and at precisely the wrong time.

'Nobody,' I said, as Leila started laughing.

Chapter Fourteen

'Right, what's next on the renovation to-do list?' asked Charlie, rubbing his hands together and looking at me expectantly. 'We might as well make the most of our final day of freedom before real life beckons again.'

'I thought I'd tackle the front steps,' I said. 'I've been reading up on some masonry techniques and Granddad's talked me through it, so I'm hoping for the best.'

He looked at me with admiration. 'That's brave.'

'Thanks for the vote of confidence, Charlie. It's actually a cowardly move because if I mess up filling in the holes in the front steps and putting new slabs down, then it's not the end of the world, whereas if I go wrong with strengthening the actual staircase inside the house, it will cause us a whole heap of problems. Filling in and replacing stonework is a simpler proposition than tackling actual woodwork. Studying carpentry techniques is next on my training schedule, although I'm hoping the stairs will hold out for a while so we don't have to tackle them for a few months.'

'You're the DIY wonder woman,' he said, watching as I set out my tools. 'You quite put me to shame with your skills. We're both willing to have a go, but of the two of us, you're definitely much more effective in your work.'

'You'll get there, if you knuckle down to it,' I said, not able to resist a slight dig at his chaotic approach to renovation.

Charlie looked around him, as if searching for inspiration. To be fair to him, there was so much to do, it was hard to know where to focus attention. 'I'm not sure there's enough room for me to try and help you. What's on the list for me?' he asked. 'I'm afraid I lost the copy you gave me.'

I forced myself to count to ten, a technique I'd usually employ in the classroom when faced with a particularly challenging pupil. 'You lost the list,' I repeated quietly.

'Yes,' he said.

'And what do you expect me to do about that?' I asked.

'Could you print off another copy?' he asked, with a smile. 'You put it together on your laptop. And I know what you're like, you'll have it saved somewhere in a folder carefully labelled 'House tasks' or similar.'

He was annoyingly accurate there.

'I don't think the list is the issue here, Charlie,' I said, walking away from him, disappointed that he couldn't see it for himself.

I settled myself down at the front steps, levered up the

crumbling slabs and scraped away the dirt and detritus that lay under them. Once I had created a smooth, clean surface I turned my attention back to the slabs, trying to work out which ones were salvageable. When I was part-way through mixing some cement to fix them back in position, Charlie hove back into view and cleared his throat to get my attention.

'You're looking sheepish,' I said, as I glanced up. 'You've got that expression on your face that used to appear when you pretended there was no chocolate left, but you'd actually stuffed the last piece in your mouth.'

'I could have my moments of being a selfish little so-and-so,' he said, with a wry grin. 'But unfortunately, perhaps I haven't changed as much as I thought I had.'

I rested on my haunches, and waited for him to continue.

'I've come to apologise,' he said. 'You're right, the list isn't the issue. We're house partners, emphasis on the word 'partner'. My books are still packed up in boxes, but I don't need my dictionary to know what that word means. We should be equals in this enterprise we've undertaken, and yet I'm falling into the habit of letting you bear the bulk of the burden by making you tell me what to do. I'm here to say that I've seen the error of my ways. I don't need your lists, Freya, and I don't want you to feel that you have to create them. We're in this together, and I promise that from now on, I will take the initiative and try harder. Although I can't promise that my efforts will be as successful as yours.'

'As long as we're both pulling our weight, that's all that

matters,' I said. He was talking the talk, but I would reserve judgment until he followed through.

'As per The Rules,' added Charlie, with a grin. 'Now let me have a go at finishing mixing that cement while you have a break. No point in you returning completely exhausted to face the kids at school. At least if I have to take a power nap during my working day, nobody is going to call me out on it.'

Between us, we spent the rest of the day working on the steps. And when I went to bed that night, I found a handwritten note on my pillow, a copy of the list of work that Charlie had compiled for himself. There was a smiley face at the bottom of it, and a rough sketch of a man and a woman juggling a bunch of work tools between them. I rolled my eyes at the childish image and scrunched the paper up, ready to throw it into the recycling. But something made me hesitate, and I found myself smoothing the paper out again and sticking it between the pages of my book.

The next morning, I experienced a pang of house separation anxiety while I was getting myself ready for work.

'Do you need some help fixing a packed lunch?' said Charlie as I whizzed around the kitchen, trying to avoid touching any of the surfaces now I was wearing my work clothes. It felt weird to be back in my trouser suit instead of my renovation uniform of ancient dungarees and a scarf wrapped around my hair.

'Kind of you to ask, but I get lunch courtesy of school. Perk of the job. And if I was doing a packed lunch, I would definitely have made it last night.'

'Of course you would have, Little Miss Organised. Well, have a good day at work, dear, and I'll see you later,' said Charlie, putting on the clipped tones of a posh 1950s housewife.

'Thank you, I'll look forward to my tea waiting for me on the table when I get in,' I said, pretending to adjust an invisible tie. Then I dropped the act. 'Seriously though, Charlie, are you sure you're going to be okay working from here today? I know it's your first day back with your normal workload, and it's not exactly going to be a comfortable working environment. We've got humane mousetraps all over the place, and it's still more like camping than anything else. Do you think you might be better off going to the local library?'

Charlie tapped the dongle which was now supplying us with broadband. 'Have Wi-Fi, can work. Besides, why would I go elsewhere when I have a home of my own to work from?'

'But there's no electricity, and only a camping chair for you to sit in.'

'Ah, but I have a power pack, and the camping chair is perfect for what I've got planned. I thought I'd sit out in the garden for a bit, make the most of the daylight. Lovely day for it.'

I peered out of the window. 'Hmm, the weather looks a bit dubious for that. And I know it's technically the summer term now, but I'm not sure the temperature has got the message about that.'

'You worry too much, I'll be fine.' He checked his watch. 'And hadn't you better run? The bus is due in less than ten minutes, which I know in Freya-time means that you're running late. Have a lovely day at school, and I'll see you later.'

It was good to be back at work, talking to people about topics other than renovation tasks, and doing nothing more physically strenuous than standing at the front of my classroom and writing on the whiteboard. But between lessons, my thoughts kept on drifting back to Oak Tree Cottage, wondering how Charlie was feeling being there by himself and whether he was managing to get the work done that he wanted to. And when, just after midday, the heavens opened, it wasn't just Charlie's work that I was worrying about. Despite it being April, a month notorious for showers, it was the first time it had actually rained since we moved in. The surveyor's report had claimed the roof was mostly sound, but what if it wasn't? I couldn't bear the thought of water pouring in, messing up the bathroom which I'd spent so many hours cleaning, and destroying all the tools and equipment we had in the house. And the space that used to be a window in my bedroom was still covered by nothing more substantial than cardboard, which would probably be turning to mush in this weather. I had visions of the rain moving in sideways, destroying the cardboard and then soaking its way through the floorboards down into the living room, seeping into the boxes of my worldly possessions that were lined up in there.

As my Year Nines settled into reading the next chapter of their textbook, I surreptitiously texted Charlie from under my desk, needing some reassurance that Oak Tree Cottage wasn't falling down around his head. But no reply came, and I couldn't even tell if he'd read the message. I told myself that he was probably busy doing his day job, but I couldn't help worrying there was some deeper meaning behind his failure to reply, my overactive imagination telling me that the house was flooding, or, worse, that the ceiling had fallen in, leaving Charlie trapped in the wreckage. I knew I was being ridiculous, jumping to conclusions and being paranoid, but his radio silence did concern me. It wasn't like he was obliged to reply to me, but he was normally very good at communicating, even if it was in the form of silly gifs and memes that he thought I'd find funny. This delay in response wasn't like him, and it fuelled my niggling anxiety that something awful had occurred.

When the bell rang for breaktime, I decided to make a beeline for the staffroom so I could phone him, but Mr Rhys pounced on me as soon as I emerged from my classroom.

'Miss Hutchinson, can we have a little chat?'

'Umm, right now?' I said, still itching to call Charlie for

a status check. Normally I wouldn't dare cross Mr Rhys, but by now I was imagining the whole house in rubble, Charlie pinioned beneath a ceiling joist, desperately calling for help but nobody hearing his cries. The last thing I wanted to do was have to negotiate a challenging conversation with my boss. Nothing good ever came out of an invitation for a 'little chat'.

'Yes, of course right now. Do you have anywhere else you should be?' He frowned at me in a manner that would normally have me bracing myself in trepidation, if my anxiety levels weren't already peaking because of my worries about Charlie and the house.

'No, of course not,' I said, pulling myself together with some effort. 'Sorry, how can I help?'

It turned out that Mr Rhys's urgent need for a chat was to make the surprise announcement that he was planning to take early retirement at the end of the next school year. Not only that, he informed me that he was telling me this before everyone else so I'd have more time to put in an application for the job he would be leaving. I gaped in astonishment. I had barely allowed myself to dream about becoming a Deputy Head of Department, let alone the actual Head of History. And for Mr Rhys to be suggesting it to me was an even more unexpected turn of events.

'I think you'd stand a good chance, Miss Hutchinson,' he said. I experienced a warm glow of pride at the unexpected praise. Maybe all my hard work hadn't gone unnoticed after all. Maybe I really was good enough to go for the job. 'After all, given that you have significantly less experience than me, your wage expectations would be much lower and you'd be better value for the school,' he added, immediately crushing the seedling of hope that had started to sprout.

And then I felt my phone buzz in my pocket. Hopefully it was Charlie finally getting back to me with a house update.

'So, you'll think about it, Miss Hutchinson?' pressed Mr Rhys.

'I uh...' I hesitated, not sure how to respond. It would have been a lot to think about even without the work at Oak Tree Cottage to factor in.

'The interviews will be held at some point in the autumn term, but as is always the way with these things, those in charge of making the decision will be watching the behaviour of any potential internal candidates most carefully from now onwards. And of course, my opinion will count for a lot.' He checked his watch. 'Right, I'm off to a meeting with a parent. By the way, the English Department needed some help clearing out the book room and moving everything into their new office. I said you'd be happy to oversee it. Have a good afternoon.'

'Thanks, you too, Mr Rhys,' I said, injecting as much positivity into my voice as possible to make up for the dilemma that was raging internally.

So, having moved house, I was now going to have to manage a move at work as well, while under the intense scrutiny of an interview panel for a job which I would apparently be perfect for because I was cheap. Brilliant.

I pretended to be heading to the English Department

office, but as soon as I got around the corner of the corridor, I fished my phone out of my pocket. Unfortunately, there was no reassuring message waiting for me from Charlie. Instead, there was a quote from the window fitters that gave me an instant headache. We were lucky that Oak Tree Cottage wasn't a listed building, with all the added rules and regulations to protect its appearance and structure, but we still wanted to do right by it, and that meant restoring it with the best-quality materials we could afford. The windows we wanted were exact replicas of the current ones, only in a much more durable material, and judging by this first quote, they were going to set us back a pretty penny.

I forwarded the message to Charlie, along with an entreaty to let me know that both he and the house were okay. Surely he'd respond to that? But my phone remained frustratingly silent throughout the afternoon, and when he still hadn't replied by the end of the day, I had pretty much decided that I wasn't being so paranoid after all. And despite knowing I should be on best behaviour given Mr Rhys's announcement, I persuaded Leila to pick up my after-school supervision, and hurried away from work as soon as the bell rang. And then I waited at the bus stop, stomach churning, fearful about what I would find at Oak Tree Cottage on my return.

Chapter Fifteen

I practically ran down the lane from the bus stop,
dodging puddles and trying to keep my umbrella from
blowing inside out, all the time wondering what would
confront me when I turned the corner. But thankfully the
house was still standing, although there was no sign of
Charlie's Land Rover on the drive. Perhaps he'd gone to the
local library to work after all, and that was the reason he'd
not replied to my messages. I felt relieved. I let myself in
through the back door and picked up my head torch from
the worksurface so I could see properly. Gingerly picking
my way through the piles of debris, I prowled around the
downstairs rooms, resting my hands on various surfaces to
check whether they were dry. And then I took a deep breath
and went upstairs, fearing that things would look very
different.

The stairs did their usual creaking and groaning trick as
I made my way up, and then I noticed another sound in the

173

mix, the distinctive clink of water dripping into a metal bucket. Okay, one bucket on the landing I could live with. But what if it was one of many? I inspected my bedroom and checked the seal on the window covering, but thankfully all was okay in there, and the bathroom was clear too. I hesitated on the threshold of Charlie's bedroom. It felt like an invasion of his privacy to go in there when he wasn't around. But then again, what if water was pouring in through a hole in the ceiling, ruining all his stuff? I took a deep breath and went in, silently apologising to my house partner. Fortunately, the room also seemed to be leak-free, but I was surprised to discover that his air bed was deflated. By the looks of things, he had been sleeping on a yoga mat on the floor. It didn't look exactly comfortable to me, but maybe Charlie preferred a firm surface. He'd made the room as homely as possible in the circumstances, with several framed pictures set up along the floor, perhaps anticipating their being displayed on the wall, once it was re-plastered and decorated.

There was one of Charlie's family, his parents looking proud, his older brothers laughing, his twin sister Alexa rolling her eyes at the person behind the camera, who I assumed must be Charlie himself. There was the scan of an old black and white photo of Oak Tree Cottage looking pristine, which Sheila had dug out of the village archive for us the day after the Easter egg hunt. I guessed the picture was there to serve as inspiration, reminding him what we were going through all this hassle for. And there was one final snap that I was surprised to see, a real blast from the past. The last time I'd seen a copy was in a photo album at my parents' house. It was of Charlie and me in our school uniform. We must have been barely five at the time, both of us looking slightly awkward and uncomfortable in our too-big uniform and shiny shoes, standing on the threshold of our classroom for the obligatory first-day photo. Charlie was gripping my hand like his life depended on it, his face slightly turning towards mine as if he was looking to me for reassurance.

Suddenly I was whisked back to that day, remembering how worried he'd been at being separated from his sister for the first time. They'd spent the whole of Nursery in the same class, and as twins they'd had an extra-special bond. My friend Charlie was a confident little boy, outgoing and full of fun, and I remembered how shocked I'd been to see him nearly in tears as his sister went one way down the school corridor and he'd had to go another without her. I'd promised him then that I'd look out for him, a normally shy little girl finding strength because she couldn't bear to see her friend in distress. He'd repaid that promise a dozen times over throughout our primary and junior school careers. And weren't we still looking out for each other now by buying this house together? I felt a surge of affection for my old friend, glad that we were by each other's side during this pivotal time.

But thinking of being by each other's side, where was Charlie and why hadn't he replied to my messages? It really wasn't like him to go incommunicado, unless something was wrong. I glanced out of his bedroom window, and that's when I spotted the collapsed roof of the outbuilding which was going to become his office. I'd walked straight past it when I'd got home from school, as the area where the roof had collapsed was at the back of the building, so it wouldn't have been obvious to the casual passer-by at ground level. But the view from above unfortunately gave all too stark a display of the destruction wrought by the heavy rain. One of the supporting beams had detached from the building. One end was sticking up towards where that section of the roof had been, while the other end was buried in a pile of debris, consisting of smashed slate tiles from the roof, and bits of rubble and brick from where the beam had sheared off.

My heart started beating more rapidly. Suddenly the fears of my overactive imagination didn't seem so unlikely after all. I disregarded all logic, forgot that Charlie's car wasn't even here, and panicked. What if Charlie had decided to work in there today after all and was now lying trapped, pinned to the floor by the heavy weight of the wreckage?

I ran down the stairs, barely able to catch a breath, the fear pressing down on my chest. If anything had happened to Charlie, I would never forgive myself. I fought my way to the back of the outbuilding, charging through the undergrowth, not even caring as the brambles tore at my clothes and the tall nettles stung every bit of exposed skin they could touch.

'Charlie, are you in there?' I yelled. I picked my way into the ruins, ignoring the ominous groaning sounds that were coming from the remaining roof struts. 'Charlie? Can you hear me?'

The raindrops were collecting on the lenses of my glasses, obscuring my vision. I took them off and shoved them in my pocket. And then I examined every inch of the wreckage, pulling piles of rubble back with my bare hands, scrabbling at the stones, terrified by what I might be about to find. Finally, I got through to ground level and only then did my heart rate slowly start to return to normal. Wherever Charlie was, he wasn't lying underneath this lot. I closed my eyes and took a few deep breaths, the sense of relief overwhelming. The thought of losing my oldest friend was too awful to contemplate.

Eventually, I found the strength to stand up, embarrassed that I had got myself into such a state, and relieved that nobody had been around to witness my panicked overreaction. I was soaked through, covered in scratches and nettle stings, and aching all over. It was stupid of me to get so wound up. I stumbled back inside and peeled off my ruined work clothes, rubbing myself vigorously with a towel to get my circulation flowing again, and cleaning the scratches as best I could. And then I pulled on my tatty dungarees and a top with sleeves so long they hid the scratches on my hands, and gingerly got on with examining the damage to the ceiling from the leak at the top of the stairs in a bid to distract myself from my ridiculous behaviour and the emotions that had been stirred in me at the thought of Charlie being hurt.

Some time later I heard the sound of a car pulling up

outside. I slowly made my way into my bedroom and peered out of the one remaining window. A sleek sports car with a sunshine roof was parked in front of the house. Of course, given the foul weather, the roof wasn't open, but I could see through it, recognising Charlie in the passenger seat from his tousled hair. I nearly opened the window to call hello, relieved all over again that he had finally reappeared, but something made me hesitate. And then I saw the woman in the driver's seat lean across and pat him on the leg. He threw his head back as if he was laughing at something she had said, then he got out of the car and stood waving it off as it sped up the lane, despite the rain still thundering down around him. I felt a pang of loss which I couldn't, or wouldn't, examine further.

By the time Charlie came into the kitchen, I was sitting on my camping chair, pretending to be completely absorbed in my marking.

'Good day at the office, dear?' he said, continuing the jokey conversation we'd had before I set off to work that morning.

'The usual,' I said, not really feeling like joining in the banter. It seemed unfair that he was in such a good mood when I'd gone through such trauma on my return from school. Rationally I knew he wasn't responsible for how I'd reacted, but the strength of my emotional response had shocked me and put me on the defensive. 'And how was your day? Get up to anything exciting?'

I stopped myself asking who the woman in the sports car was, telling myself it was absolutely none of my business who Charlie chose to spend his day with. Charlie didn't need to justify any of his friendships to me, another friend.

'I had a bit of drama at lunchtime when it started raining and the outbuilding gave up the ghost, but I think we've come off lightly in the cottage itself. As I discovered when I took a closer look, the leak at the top of the stairs is due to a couple of roof tiles that have slipped out of place, no big deal. And my dad rang asking if he could use the Land Rover while his car is in the garage. But in between all that, I actually managed to get some work done.'

'Well done you,' I said, still studiously avoiding asking him about the woman in the car. And then I remembered something else he had said. 'What do you mean, you took a closer look at the cottage roof? Through binoculars I assume?'

Charlie cleared his throat. 'Um, well actually…'

'Oh my goodness, tell me you didn't climb up there while you were at home alone?'

'It seemed like a good idea at the time,' he said.

'Jeez, Charlie. Anything could have happened. Especially in this rain. You could have slipped on the rungs of the ladder and fallen to the ground. You could have broken a leg. Heck, you could have broken your neck. And it's not like any of the neighbours are near enough to have heard a cry for help.' I jumped up and started pacing anxiously around the kitchen. 'This is exactly what I was worrying about.'

'Oh, Freya, were you worrying about me?' Charlie's

voice had softened, the huskiness of his low tones stirring a strange sense of tenderness and something else within me. I could sense him moving towards me. For a moment I longed to turn around and hug him, hold him close and feel his arms wrapped around me, reassuring me that he was still in one piece.

Instead, I spun round to face him. 'Don't be too flattered. I don't want to be lumbered with converting this place solo,' I snapped, my fear from earlier and the shock at the surprising direction my mind had just gone in converting into anger all too easily. I felt like I'd exposed yet another vulnerability to him, and I wasn't quite sure I was ready for it.

'Sure,' said Charlie in his usual happy-go-lucky manner, not rising to the bait.

He set about lighting the camping stove and putting the kettle on, while my guilt increased. He'd done nothing to deserve being on the receiving end of my quick temper, which I knew was driven by my own insecurities rather than anything else.

I steeled myself. 'Sorry,' I said quietly, then repeated it more loudly when I thought he hadn't heard me.

Charlie reached out and squeezed my hand. 'Don't worry about it. You're absolutely right. It was a silly move on my part. Hey, what happened to you?' He traced the scratches on the back of my hands, gently rolling my sleeves up to reveal more scratches and the angry blotches from the nettle stings.

'I foolishly decided to have a go at the garden,' I said,

telling half of the truth. Fortunately, he was too distracted by concern about my injuries to question why I'd apparently decided to choose the wettest day of the year to do some gardening.

'This looks really sore. Do you want me to search for some ointment in the first-aid box?'

'It's fine. I'll live. I'm more worried by your antics on the roof.'

Charlie watched me closely. I could tell he was trying to work out what was really going through my head. I forced my face into a neutral expression. Eventually he shrugged.

'I won't do it again. At least, not while I'm here by myself. Will it make you feel any better if I promise I'm not going to abandon you to do the renovation by yourself, whatever else happens?'

I forced myself to let go of his hand.

'Thanks, Charlie. Team work makes the dream work.'

But I couldn't help wondering what else he might be alluding to.

Chapter Sixteen

The summer term accelerated towards exam season in the terrifying way it always seemed to. At work I was spending every minute of the day coaxing teenagers to revise or trying to cheer them up as the stress got to them. I was still undecided about whether I dared go for the Head of Department job, but I felt the pressure, knowing that everything I did was under scrutiny regardless. And at Oak Tree Cottage, I was feeling the pressure too. As my workload increased, so had Charlie's, and we were struggling to stick to the renovation schedule which I'd mapped out. As the evenings grew brighter, I was grateful for the extra few hours of sunlight to put in work on the house, but it never seemed enough. However tired I was, I always tried to do something each day, chipping away at the tasks, but every time I looked at the bigger picture, I felt overwhelmed by how much there was to sort out.

A month after we'd moved in, the electrician finally came out, checked the wiring and declared the electricity 'moderately safe' to use. In other words, we could boil a kettle or I could use the hair dryer, but it was better not to attempt to do both at the same time, not if we didn't want to blow a fuse and have to trek down into the cellar through the dodgy hatch underneath the stairs to do battle with the fusebox. Given the expression on her face when she'd stated this small concession, which was only given after some gentle pushing from Charlie, we'd voted not to use the power if we could possibly help it. What was another month without lights? We'd booked her in to do the full rewiring at the start of the summer holiday, judging it would be the least disruptive time as I would be around all day, while Charlie could go and work in the library.

Still, not having proper electricity was at least saving us some money. And we needed to save as much as we could because we were burning through our meagre budget at an alarming rate. We were now playing host to a succession of tradespeople who were booked to do the essential work that it was simply not safe for Charlie and me to attempt, however many YouTube tutorials I studied. The army of skilled craftspeople all seemed to have the terrible habit of sucking air through their teeth and shaking their heads in apparent despair when they examined the problem they'd been asked to solve. It didn't exactly bolster my confidence in the house. But although they made it very clear that they thought we were completely deluded in the challenge we'd undertaken, they were very happy to take our money, even if some of them didn't get to work with the haste they'd initially guaranteed.

I took to wearing headphones at school when I wasn't actually teaching, so that when I was marching around the corridors or running errands for Mr Rhys, I could simultaneously ring up the workers who'd failed to arrive when promised. I soon came to realise that the scaffolder in particular was going to be my arch nemesis. However much both Charlie and I had stressed to him that we were equal partners in the renovation and would be making all decisions jointly, he didn't pay any attention at all to what I had to say, forcing Charlie into the horrible position of having to he-peat everything I'd said just so the scaffolder would acknowledge it. I gritted my teeth and endured it, purely because the guy had given us the cheapest quote, but I'll admit I got my revenge in a petty but satisfying way, by pretending not to hear his frequent requests for cups of tea.

The sorting of the scaffolding coincided with the start of the summer holidays. Once it was in place, a builder got to work on the precariously teetering chimney stack, while a team of fitters began replacing the rotten windows, i.e. all of them, with shiny new ones. Indoors, the electrician set about drilling into the walls, replacing wires and rejuvenating a system which looked like it had been originally installed when electricity was first invented. Although I was pleased we were finally making tangible progress, the constant banging, crashing and smashing was utterly draining, and now I had nowhere to escape to. I tried to continue with other tasks such as ripping up carpets and working out the best layout for the new kitchen, but I felt like I wasn't really making any difference.

Charlie meanwhile was spending more and more time out of the house. I understood and completely accepted that during working hours it made sense for him to go elsewhere so he could concentrate on keeping his business going without the distracting soundtrack of building work in progress. But despite his promise to pull his weight, he was also starting to disappear at other times of the week, not just on Mondays for his dance class, but for a couple of hours every Thursday too, and sometimes on Sundays. When I'd asked if he'd been picking up some extra shifts at the estate agents, he'd been rather cagey and changed the subject, leaving me speculating what he was really up to. I reminded myself that he didn't have to account to me for what he did in his spare time, but I couldn't help wondering if the woman in the sports car had something to do with it. I told myself that my sense of grievance was down to the fact that I was growing tired of being by myself in a building site, but if I was being truly honest, there was a niggling voice at the back of my mind that said part of the reason I was so disgruntled was that I was a bit jealous. Jealous that Charlie seemed to have a much better social life than me, just to be clear. When I moaned about it on the phone to Leila, thinking I'd get some sympathy from my friend, I was rather surprised by her response.

'Have you talked to him about it? Have you told him that you feel he's being unfair?'

'No, but I would have thought it was obvious.'

'Ah, but what is obvious to one person can be a complete mystery to another. And if there's one thing you're very good at, Freya Hutchinson, that's keeping your feelings to yourself when you choose to. We've been mates for years, and even I don't know what's going through your head half the time. I mean, I can make a good guess at it, but I don't *know* know. And that's okay, you're entitled to your privacy. But equally you can't expect Charlie to psychically glean what's on your mind. Yes, you were best friends when you were little and apparently shared everything, but friendship when you're ten years old is a lot more straightforward than as an adult, even if it doesn't seem it at the time. If you're unhappy that he's going out and leaving you to it in the house, then I suggest you sit down with him and have a chat about it.' She paused, as if she was trying to find the right words. 'But I would also say that he has been running his own business from Oak Tree Cottage while you've been going out to school, so the poor guy is probably a bit sick of being surrounded by the same old tumbledown walls. It's not really unreasonable that he's popping out for a few hours a couple of times a week to get some me time, now the tables have been turned and you're the one at home all day.'

She had a point, and I made a real effort not to feel frustrated that he was disappearing. But I still couldn't help wondering where he was going and who with.

After one such Thursday evening vanishing act from Charlie, he returned to Oak Tree Cottage to find me peering in despair at the bank balance on the app on my phone.

'Penny for 'em,' he said, in the cheery voice of someone who had spent several hours having a lovely time away from our building site.

'Yes please, that would help boost the total in my account, and frankly at this stage, every penny counts,' I said. 'Once all these bills have been paid and the deposit has gone out on the rewiring work, I have precisely £16.37 left to see me through until next payday, at which point all my wages will disappear out of my account in less than twenty-four hours on yet more vital stuff we need for the renovation. And they're only the very basics. There's so much more to do on top of that. I don't know how we're going to manage.' As if to reflect the sinking feeling I was experiencing, my phone bleeped a warning that its battery was getting low.

'That's approximately ten pounds more than I have. The trouble with running your own business is that customers aren't always as proactive about paying their invoices as they are about demanding the work is done. We always knew we were going to have to live off beans on toast for a while,' said Charlie. 'We'll find a way. We might have to go for the budget paint rather than the super swanky stuff.'

'If only it was down to simple stuff like economising on paint. But we've got bigger issues than that. Think how much it costs to fill up your car with fuel so you can get to the library to work. And the bus driver isn't going to transport me for free to the supermarket to do the weekly shop. How are we even going to get anywhere to charge our phones until the electrician finishes? You know the sockets in this place aren't to be trusted yet. And don't suggest that solar panel charger thing of yours again.'

'The seller online said it was guaranteed to work, and exactly what everyone should invest in to help give them peace of mind in today's climate. When the zombies take over and destroy mainstream systems, the people with their own power sources will be laughing.' I knew he was teasing me, but I was in no mood for levity.

'Great, well, we're sorted then,' I said. 'That seller saw you coming a mile off, Charlie. Why waste precious money on something that is yet to work properly? Mind you, the same could be said of us buying this place.' I gestured around me at the bare living room. Although the psychedelic decorations had been cleared and the grotty carpet stripped back, the surroundings weren't exactly homely. With my camping mattress still in the corner of the room, it was very much giving off halfway house chic.

'I can't help being an eternal optimist.' He hummed a few bars of 'Always Look on the Bright Side of Life'. Then he snapped his fingers. 'I've got an idea. I don't know why I didn't think of it before. I used to do it all the time when I was a teenager to make some extra cash.'

'We can't go round offering to clean cars, Charlie. It only works when you're a Scout doing it for charity. We've definitely grown past the cute factor. Everyone would think it was weird. Besides, how could I explain to Mr Rhys when the parents call in asking why a member of the History Department is knocking on doors offering to do odd jobs over the summer holidays?'

'Not that, silly. I was talking about busking. You know, playing the guitar and singing a bit while passers-by chuck coins into the case.'

'You're going to suggest you add some of your ballet moves in next,' I said, watching Charlie's expression closely, trying to work out if he was being serious. While his wacky sense of humour had seen me through a few challenging moments since we'd moved in, such was my state of anxiety about everything that was going wrong that it was starting to wear on me. 'And don't call me silly.'

'Sorry, of course you're not silly, because dancing is an excellent idea,' he said. He bowed to me and held out his hand. Then when it became clear that I wasn't going to respond in kind, he jived his way forward, his eyes sparkling with amusement, and looped his arm around my waist, gently guiding me into a waltz. He spun me around the room, skilfully avoiding the dodgy areas of the floorboards and humming a tune to accompany us. At first it was a typical Charlie funny jape, and then something changed. His musical accompaniment grew softer and I had to draw closer to him to hear it. The dance evolved into a slow shuffle on the spot, the warmth of his breath tickling my neck as he leaned towards me. The next natural step would be for me to rest my head on his shoulder and for his hand to soften on the small of my back as we swayed, and for a brief out-of-body moment I wondered how it would feel if we did just that, moving closer still so there wasn't a millimetre of space between us, our bodies curving together. And then a floorboard creaked beneath us, the sound so jarring and unexpected that it brought me back to my senses. I shook my head, and broke away from what had almost become an embrace.

'I'm no good at dancing,' I said, turning away from him and brushing at my clothes, as if I was suddenly intent on trying to get rid of the dirt that was always there, embarrassed by my momentary flight of fancy.

'I'd dispute that,' said Charlie. I could feel his gaze on me. In the silence that followed, I wondered what was going through his head, whether his thoughts were travelling in the same strange direction as mine.

Then he cleared his throat. 'You're not going to distract me that easily. If I'm dancing, playing the guitar and singing, what are you going to contribute to the busking spectacular?'

I pulled a face, struggling to navigate my way through this confusing minefield of a conversation. 'If I wasn't keen on washing cars in case parents catch me doing it, you're definitely not going to be able to persuade me to make a fool of myself parading around in the centre of town for some loose change which will make no difference whatsoever to our restoration fund. No way. I have zero musical talent, and I hate being the centre of attention.'

'You shouldn't care so much about what random

strangers think about you. I thought now you're a grown-up teacher and everything, you'd have grown out of that,' said Charlie, the lightness in his tone belying the close scrutiny he was putting me under.

'You thought wrong,' I said, pretending now to be completely focused on my dying phone so that I could escape the all too knowing look he was giving me.

'Shame,' he said. 'You should let yourself loosen up, have some fun.'

His casual comment hit a nerve and his implied suggestion that I was uptight and boring made me bite back.

'Is that what you're doing on those Thursdays and Sundays when you swan off and abandon me to pick up the work?' I said. 'Unfortunately, someone around here has to pull their weight and demonstrate a bit of responsibility and good sense.' In my head it started out as a reasonable statement, but by the time it came out of my mouth I sounded naggy and cross. I instantly regretted saying it, knowing that I was deliberately picking a fight, but at the same time, I was desperate to know why he kept on disappearing, and frustrated that I was being left out.

Charlie's normally open, easy to read expression was suddenly shuttered.

'I'm sorry you feel that way. I'd rather not say what I'm doing at the moment, if you don't mind,' he said cagily, which of course was the one thing guaranteed to ignite my curiosity even further.

'Forget I ever asked,' I said, standing up and turning away from him. 'It's absolutely none of my business.'

'Technically that's right,' said Charlie quietly, in a very reasonable tone of voice that irritated me still further.

'Absolutely. Don't mind me. Good discussion. I'm going to sand the floor in my bedroom,' I said, trying to pretend that everything was normal.

'Freya, I feel like there's something else going on here. I hate to see you upset. Let's chat about it, please,' said Charlie. 'Remember The Rules.' He said it in a light-hearted manner but it was the mention of The Rules that forced me to get my act together. He was referring to my rule about open communication but I was thinking of another rule altogether. Specifically Rule 18c: 'No getting involved'. Because despite my best intentions, I was getting involved. Not romantically, obviously, I told myself, pushing to the back of my mind the memory of that fleeting tenderness as we danced. But couldn't it equally apply to getting involved in each other's lives and feeling we had the right to express an opinion about what each of us did or didn't do in their spare time? In which case I had come dangerously close to breaking that. I forced a smile on my face and told myself to stamp down on the resentment that was still burning away at the back of my mind.

'Absolutely. I'm really sorry, Charlie. What you do in your free time is totally up to you. I hope you're having fun. Now if you'll excuse me, that floor is not going to sand itself.'

'Freya, please,' called Charlie after me, but I pretended

not to hear him. Sanding the floor was a futile exercise because I'd be doing it by hand as we hadn't got round to sourcing an electric sander yet. But it would do me good to focus on a mind-numbing, physically painful task. I knew I had crossed a line in my relationship with Charlie, and I wasn't sure what it all meant.

Chapter Seventeen

I did my best to avoid Charlie the next day, continuing the fruitless task of trying to strip the floorboards in my bedroom with the door firmly closed. I knew I was only fuelling my frustration at his mysterious behaviour and my own confusing response to it, but perhaps it was better not to allow myself to examine that further.

As I worked, I tried to ignore the sound of Charlie clattering around elsewhere in the house. He seemed to have the ability to make copious amounts of noise, however minor the task he was involved in. It was one of the things I had started to miss when he was out on his jaunts, but today, rather than being comforting, its presence seemed pointed, as if he was doing it deliberately to prove wrong my suggestion that he wasn't pulling his weight. I turned some music on to try to drown it out and when he knocked on my door around lunchtime, I pretended not to have heard him.

In the afternoon, the noise stopped and I assumed he'd gone out again. Taking the opportunity to venture out of my room in search of a cup of tea, to my surprise I encountered Charlie at the bottom of the stairs waiting for me with a rucksack and my walking boots.

'I knew you'd emerge eventually,' he said, a note of triumph in his voice.

'Are you trying to ambush me?' I asked, embarrassed at being called out for hiding away.

'Yes,' he admitted freely. 'I was wondering if you'd had enough of sanding and fancied going for a walk instead? It's far too beautiful a day to be stuck indoors. And before you say anything about not being able to afford the time to go out and have fun, well, we'll make time for it.' He was acting as if the almost-row had never happened.

'You make me sound so dull,' I said, hurt all over again. 'I don't want to be the fun police. It's just that the school holidays only last so long. Before we know it, it'll be autumn, the nights will be drawing in, I'll be back at work, and the house will still be in such a state that we'll both…' My voice trailed off as Charlie persisted in holding my walking boots out towards me, an exasperating smile on his face. 'You're going to say I should relax and not worry so much, aren't you?'

'Yes, I am,' he said. 'But I'm glad you said it instead. And you're anything but dull. Look, if you'd really prefer to stay here and carry on working, I'm not going to get in the way, and I will work by your side. But if you fancy a break, I am offering my services as chauffeur to take you wherever you'd like to go. I know it's much easier for me to get out and about because I have a car, but I hope you know I'm always happy to give you a lift. If I've not been clear enough about that, I apologise.'

I surveyed the piles of rubble and rubbish that surrounded us, and once again experienced the jolt of panic which seemed to grip me whenever I thought too hard about how much work we had to do. And then I told myself to take a leaf out of Charlie's book, and go easy on myself for once. I'd complained about him disappearing all the time. I should at least give him the chance to try to make it up to me.

'Perhaps a change of scenery might be nice. Fine, you've got yourself a deal. But only if we stop by and collect Ted. I've been finding it hard to keep up with my turn on the walking rota since term ended. He could probably do with a proper run out.'

'Let's go,' said Charlie. He made as if to throw my walking boots towards me, then made a great show of juggling them instead.

'Give over,' I said, smoothly snatching one of them out of the air as he chuckled.

Ted greeted us at Granddad's by spinning around with delight on the spot so fast that he landed on his backside.

'Careful, Ted lad, you'll wear yourself out before your W-A-L-K,' said Granddad, carefully spelling out the word in a pointless attempt not to get him any more excited. 'Freya, love, you're looking a bit washed out, if you don't mind me saying. It'll do you good to get out in the fresh air.' He squeezed my arm. 'I hope all this building work isn't tiring you out too much. And Charlie, how are you getting on with the l—?'

'Everything's going well, thank you,' said Charlie, answering before Granddad had even finished the question. I thought I caught the two men exchanging a look, but before I could ask what they were talking about, Ted distracted me by depositing a ball at my feet to be thrown, and by the time I'd done the honours, their conversation had moved on.

'Are you sure you don't want to join us? We could head to the park,' I suggested, trying to think of the most accessible destination for my grandfather without making it too obvious that's what I was doing. Of course, there was no point in trying to get anything past him.

'I'd only get in the way of you young ones, and I've got a busy afternoon with the crossword planned. Off you go and enjoy yourselves, and make sure Ted doesn't wear you out.'

Without really discussing it, we headed up towards the moors, me navigating while Ted let out the occasional woof of support from the boot where he was safely ensconced behind the dog guard.

'It's a while since I've been here,' said Charlie, as we pulled up in a small car park at the bottom of Sutton Bank in the national park. 'They must have repainted the horse recently. I'm sure it wasn't that white last time I walked here.' He gestured at the huge shape that had been cut into the hillside back in Victorian times. 'You know, when I was travelling and feeling horribly homesick and lonely, I always used to imagine this walk and it made me feel better.'

I glanced across at Charlie. He always seemed so happily sure of himself that it was hard to imagine him being homesick. But then again, I supposed his ready admission that he had low moments was another demonstration of that self-confidence. It was a quality of his that I both admired and envied.

'Mr Rhys always makes a big point of telling the kids that it was a schoolmaster and his pupils who originally marked out the horse. I live in fear of him suggesting we do something similar, not that there are any suitable hills near school, but it's exactly the kind of "little project" that he'd suggest in the guise of helping my promotion opportunities.'

'Promotion opportunities?' asked Charlie casually as he finished tying his laces and waited for me to check that Ted's harness was properly done up.

'Oh, it's nothing really,' I said. 'Do you want to do the steps up the hill, or take the path through the woodland?'

'Woodland path, no contest. Although I will protest loudly if you let Ted do all the hard work by dragging you up the slope.'

I laughed, already starting to feel more relaxed as the different surroundings worked their magic on me. 'You're welcome to take him, although I warn you, you'll have one arm longer than the other by the time we arrive at the top. He may only be a little dog but he's determined when he wants to be.'

I handed over the lead, and Ted set off enthusiastically, nearly sending Charlie flying. We headed into the woods, the pace thankfully slowing down as Ted took frequent pit stops to sniff out all the interesting smells. While he was more interested in the mud and occasional rabbit droppings, it at least gave Charlie and me the time to enjoy the sweeter scent of the honeysuckle that was trailing its way through the undergrowth. It was good to get away from the house, and although we were surrounded by trees, the soft whisper of their leaves moving in the breeze helped to create a sense of space and peace, easing the claustrophobia that I'd started to feel from being trapped by all the renovation work at Oak Tree Cottage.

Charlie waited until we'd got to the top of the escarpment and had paused to admire the view (for that, read: take a breather) to ask the question again. 'What is this promotion opportunity?'

I watched as a glider from the nearby flying club silently soared overhead. The view from the cockpit would be even better than ours, although I didn't think I'd be brave enough to get in one and put my entire trust in the movement of the air with no safety net of an engine. Should I answer Charlie's question? I hadn't even discussed the idea with Leila, not daring to say the words out loud in case others confirmed my secret fear that the job was way out of my league. But despite his infuriating moments, I knew Charlie was a good listener and would be happy to act as a sounding board.

'Mr Rhys told me in confidence that he's going to retire at the end of next year. He suggested I apply to be his replacement.'

'Freya, that's fantastic news,' said Charlie, sounding for all the world as if I'd already got the position.

'He only said it because I'd save the school money,' I responded, explaining the full conversation my boss had had with me.

'Utter nonsense,' retorted Charlie. 'For a start, you'd be amazing at the job. I've never met anyone with such enthusiasm for what they do, plus I've seen you working all hours to make sure that your students get the very best teaching. And if you'll allow me to address the frankly ridiculous suggestion that he's only pushing you to do it for the school's financial benefit, think logically about that. He's retiring. Why would he care a jot how much money the school does or doesn't spend on staffing? Presumably he'll be getting his nice pension regardless. Don't do yourself down.' His entreaty was so earnestly delivered that I found myself nodding in acknowledgement that he had a point. 'You will go for it, won't you?' he asked, as if it was the simplest thing in the world. I felt a warm glow of happiness at his easy belief in me.

'It's not that straightforward. I mean, of course it's the dream job. I always hoped I'd get there one day. But maybe not quite at this stage of my life. It's come at a really bad time. There's the house to think about. I'm not sure I can give the application the attention it deserves and needs, as well as juggling all the renovation work. Oak Tree Cottage has to be my priority. That was the deal we made. We do it up as quickly and efficiently as possible so that we can sell up, move on and find our own places. That's what we both want.' I experienced a pang of uncertainty as I said the words. Were they still true? Or had I started to get so used to being at Oak Tree Cottage playing at house with Charlie that part of me wanted to carry on?

Charlie reached down to scratch the top of Ted's head. I got the impression he was thinking carefully before he responded to me.

'You must do what you think is best for you,' he said eventually. 'But don't rush into any decisions that you might regret later. Remember what it's like being on this walk. The path up through the woods is tough, but then you emerge at the top and you can see the bigger picture with the breath-taking view, and it makes the earlier challenge all worthwhile.'

I thought about Charlie's words all the way back home to Oak Tree Cottage. And then I began asking myself when I'd started to think of Oak Tree Cottage as 'home' rather than merely a project. Because despite all its quirks and frustrations, I did feel at home there. I decided it was probably best to ignore the annoying voice at the back of my head that wondered if a similar view could be taken of my relationship with Charlie. It was safer not to stray into that kind of territory.

Chapter Eighteen

'Hello,' I said to the petite woman on the doorstep. The surprise in my voice and the startled expression I knew must be on my face were mostly due to the fact that I didn't even realise we had a doorbell, let alone a functioning one. Charlie must have sorted it out, a task ticked off on one of the lists that he'd started regularly making, joking that my organisational skills were rubbing off on him. 'Can I help?' I asked, assuming she must have taken a wrong turning and be intending to visit our neighbours, who lived in much more civilised surroundings.

'Thanks, Freya, I'll take it from here,' said Charlie, brushing past me and ushering the woman into the house. As she walked inside, I had a spark of recognition. If I wasn't very much mistaken, this was the mysterious woman who had dropped him off the other week. I put two and two together. Was I meeting Ms Thursday Night Out?

And if so, why hadn't Charlie warned me that she was coming round? I felt at a distinct disadvantage, greeting someone who appeared so put together and elegant in her pristine white plimsolls and immaculate jumpsuit, when I knew I looked like I hadn't had a change of clothes in the last month. Standing next to her, I felt like a gawky, grubby giant.

'Aren't you going to introduce me to your friend?' I asked, mostly because I was getting a very clear impression that he had no such intention. I couldn't help feeling rather put out.

'This is Serena, she's a…work colleague,' said Charlie in such a false tone of voice that I was immediately convinced she was anything but. I experienced a moment of hurt that although I'd confided in him about my secret on our walk, he hadn't been open with me in return.

The woman held her hand out and shook mine, seemingly unbothered by the fact that my palms were covered in bits of paint. But before she could elaborate further on Charlie's introduction, he had somehow engineered it so he was standing between us and was practically herding her into the dining room away from me, clearly desperate to stop me continuing the conversation. Or maybe he was just desperate to be alone with her.

'Hi, Serena, nice to meet you,' I said to her departing form. She looked back towards me and smiled briefly before she was swept out of the room by Charlie. I stood in the living room and wondered what I was meant to do now. Carry on with renovation work while Charlie enjoyed a cosy afternoon in with the lovely Serena? I mean, of course he was entitled to entertain a guest in his own house. But it would have been nice to have had some warning about it. That way I could have made myself scarce, or maybe invited a friend of my own round to keep me company. I told myself that the lack of consideration was the only reason why I was feeling so irrationally irritated by it.

I strode into the dining room, only wondering once I'd got in there whether I should have knocked first. Charlie leaped away from Serena. I'd merely got the briefest glimpse of them standing by the window, but their heads had been bent closely together, and I got the distinct impression that they'd been deep in conversation, or perhaps something else.

'Sorry to interrupt,' I said.

'It's no bother,' said Serena in her soft Scottish accent, neatly tucking her hair behind her ears in a manner that made me feel even more chaotic and messy.

Charlie on the other hand looked distinctly embarrassed and shifty.

'What is it, Freya?' he asked, clearly desperate for me to leave the room. He kept on glancing nervously towards Serena and then the door, every bit of his body language uncharacteristically awkward and uncomfortable with my presence. I felt a stab of pain at this strange new attitude towards me.

I'm not proud of what I did next, but there was something about his eagerness for me to get out of the way that made me perversely decide to do the exact opposite. I wandered over to the window where the pair of them had been standing close together and pretended to enjoy the view.

'I love the way the sunlight comes into the room at this time of day. What do you think, Serena?'

To be fair to her, she didn't seem to be surprised to be engaged in random chitchat about the sunshine.

'It's certainly a beautiful outlook,' she said. 'In my w—'

But before she could finish her sentence, Charlie had arrived at my side.

'Sorry, Freya, but what was it that you were after?' he said, abruptly speaking over Serena.

'Charlie, that's a bit much. Let the poor woman finish what she was about to say.'

I caught the warning expression he threw in Serena's direction, which made me even more curious about what was going on.

'Don't worry, it was nothing important,' she said, giving Charlie a slight nod. What was it that she was reassuring him about?

'Freya, what do you want?' Charlie asked again.

'I was wondering if you two would like a drink. Maybe an orange squash or something? We're still having to be careful with the electricity, Serena, otherwise I would offer you a cup of tea. It's all candlelit evenings around here, I'm afraid, until the rewiring's completely finished.'

'Candlelit evenings, how romantic,' said Serena.

'Hmm, not really,' I said, noticing Charlie's stony expression.

'I think we're okay for drinks, thanks for offering, Freya,' he said. 'Don't let us keep you.'

I pretended not to hear him and wandered over to examine the cupboard housing which boxed in the door between the kitchen and the dining room.

'We really need to look at tackling this soon. It's plain weird having to stride through a cupboard to get into a room. What do you think, Serena?'

'Freya,' hissed Charlie. 'Do you mind?'

'I'm sorry, I didn't realise I was getting in the way,' I said, although I guiltily acknowledged to myself that was exactly what I had knowingly been doing. 'Don't mind me, I'll work around you.'

'Would you mind giving us some privacy?' asked Charlie, finally going for the direct approach.

He couldn't have made it clearer that I was an unwanted third wheel. Suddenly everything turned even more awkward and I felt childish about the silly game I'd been playing.

'Sorry, I'll leave you to it,' I apologised hastily, and practically ran out of the room, my face flaming with embarrassment. I was confused by my own actions. Why had I made such a fuss about Charlie entertaining a female guest when he had every right to do what he wanted? I knew the way I had acted would have made me look strange or, worse, jealous. I wasn't that, was I? Had I got so used to how we'd evolved from Hutch and Humph, the Terrible Twosome, to Freya and Charlie, partners in house ownership, that I was scared of what might happen when he moved on from it?

I didn't want to examine that thought more closely. I put on my headphones and turned the volume up high so I couldn't hear anything of what was going on in the dining room, although Charlie and Serena wouldn't be able to escape the soundtrack from the DIY that I then went on to carry out. But what did they expect if they chose to cosy up together at what was essentially a building site? I spent the rest of the afternoon dismantling the plywood units in the kitchen, prising apart the frames and working out my frustration with myself by stamping on the longer sheets of wood until they snapped.

When finally my stomach told me it was dinnertime, I decided it was also time to be a better person and apologise to Charlie for my earlier odd behaviour, ashamed of myself for acting up like that. I hesitated on the threshold of the dining room, practising what I would say. I knocked loudly and waited, giving them plenty of time. When there was no answer, I knocked again, then eventually I pushed the door open and went in. There was something different about the room, something I couldn't quite put my finger on, and that wasn't only because there was no sign of either of them in it. I hurried over to the window and saw that Charlie's Land Rover and Serena's swish vehicle had both gone. I felt hurt all over again. Normally when Charlie went out, he told me he was leaving, not because he had to, but because he wanted to. Things were clearly changing, and I didn't like it.

. . .

I didn't know what time he got back after Serena's visit, whether it was later that night or perhaps not even until the next morning, because I'd once again put my headphones on and kept on listening to music in bed until I finally drifted off to a sleep full of weird stressy dreams. But I did know that, after that visit, things were different between us.

I found myself overthinking every comment, worried about inadvertently exposing something that I wasn't even sure of myself. I knew it was making me act stiff and standoffish, but I couldn't work out how to stop myself. I missed the relaxed bantering fun we used to have, the way we would tease each other and laugh together. Now, on the rare occasion when I attempted to banter with Charlie, it came out wrong, like I was sniping at him, which he reacted to by becoming careful around me, almost distant. It was like living with a stranger. Even though the house was becoming slowly more habitable, I was feeling more uncomfortable than when we first moved in. I wanted things to go back to how they had been.

It got so bad that I volunteered to help Leila out at the school's holiday club, just to get out of the house again for a few hours. It proved to be a welcome escape. We spent a lot of time hanging around by the bike sheds, ostensibly to catch any holiday club participants who were planning to slope off there and get up to no good, but really because it was the place with the best chance of privacy in the grounds.

'How's life in the funhouse?' Leila asked, opening a packet of crisps and settling in for a good gossip. She always felt she couldn't eat junk food in front of the pupils because she had to maintain the illusion of the fit and healthy PE teacher whose body was a temple. I leaned over and helped myself to a couple while I thought about my answer.

'It's fine,' I said, although I knew there wasn't much conviction behind my words. Leila raised an eyebrow. 'Okay, so maybe it's not exactly fine. It's…different. I can't really explain it. Instead of getting on with things and being relaxed around each other, we're just being super polite.'

'Polite. Sounds ideal. Better than killing each other, which you'll recall is one of two big dangers I warned you about before you embarked on this house-buying malarkey. And remind me why this isn't a good thing?' asked Leila in a tone of voice that suggested she had a whole lot of ideas about what the answer really was.

'Because it feels so strange. So unnatural. Charlie and I have never been polite to each other because we're old friends. Old friends who don't need to worry about skirting around the important stuff, who can laugh and joke and say whatever comes into our heads without worrying about what the other one thinks, because we know that they're probably of the same mind. I'm not saying that we're rude to each other, don't get me wrong. But we are at ease, relaxed in each other's company. Or at least, we were. Now I'm worried that whatever I say will come out wrong and Charlie is acting like I'm a client he needs to be scrupulously formal with. It's weird. And I still don't really understand why things have changed.'

That last bit was a lie. Because I had a fairly good idea that I was the reason why things were so different between us.

'But surely polite formality is better than yelling at each other and falling out all the time?' said Leila.

I scratched my heel in the dirt, sketching out a serious of wobbly lines while I thought about my answer.

'Obviously shouting at each other would be horrible. But this coldness in our communication, it's not like us. It's as if we're strangers. Only it's worse than that because I know how things were before. I might as well be back in a house share, the way things are now.'

Leila chomped another handful of crisps before she replied. When she did, I wished she'd carried on eating. 'But when you boil things down, isn't a house share exactly what your arrangement is? Yes, you have some history as friends, and living together while doing the renovation work is obviously creating a more intense environment, but ultimately you clubbed together to buy a house for purely practical, financial reasons. It was essentially a cold-hearted business decision. However you act towards each other while you're doing it up, it's not going to change the outcome; that you're going to sell up, hopefully make a nice tidy profit apiece, and then go your separate ways, to live your own lives, and probably gradually fall back into the state of your friendship before you bumped into each other in the pub. Which was that you were pretty much just acquaintances. Unless...' Leila tailed off and fixed me with her stern teacher look. 'Unless there's something else going through your mind that you've not confessed to me?'

'What do you mean? There's nothing else going through my mind, absolutely nothing at all,' I said, knowing that I was protesting too much at what she was obviously implying, but not able to stop myself. 'I'm merely frustrated by the situation, and wondering how to resolve it. But you're absolutely right. The state of our relationship doesn't really matter one way or the other. What does matter is that we finish the renovation and get to move on with our lives.'

'Yes indeed,' said Leila, 'and say it once more, but this time with conviction behind the words. I find it interesting that you said "relationship" rather than "friendship", by the way. Freud would have a field day.'

I shot her a warning look.

'Okay, okay, so you're not ready to talk about it yet,' she said, holding her hands up in mock surrender. 'But when you do feel like sharing with your Aunty Leila, remember I'm here for you, day or night.'

Chapter Nineteen

Determined to prove to Leila that I wasn't turning into someone who spent all her time doing building work and overanalysing the state of play with my housemate, I took up her invitation to go out for a few drinks after our shift at the holiday club ended. I knew it was a mistake as soon as we walked into The Taps and she turned to me with a faux misty-eyed expression and asked whether they should install a plaque to commemorate it as the location where Charlie and I were reunited. I realised that protesting any further was just going to encourage the teasing so I changed tactics to ignoring it completely, which in reality meant she indulged even more.

Thankfully Nim turned up shortly afterwards and succeeded in distracting her from tormenting me, while I enjoyed the novelty of being in a civilised environment where I could walk around on a carpeted surface and not have to breathe in clouds of dust. Doing the house renovation was like living in a bubble, everything within it amplified to huge importance, making me forget that there was a real world out here where most people's lives carried on as usual. Maybe Charlie had the right idea, getting out and about a couple of times a week. Maybe I should do the same. That way I might be able to keep everything in perspective, both the state of the house and the state of my dealings with the person I shared it with. I pushed that thought away, still unwilling to examine my emotions towards Charlie more closely. Instead, I threw myself into socialising, enjoying the novelty of being out. And although I only nursed one drink for the whole of the evening, when last orders were called I found myself reluctant to return to the awkwardness – both atmospheric and physical – of Oak Tree Cottage.

'Are you sure you don't want to come and camp out on my sofa for a bit, have a break from life on a building site?' said Leila, as she and Nim waited with me at the stop for my bus back to the village.

'Thanks, but I don't want to get in your way. I've made my camping bed, and so I will lie in it, however uncomfortable it is.'

'You know you don't have to put yourself through all this overthinking and second-guessing what's happening,' said Leila. 'I know I was teasing you earlier, but I'm going to be serious now. I think you should talk to Charlie about what's going through your head.' She held up her hand to stop the interruption I was going to make. 'Yes, I know you're not sure yourself how you feel and what's going on here. But he's not stupid. If you think things have changed between you, he'll have recognised that too and would probably welcome the opportunity to get stuff out in the open. It's better to talk about it than live in uncertainty. Just my opinion, of course.'

The arrival of the bus spared me from answering her. But when she gave me a hug goodbye, she whispered 'Good luck' in my ear.

I waved cheerily at Leila and Nim until they were out of sight, and then I spent the journey back to Oak Tree Cottage wrestling with the confusing thoughts whizzing around inside my head. I experienced a pang of nerves when the bus eventually dropped me off in the village, still wondering if I dared follow Leila's advice. And when I finally walked down the lane and let myself into the house, I told myself I was relieved that although Charlie's car was parked on the drive, Charlie himself was nowhere to be seen. Whatever conversation I needed to have with him could wait until the morning. Before I could chicken out completely, I scribbled a quick note asking him for a chat and left it by his coffee mug in the kitchen. I would decide in the bright light of the day how far that conversation would go.

I woke with a start, my heart pounding. Thankfully this time I wasn't being woken from a deep sleep by someone creeping around my room, but something else had dragged me from my dreams, something potentially just as worrying. My phone was buzzing insistently. I'd set it on the 'do not disturb' mode before I eventually went to sleep, so for it to be buzzing now, the person at the other end of the line must have rung several times to have overridden it. I scrabbled around in the dark, trying to feel where it was without sitting up, as I was still half-asleep. It must be the middle of the night still. And with that my sense of foreboding grew stronger. A phone call at this time was never a good thing.

Somehow I managed to answer the call, still struggling to prop myself up on my slightly deflated camp bed and get my bearings.

'Freya, the important thing is not to panic,' said my mum, but what she said and how she said it immediately made me do the exact opposite.

Suddenly I was bolt upright and as wide awake as if I'd never been to sleep.

'What's happened? Are you all right? Is Dad okay?'

'We're both fine. It's your granddad.'

Icy fear gripped my insides. Not Granddad Arthur, my sweet lovely Granddad.

'He's not...he's not dead, is he?' I asked hesitantly, the word 'dead' coming out in a whisper. I immediately wished it unsaid, as if I was going to make it true by saying it out loud.

'No, he's not dead,' said Mum, putting on the straight-talking voice, kindly but firm, which she normally used in the most serious of situations. 'But he's not in a good way.

He had a fall yesterday morning, and instead of using his alarm straight away to call for help, he thought he'd be able to get himself back up again and nobody would be any the wiser. In fact, I have a horrible feeling he wasn't even wearing his personal alarm, and he certainly didn't have his mobile on him. He spent most of the day on the floor, and it was only when a parcel delivery arrived late in the evening that he was found. The guy doing the delivery says he was concerned by the way Ted was barking at him, because Ted isn't normally a barking dog.'

'Oh, poor Granddad, couldn't he even reach the phone? How terrifying for him. Thank goodness for Ted.'

I could imagine the scene now, Granddad Arthur trapped on the floor and in pain, torn between wishing someone would find him and longing not to be discovered so no one would learn about his moment of helplessness.

'You know what he's like, stubborn as a point of pride. And by the time he realised he was in serious trouble, there wasn't really anyone around to call. I'm not sure he was even making any noise when the delivery guy got there. The man deserves a medal because he tried to get into the house. Anyway, it turned out to be a rare occasion on which your granddad had locked his front door, so there was quite a delay in getting help because the ambulance crew had to wait for the police to break in to get to him. And then it took a while to notify us as his next of kin because he was in too much pain to be able to get the information across.'

Mum was being very factual but I felt myself shaking in shock at the impact.

'Poor, poor Granddad,' I said, a sob in my voice.

And then I felt a strong arm going around my shoulders. Charlie sat down beside me on the camping bed, saying nothing, but letting me lean on him and draw strength from his proximity. Although he couldn't hear everything that Mum was saying, he knew I was upset, and didn't want me to be alone to deal with it.

'The doctors say he's broken his hip,' she continued. 'They're going to take him in for surgery first thing, and then we'll have to wait and see.'

'Surgery, at his age? That's really not good.' Once again my imagination was running wild, calculating the risks, itching to Google the outcomes, but fearing what I might find out.

'It is what it is,' said Mum, and this time I could hear the pain in her voice.

'Are you okay, Mum?'

'Not really.' She paused, and I could hear her taking a deep breath, trying to pull herself together so that she could be strong for me. 'But I'm with him now, and he's in the best place. I've just snuck out into the corridor to call you.'

I in turn tried to pull myself together to be strong for her. 'I'll come over right now. Which hospital is he in?'

I didn't even have to see Charlie's face to know that he would be more than happy to jump in the car and drive me wherever I needed to get to.

'That's very kind of you, love, but he's sleeping now, and it's probably best to wait until morning. I'll let you know when I've got more information about the surgery.'

'What about Ted? Is he okay?' The pair of them were normally inseparable and I knew the little dog would be upset being without Granddad.

'He's still at Granddad's. The neighbours are going to keep an eye on him in the morning, but we'll need to work out what happens after that. Your dad and I can't take him because our lease says we need written permission in advance before a pet can move in.'

'We'll take him,' I said, not even hesitating. I wasn't sure how much of Mum's end of the conversation Charlie could hear, but I could tell from the way his arm tightened around my shoulders that he was in agreement with what I'd said.

Mum sighed. 'I must say that would be a huge relief, love. The ambulance crew said your granddad was all for refusing to be taken off to hospital because he was afraid Ted would be left behind. I know he's terrified of him ending up in kennels or a rescue shelter.'

'That is never going to happen. Ted can stay with us for as long as he needs to. The house is mostly cleared of rubbish now, and the worst of the rewiring and window refitting is done, so it's not as hazardous as it was when we first moved in. We can whizz around the garden and borrow a strimmer from the neighbours to clear a patch for him to play in.'

'Thanks, love. At least that's one less thing to worry about, and I know your granddad will be relieved when he hears it. Now you try and get some sleep for what's left of the night, and I'll give you another ring when I know more.'

'Thanks, Mum. Give him a big kiss from me, and send

him my love. And tell him not to worry a second more about Ted.'

When the call ended, I carried on gripping the phone as if my life depended on it. Suddenly the problems I'd been worrying about when I went to sleep felt so petty and insignificant. I felt chilled to the bone, unable to escape the mental image of the sheer trauma my beloved granddad had been through. And that was only the beginning of it. Who knew what challenges would lie ahead for him? One thing was certain, his life wasn't going to be the same again. I'd heard too many horror stories in the news to be naïve enough to think his recovery and return home would be straightforward.

'Don't,' said Charlie quietly.

'Don't what?'

'Don't let your thoughts go there,' said Charlie. 'I can practically hear the cogs whirring as you work out Arthur's odds and worry about what's going to happen next.'

I half-heartedly tried to shrug out of his embrace, but was quite glad when he gently squeezed my shoulders tighter, indicating that he wasn't going anywhere. There was something comforting about the warmth of his arm around me.

'It's hardly surprising I'm worried,' I said.

'You're a natural-born worrier, Freya,' he said softly. 'But a wise person, who also happens to be your granddad Arthur, once told me that by worrying, we're only torturing ourselves twice over, because we experience the anticipation of the pain, and then the pain itself, if it happens. And it's still an 'if' at this stage, isn't it? Worrying isn't going to change anything for the better or the worse, so it's better to try not to do it.'

'Easier said than done,' I muttered.

'I know,' he said. 'Of course you're going to worry. You're a kind, caring woman, and that's your natural response. But don't let it take over. You're going to need to be strong for Arthur.' He pulled me closer still. 'You're shivering.'

'I can't imagine being warm ever again,' I said somewhat melodramatically.

'You will. When the sun rises in the morning, you'll find the strength to get through this. You'll find the strength to support Arthur, because that's what you need to do. And in the meantime, let me go and get you a hot drink and an extra blanket so you stop shivering,' said Charlie. 'Then you can try and get some more sleep.'

'Please don't leave me,' I whispered, scared to be alone with my thoughts.

He hesitated.

'Please,' I said. 'Stay with me. I feel better when you're with me.'

When he finally answered, there was a huskiness in his voice, and I wondered if he was doing a bad job of following his own advice about worrying.

'I'm here as long as you need me, Freya,' he said. 'Come on, let's try to get some sleep. Kick me if I take up too much room.'

I didn't think I'd stand a chance of getting another wink

that night, but there was something comforting about lying there with Charlie next to me. My camping bed was a single, so we had to snuggle up close, his breath tickling the back of my neck. Slowly I felt the warmth return to my body and the tension in my limbs begin to ease. As I started to drift off, I thought I heard him say my name quietly, as if he wanted to ask me something, but by that point I was too sleepy to really register it or respond.

Chapter Twenty

I woke the next morning feeling warm, contented and like everything was right in the world. I stretched out and was surprised to hear someone let out a groan.

'Eurgh, thanks for the elbow in the ribs, Freya,' said Charlie.

I rolled over and found myself face to face with my house partner and everything came flooding back. The late-night call from my mum with the news about Granddad Arthur, my shocked reaction, Charlie's response of calm, solid support.

'Oh, Granddad,' I said, sick all over again as I wondered how he was doing.

'Not the response I normally like to hear when I wake up next to a woman,' said Charlie with a wink.

I elbowed him in the ribs again, this time deliberately.

'Don't be disgusting, Charlie,' I said, suppressing a smile.

'Just trying to lighten the mood.' Then his expression grew serious. He reached out and tucked a stray lock of hair behind my ears. Despite my worry for my granddad, I couldn't help noticing the tingle that Charlie's touch ignited in my skin. How could I be thinking such things at a time like this? 'He'll be okay, you know, Freya. If anyone can get through this, Arthur can. I've never met anyone so determined and stubborn.' He paused. 'Well, maybe except his granddaughter.'

'I think that's probably the nicest thing you've ever said to me,' I said, my eyes tearing up all over again.

'Then I probably need to work harder with my compliments. But seriously, no more tears,' he responded, blotting them before they could fall onto the bedding. 'Now we need to put on a brave face for Arthur. He'd hate to see you crying.'

'I know. And thank you.' I gestured vaguely between us, hoping to convey my gratitude to him for taking pity on me and staying by my side through the night, even though it couldn't have been particularly comfortable for him.

Charlie cleared his throat. 'No thanks needed. It's what friends are for.'

Friends. Of course.

'Well, thank you anyway.'

I forced myself to sit up, even though I would quite happily have stayed there snuggled up with him for the rest of the day.

'Now that's what I call a bed head,' said Charlie, laughing.

I reached up and felt the tangle of my hair.

'You can talk, Mr Hairy Features.' It felt good to be bantering with Charlie again, distracting myself from worrying about what was happening in the hospital.

'Just another of my talents. Right, well, I might as well put this to good use,' said Charlie miming lighting a match on his stubble. 'I'll put the kettle on if you want to jump in the shower first.'

'What a gent. By the time I've finished there might be some hot water coming through for you to use.'

'Darn, you've seen straight through my wicked plan.' He shook his head in faux disappointment.

I hopped out of bed, in a much brighter mood than I would have imagined possible. As I reached the bathroom door, I turned round.

'Charlie, if…'

But he didn't even need me to finish my sentence. He held up my phone.

'If your mum rings, I'll answer it for you. Unless you want me to rush into the bathroom with the phone while you're showering.'

I pretended to consider. 'Nice try. I'm sure you're perfectly capable of taking a message for me.'

He grinned. 'It's good to see you smiling. Now hurry up, or I'll have drunk all the tea by the time you're done.'

As Charlie had promised, I felt better still once I'd had a shower and got dressed. While he disappeared to get ready, I prepared our favourite veggie sausage sandwiches, and then forced myself to go outside for some fresh air rather than anxiously pace indoors, willing my phone to ring and dreading it at the same time. Whether I was staring at the screen or had left it by the camping stove in the kitchen, it wouldn't make any difference to the outcome.

The long grass was shimmering with droplets of dew while the flattering shadows of the early morning made the garden look wild and lush rather than unkempt. Somewhere among the branches of the oak tree, a robin was greeting the new day with a melodious tune. Its song was accompanied by the low hum of bees busily inspecting the wildflowers and weeds for nectar. Despite everything that was going on, I could still appreciate the peace, standing out here in my garden, my home glowing in the sunrise behind me.

I slowly fought my way around the boundary, inspecting it for gaps or holes which would prove tantalisingly inviting to a small and excitable dog. I knew Ted had a track record of disappearing to go exploring and I didn't want to have to explain to Granddad that he'd gone missing on my watch. We'd have to rig up some kind of barrier at the end of the drive, as the gaps in the rotting five-bar gate that currently stood there would prove no obstacle to Ted, who had got himself through spaces far smaller. And we'd have to find some way of stopping him running into the ruins of the outbuilding, as the remains of the roof were still piled up in the middle of the floor. But at least there would be plenty of interesting places to take him for walks around here, and I was sure once we'd set up his bed and created a cosy nook in each room for him to curl up in, he'd be content enough, although I knew he'd still be missing his master.

'Freya, your mum's on the phone.'

Charlie stuck his head round the back door to call me. He was in his dressing gown, hair still wet from the shower, the droplets of water glistening as they dripped down onto his shoulders in a way that could have been thoroughly distracting if I hadn't had much more serious issues on my mind.

'Give me two seconds and I'll be right with you,' I called back, beating my way through the jungle garden, my heart pounding as my anxiety returned at full throttle. I wasn't sure I was ready to hear what news she had to share.

'No need to rush, there's been no serious change,' said Charlie, recognising my urgent need for reassurance. 'Arthur had a good night and they seem to be managing his pain effectively.'

I let out a breath I didn't even realise I'd been holding.

Charlie passed the phone over to me and hovered in the doorway, clearly unsure whether to give me some privacy or to stay in case I need his support. I answered his unspoken question by moving to stand next to him and putting the phone on speaker so he could hear both sides of the conversation. He and Granddad went way back, and I knew he'd also be very concerned about him. Besides, it was always good to have a second pair of ears when important information was being conveyed, in case I didn't take everything in.

'I think Charlie already passed on the good news that

your granddad had a decent night's sleep. But the other bit of news is that he's about to go into surgery. They've decided the most efficient way to treat the break is by doing a hip replacement, as they think it will give him the best chance of getting moving again.'

'That sounds pretty drastic, but if it's what's best for him…'

'The surgeon sounded confident. I think your granddad's quite pleased about it. He managed to crack a joke about becoming the Bionic Man anyway, before they wheeled him into theatre. Of course he's going to have to do a lot of rehabilitation work, and I dread to think how he'll manage in that house of his.'

'Mum, let's take one thing at a time. There's no point in worrying about how he'll manage to get home until he's at that point in his recovery.'

Charlie reached out and squeezed my hand, smiling as I passed on his advice about worrying.

'You're right. But it's a lot to think about. I've always said there are far too many stairs in that house of his.'

'Now we're dab hands at building work, we're always happy to help with adaptations,' said Charlie.

'Hmm, not so sure about that,' chorused Mum and I, which at least made us laugh. If I wasn't much mistaken, that had been Charlie's intention in saying it.

By the time I'd finished the conversation, I did at least feel more reassured about Granddad's prospects, although I knew I wouldn't be completely at ease until he was safely out of hospital and on the road to recovery.

'Right, I'll go and get dressed and then shall we fetch Ted?' said Charlie, once I'd hung up the phone.

'Thanks,' I said, knowing that he would be sacrificing important work time to do me this kindness. Charlie would help me to keep the anxiety at bay.

As we trundled along the country lanes towards Granddad's house, the Land Rover bouncing over the potholes, Charlie suddenly asked, 'What was it that you wanted to talk to me about, by the way?'

For a moment, I couldn't think what he was referring to.

'The note,' he prompted. 'The one you left by my coffee mug. It said, "We need to talk." One of the most ominous phrases in the English language, if you ask me,' he added lightly.

'It is rather,' I agreed. With everything that had happened, I had completely forgotten about writing it, and it had definitely slipped my mind how melodramatic the note had been. Now I wondered what had possessed me. There was too much uncertainty and change in my life already without adding anything like that into the mix.

'So, let's talk,' invited Charlie. 'We might as well pass the journey by chatting, rather than by wondering about Arthur's surgery.'

I opened my mouth, ready to say...what exactly? Because my earlier concerns about Charlie vanishing and not pulling his weight in the house renovation had faded into insignificance given his solid support over the last twelve hours. And as for the other thing that had been on my mind – well, that was a ridiculous distraction. It was probably just a reaction to the amount of time I'd been spending not looking beyond the boundaries of Oak Tree Cottage. It was time to get back to business, and focus on staying strong for my family and taking care of Ted.

'So, what was it that you wanted to talk about?' Charlie pressed.

'Do you know, it's completely slipped my mind,' I said. 'It can't have been very important. And if it was, it'll probably come back to me when I'm not thinking about it.'

'Hmm,' said Charlie. He didn't sound convinced, but to give him credit, he didn't push me further, although I could tell my evasive response had only increased his curiosity. We both knew that I was too organised a person to forget important things.

I responded by reaching out and turning the radio on. The news headlines didn't exactly make me feel any better with their tales of cruelty and misery, but at least it put an end to what could have developed into a very awkward conversation.

Ted was in a particularly bumptious mood when we opened the door of Granddad's house, spinning around on the spot, and then running across to pick up his dinner bowl, so we could be in no doubt that he was hungry. It felt wrong to be crossing the threshold knowing that Granddad wouldn't be here to meet us with his usual cheery greeting. Ted's noisy exuberance somehow amplified the quiet elsewhere in the house. Granddad normally kept the place immaculate, but I could see spiderwebs in the corners of the room, and when I opened the cupboards to find Ted's essentials, a collection of junk mail and recycling fell out of them. Granddad had obviously been finding things tough for a while, but had preferred to conceal it rather than lose face by asking for more help. I could have kicked myself for not paying better attention and noticing it sooner.

I set about clearing up so that Granddad would have one less thing to worry about on his return. Charlie opened the fridge and started checking the items within.

'I think we're going to have to take the veg and milk with us. They'll only go off if we leave them.'

I nodded. There was no point in me pretending that Granddad would be coming back in the next few days. The road to recovery that lay before him was going to be long.

'Chin up, for Ted's sake,' said Charlie, gently squeezing my shoulder as I helped him put the food into bags. 'Let's drop these off at the food bank on our way back. I think Arthur will appreciate the gesture, and at least we'll be doing something positive.'

'Good idea. Right, I'd better get Ted's stuff together. You're missing him already, aren't you, Teddy boy?'

Ted responded by thudding his tail loudly against the radiator, beating a rhythm like he was a drummer in a band.

'Your master is going to be okay. And you're a very good boy for getting help to him,' I said. 'Lassie had better watch out.'

Charlie gave a final check around the kitchen. 'You don't travel light, that's one thing for certain, Ted.' He reached down and scratched the top of his head. Ted gave a grunt of approval in response. 'I think I've gathered all his toys.

Apart from his bed, food and bowls, is there anything else we need? No medication or anything?'

'No, I think we're good. I've got his harness and lead. Right, Ted, are you going to come with us?'

When I was describing what happened next on my return to school, Leila almost couldn't believe me. Because as soon as Ted realised we'd packed up all his stuff, his whole demeanour changed. He went from wiggling with fun to worn down with worry, his tail between his legs, looking between us sadly as he dug his claws into the kitchen floor and refused to move.

'I think he's concerned about abandoning Granddad,' I said, my heart aching all over again. How could I explain the situation to him? 'I promise, we'll take you to see him, Ted. He's going to be okay. But you're going to have to come and stay with us for a while until he gets fully better.'

Ted wasn't having any of it.

'Look, Ted, what's this?' Charlie tried the other, usually foolproof, method of bribing him with a treat. But Ted only gave it a half-hearted sniff before he returned to the spot where his bed had been and continued his sit-in protest.

Eventually, when it became clear that neither persuasion nor gentle coercion was going to work, Charlie bent down and picked Ted up.

'Good thing you're a Border Terrier and not a Labrador or larger, old boy,' he said. To be honest, I think that's what Ted had been angling for the whole time. Charlie cuddled Ted to him and muttered comforting nothings in his soft ears, which also made me feel a bit better. Thankfully Ted perked up once we got in the car, and by the time we returned to Oak Tree Cottage, he was once again acting like the big dog in a little body that he was.

When we got the call to say that Granddad was out of surgery and doing well, Charlie had already fixed Ted up with his own dog-safe run. I say dog-safe, but what actually happened was that Ted solemnly watched Charlie working for several hours to construct a vast pen for him in the garden, cutting back the weeds and fencing off a sizeable run, and then as soon as Charlie declared it completely dog-proof, Ted calmly hopped over the fence and started pottering around the rest of the garden without a care in the world.

'I swear he did that deliberately,' said Charlie, wiping the sweat from his brow, and shaking his head at the pooch's antics.

'You know Ted, he doesn't let anything stand in his way,' I said, glad to have something to laugh about. Although Granddad was out of imminent danger, I knew there were still many post-surgery complications which could affect a man of his seniority.

'I honestly thought I'd built the fence high enough. The guy on YouTube said it would create a secure space for a dog twice Ted's size.'

I smiled. 'Ah, so you've finally caught the YouTube tutorial bug too?'

Charlie looked embarrassed. 'It seemed to be working for you, so I thought I'd give the more methodical approach a go. I don't understand where I went wrong.'

'For a man who works in social media, you seem remarkably naïve about how these influencers work. I'm beginning to believe that it's all in the edit, and the bits where they go wrong or get stuck end up on the cutting-room floor. Besides, Ted's a bright boy. If he's determined enough, he'll find a way.'

'Ted might be determined, but I'm even more so. I won't let him get the better of me.'

True to his word, Charlie spent the rest of the afternoon battling with the dog run. It grew more and more elaborate, as he fished bits of the old kitchen units out of the skip to help the construction process. Finally, he declared himself satisfied, and so I brought Ted back out from where he'd been 'helping' me choose paint for the kitchen, aka snoring on his back with his legs in the air.

With a great sense of theatre, Charlie scooped Ted up and deposited him in the run, and gave a bow.

'Your domain, my lord,' he said.

Ted scampered around the boundary, sniffing the escape-proof solid walls with determination. When he finally realised that there was nowhere to get out, he sat in the middle of the run and gave a plaintive howl.

'Give him a second, he'll get used to it,' said Charlie, the uncertainty in his voice contradicting the confidence of his words.

Ted let out another 'haruuuuwl' of despair and anguish. I couldn't bear it any longer. I clambered over the barrier and picked him up, burying my face in his warm fur.

'I'm sorry, Ted. Mean Charlie won't make you stay in it any longer, I promise.'

'I swear he just winked at me,' said Charlie with a laugh. 'I've got to hand it to you, Ted, you managed to get out of the escape-proof run. You're definitely going to add to the laughter in the Hutchinson–Humphries household.'

Chapter Twenty-One

'I think it's time to move some furniture in,' declared Charlie, as we watched a skip-load of rubbish and renovation detritus being raised onto the back of a flatbed truck, another empty skip replacing it. Granddad's gift really was the present that kept on giving.

'Do you think? But I was getting quite used to my air bed. Minimalistic living is all the rage, don't you know?'

Since the drama of Granddad's fall, Charlie and I had reverted to normal, our behaviour business as usual, which was helping me to cope with the worry, even if it made other niggling thoughts harder to ignore.

Charlie laughed. 'You might be getting used to it, but I'm growing a bit sick of my yoga mat. It felt very virtuous to begin with but I'm starting to develop some serious aches and pains.'

'Guessing you're a way off guru status then?'

'Most definitely. Give me a memory foam mattress with crisp white sheets any day.'

The image of Charlie sitting up in bed and running his hands over the sheets, inviting me to join him, suddenly intruded on my mind. I swallowed, feeling myself blush.

'You all right, Freya?' he asked. 'The sun getting too much for you?'

'If that's an attempt at a redhead joke, Charlie Humphries, I'm not having it,' I said, deciding it was best to go on the offensive.

Charlie held his arms up in surrender. 'I wouldn't dare. I've still got the wound from the last time I tried it. You threw a wellington boot at me.'

'I didn't throw it at you, you just happened to be in the way when I flung it. There's a big difference. And you know I still feel guilty about that.'

My eyes sought out the tiny scar on his forehead which I had unintentionally been the cause of when we were both six years old. It had been bad luck that there was gravel stuck in the tread of the boot, which I had chucked in general exasperation rather than deliberately aiming it at him. Another little boy in our class had been taunting me for weeks about being a 'carrot head' and having 'ginger pubes', a phrase which I didn't really understand at the time, but which I knew was probably not nice given the nasty expression on his face every time he said it, which was several times a day. Charlie had happened to wander over at the wrong time offering me a copy of *Anne of Green*

Gables because it had a picture of a girl with red hair on the cover, and I had absolutely lost it.

The cut had only been tiny, but as it was on his head, it had bled copiously, and I had been convinced I'd killed him. He'd been the one who'd ended up comforting me as I sobbed my heart out, urging the teacher to send me off to prison, because I deserved to be there for causing so much damage to my best friend. Afterwards, Charlie had insisted he was proud of the scar, like it was a war wound which joined us together for ever. I wasn't so sure about that, but I had been greatly relieved to see the smile on his face.

Grown-up Charlie grinned at me, and rubbed his head as if it was causing him pain. 'I've learned my lesson, never you fear. Anyway, stop distracting me – what do you think about furniture? I reckon we can do a lot better than camping kit and upturned cardboard boxes, even if you have covered them in wood-effect laminate. We are allowed to have some comfort while we're doing the renovation work, you know. Now the worst of the dusty stuff is done, it makes sense to do it. It would be good to make the place feel more homely. And it would make it look more inviting to potential buyers,' he added, his casual afterthought a jarring reminder that I needed to focus on Oak Tree Cottage as our investment, rather than our home.

'A proper bed would be nice,' I said. 'And maybe a chest of drawers or a wardrobe so I could put my clothes away instead of living out of a suitcase. My parents did promise us a sofa. If we hired a van, we could go and collect it from them. They've got enough on their plate with Granddad still in hospital.'

'That sounds like a plan. We'll swing by the farm as well and check out the bits and pieces my parents have stored away in a barn. I can't promise the stuff will be any good, but we can have a look, and anything's better than nothing, right?'

Despite declaring myself perfectly confident about driving the van, I'll admit I felt very nervous when I hauled myself up into the cab and sat in the driver's seat. We'd decided it would be best to travel separately, Charlie following on in the Land Rover, so we could transport more stuff and make the most efficient use of the time. It had sounded good in theory, but in practice I realised how much I'd underestimated the stress of driving for the first time in a couple of years, and driving a van no less for the first time in forever.

'Being a van man suits you, Hutch,' said Charlie, standing by the door of the cab.

'I'm not sure that's a compliment,' I said. 'Does this mean I'm now obliged to wolf whistle at strangers and loudly commentate on other people's bad driving?'

'Whatever floats your boat.'

'Hmm, I'm not sure that's an appropriate metaphor for van driving. Anyway, no time for chatting, we've got some serious furniture removing to do.'

After a couple of dodgy moments trying to find the bite on the clutch, I soon got the hang of van driving and started to appreciate the elevated view I had of the road. I could see how van drivers could get carried away with their position of power, feeling so much bigger than the small hatchbacks that the vehicle towered over.

Mum and Dad had put the sofa in the garage and left the door open for us as they were having a meeting with Granddad's doctors. I parked on the road, doing my best not to block anyone in, and Charlie pulled up behind me.

'Ready to put those developing muscles of yours to good use, Charlie?' I teased him.

'It's not the size that counts, but what you do with them,' he said.

'Yes, of course,' I said, laughing. 'Anyway, I'm sure between us we can manage to carry a sofa. How hard can it be?'

The weight of the sofa was not a problem in the slightest, but what I hadn't taken into account was its awkward shape and the distribution of said weight. The fabric also didn't help. The cover was a soft, velvety material in a peacock blue, pleasingly silky to the touch, and undoubtedly extremely comfortable to sit on, but also very challenging to get a grip of.

We hauled the sofa up and tried to manoeuvre it into a comfortable carrying position for both of us. Somehow I ended up in the position where I was going to have to walk backwards.

'Are we about to re-enact that scene from *Friends* where Ross yells, "Pivot, pivot" while they get the sofa stuck halfway up a flight of stairs?' I said. 'You're going to have to let me know if I'm about to bump into anything.'

'Don't worry, Freya, you're safe in my hands,' said Charlie. We walked a few steps before he added, 'Maybe this is my opportunity to get my long-planned revenge for the welly wanging incident?'

'Ha ha. Any more of that, and I'll leave you to carry it by yourself.' I would have pulled a face at him, but I suspected my features were contorted enough already from the effort.

The banter distracted us from the difficulty of the task and we eventually managed to haul the sofa into the back of the van.

'A job well done,' said Charlie, slapping himself on the back, and then repeating the gesture on me.

I pretended to stagger forward. 'I hate to tell you, but that was the easy bit. The real challenge will be when we get it back to Oak Tree Cottage and try to get it through the doorways.'

Charlie's face fell. 'Hmm, maybe we should have measured the gap before we collected it.'

'Charlie, what do you take me for? Of course I measured the gap before we collected it. It's going to be a tight squeeze, I warn you now, but I have faith in the pair of us.' I checked my watch, and realised to my horror that we'd already fallen behind the schedule I'd mentally sketched out. 'Right, we've only got the van for another couple of hours, so we're going to have to get a wiggle on if we're going to pick up stuff from your parents' place as well.'

'Let's hope they're out on the tractor then when we arrive, otherwise they'll keep us chatting for ages,' said

Charlie, the affection for his mum and dad obvious in his voice.

'Although it would be good to have a couple of pairs of extra hands,' I pointed out. 'See you up there.'

It felt like a trip down memory lane driving along the road to Charlie's parents' house, even though it was the first time doing it when I was in the driving seat rather than being dropped off by my dad for a play date. It hadn't changed much since I'd last visited as an eleven-year-old, the paintwork perhaps slightly more faded and the outbuildings more weathered. But it still felt welcoming and comforting, the place that I used to regard as my second home.

Charlie's mum came rushing out from one of the barns to greet us, a smear of oil on her face.

'There you are, I was wondering when I'd be seeing you two. Excuse the mess I'm in, I've been tinkering with the trailer again. Your dad keeps saying we should get a new one, but I know I can fix it. How are you, Freya my love?' She gave me a huge hug, then stood back, holding me at arm's length, regarding me closely. 'Haven't you grown?'

'It's to be expected, Mum,' said Charlie. 'We're not kids anymore.'

'You'll always be my baby, you big brute,' she said, ruffling his hair. 'Do you two have time for a cuppa?'

'Sorry, Mum, we could only hire the van for a few hours, so we're rather up against it,' said Charlie. 'Freya's keeping me on a tight leash.' He winked at me, which somehow made me interpret his comment in a rather suggestive manner. I felt my face go fiery again. Charlie's grin grew broader.

'In which case, I'll summon your father and we'll help you carry the furniture.' She tapped out a message on her phone and then beckoned us into one of the barns. 'Help yourself to whatever you fancy. They're nothing special, just a few pieces we've picked up over the years and grown tired of, or replaced. Generally items my troublesome children simply had to have in their bedrooms and then quickly fell out of love with,' she told me. 'Charlie's dad is a terrible one for keeping hold of things "just in case". Hopefully they will prove to be of use to you.'

'It's very kind of you, Mrs Humphries,' I said.

'It's Sara, you don't have to "Mrs Humphries" me. It makes me feel ancient.'

Charlie put his arm around his mum. 'Come on, Aged Parent, let's get on with it.' She pretended to slap him away as Charlie laughed.

The barn was a veritable treasure trove of items, and Charlie and I had great fun picking out some chairs, a wardrobe and a couple of chests of drawers. We even struck lucky on the bed front, finding two rusty old bed frames, a double and a single.

'A bit of sanding and maybe some painting, and these will be good as new,' I said. 'Thank you so much, Sara, you're saving us a fortune.'

'Ah, but how are we going to decide who gets which bed?' Charlie said. 'Unless we share the double of course.'

He waggled his eyebrows suggestively. I knew he was joking but I wished he wouldn't.

'We'll Rock, Paper, Scissors for it,' I said. 'Only this time it'll be the classic form of the game, no flamethrowers allowed.'

'Nothing changes with you two,' said Charlie's dad with a grin. 'Are you sure you don't want our help carrying things at the other end?'

'We've taken up enough of your time already. Thank you so much, Mum and Dad. We'll invite you and Freya's parents round for dinner once the house is in a more habitable state.'

'We'll look forward to it,' said Sara.

Once we got back to Oak Tree Cottage, we both seriously regretted Charlie's refusal to accept his parents' help. As time was not on our side, we decided to unload the van first so we could return it to the depot, and then worry about the furniture, which we left stacked up at the side of the house.

'The neighbours are going to start a petition about the state of the place,' I said. 'Please don't let it rain this afternoon.'

By the time we arrived back from the depot, the clouds were gathering, and Ted was expressing his indignation at having been left behind by chewing on the kitchen door.

'Ted, stop it, that's not like you at all,' I said, feeling guilty. I felt even worse when I had to deposit him in his run in the garden so we could carry the furniture in without him getting underfoot. I promised him an extra-long walk as compensation and then hurried round to the furniture pile, feeling his baleful eyes watching my every move.

Charlie glanced up at the sky. 'I think perhaps the sofa should come in first. That's most likely to get damaged if it rains. The rest should be okay. A bit more rust won't make much of a difference to the beds.'

Despite my fears, we made a much better job of bringing the sofa into the house than Ross Geller would have done. I took the precaution of unscrewing the feet, which gave us a vital centimetre or so clearance between the frame of the front door, and we picked our way up the steps to it between the beautifully planted flower pots that had appeared there while we were on our travels. Stuck to a hanging basket I'd found a note from my parents, saying they were a present, and apologising that they couldn't be here in person to hand them over. The generous donations from our parents felt like housewarming gifts, like we were a real couple, planning on staying at Oak Tree Cottage long term. I allowed myself to briefly indulge the fantasy, before sensibly squashing the idea.

It was amazing how much difference having a sofa made to the living room. Even though the walls were still rough and the floor was bare, it was so much more homely having one comfortable item in there. I could picture relaxing on it on a winter's evening, Charlie jokingly complaining about me taking up all the space, before doing exactly that himself.

The wardrobe proved much more of a challenge to manoeuvre than the sofa had been, and both Charlie and I ended up with bruised fingers as we tried to get it up the stairs, which were creaking horribly throughout the whole process. For one terrifying moment I thought I wasn't going to be able to hold the thing for any longer, which would have put all the weight on Charlie, probably sending him tumbling down to the bottom.

'You've got this, Freya,' said Charlie, fixing me with a confident look which gave me enough strength to make it up the final steps. We dumped the wardrobe at the top of the stairs and stood back, the pair of us short of breath from the effort.

'I'd offer you a puff of my inhaler if I wasn't worried about the side effects,' I said to Charlie.

'You and your rules, Freya, always looking out for me. Don't worry, I'll live. Probably.' He pretended to gasp for air. I played along by rubbing his back in a comforting manner, wondering if his skin was tingling from the touch as much as my fingers were. Slowly, without me consciously thinking about it, my movement changed from teasing to more sensual as his back arched under my hand. I was even tempted to pull him closer and explore further, emboldened by the way he was watching me closely.

I leaned forward and whispered in his ear. 'When you've finished being melodramatic, do you want to come to my room?' I said, my heart beating rapidly as I issued an invitation that I knew was open to misinterpretation. Blame the fact that so many conversations today had involved talking about our plans for the future, as if it was a given that that future was still together. I decided for once to be spontaneous and daring, to act on that impulse of desire, and see what happened. Charlie gazed at me intensely, then reached forward. I tensed in glorious anticipation of his hand on my body, of his voice replying with a husky 'Yes', but instead he reached past me and plucked something out of mid-air.

'A spider was about to land on your head, Hutch,' he said.

And all at once my courage disappeared and embarrassment replaced it. I hadn't seen a spider scuttling away, so for all I knew it was a convenient excuse of Charlie's to prevent an awkward moment. I was letting myself get carried away. I cleared my throat, the sound unnaturally loud. 'Do you want to bring the wardrobe into my room?' I said, as if that had been what I'd intended all along. 'If you're still sure that it's okay for me to have it.'

Charlie's features relaxed into their usual cheery expression. 'You have more posh clothes than I do. Besides, I'm hoping it gives me leverage on getting the double bed.'

'What happened to Rock, Paper, Scissors?' I said in mock indignation, determined to act normally. 'Go on then, I suppose it's a fair exchange.'

'All's fair when it comes to furniture.'

'Won't you get lonely, having all that space in a big double bed?' I could have kicked myself as soon as the words were out of my mouth.

Charlie put his head on one side. 'I'm not planning on sleeping in it by myself for the rest of my life,' he said. For a moment, I hoped his comments were directed at me. And then I thought about the spider that might not have existed, and remembered the presence of Serena in Charlie's life, and the thousand other reasons why complicating our house partnership would be a really, really bad idea, and reality came crashing back.

I turned back to pretend I was intent on examining the wardrobe.

'Do you think it'll fit through the doorway?'

'We got it into the house, so I don't see why not. I can always remove the door if we need a bit of extra space.'

'If you're promising a re-run of when you "removed" my bedroom window, then I'd rather you didn't.'

Charlie laughed. 'I like to think my house skills have improved since then. Come on. I know what you're like, you're trying delaying tactics. The sooner we get this into your room, the sooner we can take a break.'

'Or get started on sprucing up those beds. Now the prospect of sleeping in a comfortable bed has been dangled in front of me, I want to get on with it.'

'You and me both,' said Charlie. I turned my face away so he couldn't see my expression.

Once the furniture was in place, basic as it was, the house seemed to transform from a building site into something that actually resembled a proper home. I could overlook the crumbling plasterwork when there was a comfy sofa ready to collapse on in front of it, and the bare floorboards were significantly improved by the addition of some mats and rugs that I found in the bargain bucket at a charity shop. It was still a long way off being perfect, but it was getting there.

Charlie and I had never formally discussed it, but those times when we weren't working on house renovations or popping to the hospital to visit Granddad were now spent together in some kind of shared activity, almost as if we were an actual couple, although I kept telling myself not to think like that. And despite his comment about the double bed, he showed no sign of inviting Serena around to share it, even after we'd spent an afternoon in the garden rubbing the metal down and treating it until it was shining again. When we installed it in his room, I thought I caught his eyes on me and felt a burst of longing, but when I looked back, he was apparently concentrating on fitting the frame together, at which point I firmly reminded myself to keep a handle on any wayward feelings.

The transformation of my single bed was much less successful, but even though I couldn't get rid of all the rust, it was strong enough to hold a proper mattress, and that was all that mattered to me. But the first night I slept in it, I struggled to drift off. I'd obviously grown far too accustomed to the privations of the camping lifestyle. Or perhaps it had something to do with the fact that it was another milestone in our house renovation, and therefore another milestone closer to the day when we would be selling up and going our separate ways.

Chapter Twenty-Two

As well as having to keep a close eye on Ted when he was outside, it turned out we needed to watch him when he was inside too. He might be a small dog, but he certainly had a big presence and didn't allow us to forget he was around. On the plus side, at least it provided me with plenty of funny stories to share with Granddad, but it was definitely to the detriment of the renovation schedule.

We'd reached the momentous point of being able to paint the kitchen. Despite its initially unpromising appearance, it had turned out to be the only room that didn't need completely re-plastering, even after the electrician had done her worst. The plan of work I had drawn up went as follows: paint kitchen, build and install new kitchen cabinets, fit white goods, put flooring down, kitchen complete. It looked so simple on paper, but I should have known better; nothing to do with renovating Oak Tree Cottage was ever simple.

'You look like one of those poster girls from the 1940s, you know, the ones where they're flexing their arms and saying things like "We can do it",' said Charlie, reaching out and tweaking the headscarf which I'd tied over my hair in an attempt to protect it from paint. If there was one thing I'd learned from the step-by-step guide to painting your ceiling I'd read last night, it was that paint drips went everywhere.

'Yes, you're definitely giving off sexy 40s pinup vibes, Freya,' said Leila, who'd invited herself round to assist. 'What do you think, Charlie?' she asked, a wicked grin on her face. I shot her a warning glance, knowing she was trying to stir things up.

'I stand by my original statement,' said Charlie, enigmatically.

Leila rolled her eyes, disappointed not to have got a direct agreement out of him.

'When you two have finished gossiping about me, do you think we could get to work?' I asked, deciding it was time to move the conversation along. 'What do you think of the colour, Leila?'

Using a screwdriver, I levered the lid of the paint tin open to reveal the contents.

'Ta dah,' chorused Charlie and I, both of us caught up in the moment. We'd spent hours robustly debating the merits of various different shades, trying out patches on the walls and shining lights on them at various angles until we were completely satisfied. The discussion about the tiles had gone on even longer, until eventually I'd admitted defeat and conceded that Charlie's idea of green and cream ones in a chequerboard pattern looked better than my suggestion.

'You spent how long picking this?' said Leila. 'What is it, magnolia?'

I knew she was only teasing but I felt rather hurt by her underwhelmed response.

Fortunately Charlie defended our decision.

'Magnolia? How dare you! This is so much more than magnolia,' he said, threatening her with the paintbrush.

Leila wafted it away. 'I take it back. What do I know? You guys have taste. We all know that I have none and lazily relied on my relatives to pay for an interior designer to style my flat, like the poor little rich girl that I am.'

'Woe is you indeed,' I said, passing a paint roller across to her. 'As punishment for that blatant attempt to play the emotionally deprived childhood card, you can have fun with the ceiling. And for future reference, this colour is "Grecian Skies", a warm white which has undertones of the yellow sun and blue seas of summer in the Greek islands.'

'Fancy,' said Leila. 'Who knew that such an apparently neutral colour could deliver so much?'

'And it was fifty per cent off in the end-of-line sale, not that that in any way influenced our decision, ahem,' I added.

'Even better.'

'I think we've done enough hanging around talking about it. Let's get on with the task before us,' said Charlie, rubbing his hands together with infectious enthusiasm. I had to admire his newly improved work ethic. Since

Granddad's accident, he seemed to be consciously making more time to help me with the renovations, even though I knew the workload from his business had increased as he picked up the marketing slack for companies while their employees went off on their summer holidays.

'I call dibs on the stepladder,' said Leila. 'You two tall beans can practically reach the ceiling without any help.'

Charlie turned the radio on, and then we set to work. I was ashamed to admit that this was my first time painting a room. Unlike many teenagers, I hadn't gone through a phase of wanting to paint my bedroom black, and since I'd moved out, I'd never been given the option of redecorating the series of depressing rental rooms I'd called home. Judging by the videos I'd watched online, it would be an extremely satisfying, and hopefully quite speedy process, with the colour smoothly going on the walls and making them dazzle with their fresh new look. Of course, what I'd failed to take into account was that most of the videos I'd watched had been timelapses with the sound turned off. Because it quickly became clear to me that anyone who could paint a room without feeling the need to swear out loud in frustration must be some kind of saint. Every time I tried to mimic the long, smooth brush strokes of the tutorial, I ended up depositing huge dollops of paint on the wall which then started dribbling down onto everything. And as for the claim on the side of the can that 'One coat covers all', well, I was distracting myself from the rapidly developing ache between my shoulder blades by mentally composing a letter of complaint to the manufacturers pointing out that their claim was complete fiction.

'The paint's meant to go on the wall, not on you,' said Charlie, as yet another splatter landed on my face. I'd long since put my glasses away, fearing I was going to do irreparable damage to them. Painting in a short-sighted state wasn't really helping the process, but at least it was giving a flattering soft-focus effect to my feeble attempts.

'Hold on, what's that on the end of your nose?' I asked, pretending to lean forward to inspect Charlie's features, then daubing him with the paintbrush.

'Oh, you asked for it,' said Charlie, coming at me with the roller. I squealed and tried to run away, ducking down so that he couldn't reach his intended target. Unfortunately, Charlie couldn't stop the momentum of the roller, so Leila ended up with a great big streak of paint all the way down one leg.

'Children, behave yourselves, please,' she said, shaking her head at the state of her attire.

'Sorry, Leila,' chorused Charlie and I, pretending to be shamefaced.

'And apologise to each other,' she pressed, engaging teacher mode.

Charlie fixed me with a look that was quite devastating in its intensity. As I gazed back at him, I found myself taking a step closer, suddenly hypnotised by the warm expression in his eyes. Was it my imagination, or had his gaze briefly lowered to my lips? He reached towards me, his eyes once again gazing deep into mine.

'Freya...' he breathed, his voice doing that husky thing that instantly set something zinging within me, despite myself. Then he cupped my chin with his hand and ever so slowly and ever so gently smeared paint across my cheek.

'You devious bastard,' I said, trying to grab the roller from his hands before he could inflict more damage on me.

Somewhere in the back of my mind, I registered Leila saying she needed to get something from her car and swiftly exiting the room, but I was far too wrapped up in trying to get my own back on Charlie to take it in. I caught hold of his wrists and pulled his hands close to me, trapping them between us so he couldn't move them without causing equal paint carnage on himself.

'Are you sure you want to continue this battle?' said Charlie, his eyes glinting with amusement. Somehow he managed to pull me closer so that now he had the advantage. Suddenly I was very aware that the only thing between us was the paint roller, and I could already feel the coolness of the wet paint soaking into the top part of my dungarees. I knew that Charlie would have the mirrored mark on his boiler suit. The warmth of his breath tickled my mouth, and I couldn't help slowly tracing my tongue around my lips in response. Charlie's expression intensified and I found myself closing the millimetre of distance between our faces. My eyelids fluttered shut in blissful anticipation of his mouth on mine. No matter that my face had a 'Grecian Skies' foundation covering half of it, that the strands of my hair which had escaped from their scarf looked like they'd been in a dip-dye experiment gone horribly wrong, and that this was a seriously bad idea. In this moment, all I cared about was the way Charlie had been looking at me, like he couldn't take his eyes off me, like I was the only person in the world. I couldn't wait for what must be about to happen.

'Ted, no! Put it down, droooop it,' said Charlie.

Unfortunately, the reality was very different from my imaginings. The front of my body felt cold now that Charlie's was no longer flush against it. He sprang away from me in pursuit of Ted, who was holding his tennis ball right above the open can of paint.

'Don't say "drop it",' I said desperately, the lust-induced jet lag of my mind finally catching up with me as I realised that this must have been what Charlie had actually been looking at so intently.

Ted, for the first time in his life, did exactly as instructed and deposited the tennis ball in the paint can. In slow motion I saw the paint slop up the sides and then slosh onto the floor.

'Leeeeave it, Ted, there's a good boy, leeeeeave it,' said Charlie, speaking slowly and carefully, and holding his hand out in a stop sign while he inched towards Ted.

Ted put his head on one side, as if considering his options. He glanced between Charlie and the ball. I swear the little minx was pondering what would get the best rise out of us. He lowered his muzzle towards the can.

'Nooo, Ted,' we both chorused.

He wagged his tail and swaggered away, leaving a trail of paint paw prints behind him. Fortunately he also left the ball in situ. It was going to be difficult enough trying to get the paint off his paws. I thanked my lucky stars we weren't going to have to tackle his head as well.

Charlie and I looked at each other and burst out laughing. The tension had gone, and suddenly everything was back to normal. As Charlie captured Ted and exited the room to deposit him in the pen in the garden before he could do any more damage, I started to wonder if the whole moment-of-magic thing had yet again been a one-sided figment of my unruly imagination.

'I'm not interrupting anything, am I?' Leila poked her head around the dining-room door, obviously having been hiding out there until the coast was clear.

'You're not,' I responded with a sigh. 'Although I'm pretty certain that there wasn't actually going to be anything for you to interrupt.'

'I'm not so sure about it. If you could see the way he looks at you when you're not aware of it...' Her voice tailed off as she saw the expression on my face, which very clearly said that I didn't believe her. 'Fine, think whatever you want to. But if you take my advice, you should talk to him at some point soon. I for one can't handle much more of this simmering tension,' she said.

'I'll think about it,' I replied, knowing I'd think of little else. She made it sound so simple, but I knew the situation was far from that. 'But in the meantime, I'm going to Google how to remove paint from a dog's paws and go out to help Charlie with the critter. It's definitely going to be a two-person job.'

'Rather you than me,' said Leila. 'I'll carry on with the ceiling, I think. I'm finding it strangely satisfying. It's bringing out an artistic side that I didn't know I had. And it's going to do wonders for my muscle tone.'

Armed with the answers from an internet search, and a large bucket of warm soapy water, I went out to join Charlie and Ted in the garden.

Ted inevitably did not want to cooperate and the contents of the bucket mostly ended up on Charlie and me rather than him. When eventually we'd managed to remove the last traces of paint from his paws and put him back down on the ground, he did several zoomy laps of his pen in protest, his backside lowered to the ground as he accelerated out of reach of the hateful bucket. We left him to dry off and returned to the kitchen, where Leila was crooning along to the Top 40 on the radio.

'You two took your time,' she said. 'I warn you, I'm going to start charging by the hour.'

'Wow, you've nearly done the first coat of the ceiling, that's so impressive,' I said, genuinely in awe at her painting skills, which certainly put mine and Charlie's to shame.

'You can thank me by naming your first-born child after me,' she said. Fortunately, Charlie's back was turned so he couldn't see that she was addressing her comment to both of us. I raised a warning eyebrow at her, and although she mimed zipping her lips, I knew it was only a matter of time before she said something else equally tactless. I marched across and turned up the radio to make chatting difficult.

And then the three of us spent the rest of the afternoon carrying out the hard labour of completing the first new paint coat in the whole house.

'I think I'm beginning to get the hang of this,' I said as we eventually stepped back to survey our work. The ceiling and every wall in the kitchen had a layer of 'Grecian Skies' on it. Yes, I could still see the dark shadow of the plaster through it, but it was looking significantly fresher than it had done.

'By the time we've done another two coats, we'll have completely mastered it,' said Charlie, who had also discovered that his painting talents did not match those of Leila. She had managed to remain pretty much pristine throughout the whole process, apart from where she'd been an unlucky bystander in the paint fight, of course. I tried to tell myself that the state of Charlie and me was mostly down to the paintbrush battle we'd had, but the reality was that we were still pretty ham-fisted as decorators. Hopefully we'd make up for it when we got to the cupboard construction stage, although I could already anticipate heated discussions over Allen keys.

Charlie leaned down and rummaged among the bags from our latest foray to the DIY store.

'Here we go,' he said, producing a bottle of Prosecco with great aplomb. 'Payment for the workers.'

'Finally,' said Leila. 'This is what I'm talking about. Although as I'm driving I will have but the smallest sip, then I'll leave you two to it. I'm sure you've got much more important things to be doing than entertaining me.' She shot a significant look in my direction which I did my best to appear oblivious to.

True to her word, after having a thimbleful of Prosecco, Leila took her leave.

Charlie and I clinked our glasses.

'And then there were two,' he said.

'Three, don't forget Ted,' I said automatically.

'How could I forget Ted? Three makes a proper family unit,' said Charlie. I couldn't decide whether there was a greater meaning to his words or he was making one of his jokes.

Kicking myself for being a coward, I decided it was safer to interpret it as the latter.

'Yep, the classic dysfunctional family. The sensible bossy one, the fun impulsive one, and the glue that holds them both together.'

Charlie leaned down and scratched Ted, who had finally been allowed back in the house as long as the kitchen remained out of bounds to him.

'I reckon in that interpretation you're the sensible bossy one, matey,' he said.

Of course I'd meant myself, but I think I preferred Charlie's way.

'As you've provided the liquid refreshments, I'll sort out the food for tonight,' I offered. 'Why don't you go and have the first shower?'

'And let the Prosecco go flat?'

'If we stick a teaspoon into it, it'll stay bubbly, don't you worry.'

'Another tip from your online videos?' said Charlie.

'Oh no, this is all mine,' I said pretending to be indignant. 'Now off you go before I change my mind and go in first.'

I half hoped Charlie would make one of his jokey invitations for us to share a shower, but of course he did no such thing.

I decided to take the camping stove out to the garden and cook in the fresh air, not wishing to taint the food with paint fumes or conversely somehow trap the scent of melting cheese in the new decor. When Charlie returned a short while later wearing a pair of smart new jeans and a top that brought out the colour of his eyes, I gave myself a little shake and left him with strict instructions not to let the mushroom risotto dry out, while I zipped upstairs to effect what I hoped would be a similar transformation.

Inevitably my hair wouldn't play ball, and I ended up tying it out of the way in a messy bun which I hoped would conceal the worst of the paint clumps that were still stuck in there. If I continued at this rate, my hairdresser was going to cry next time I managed to get an appointment.

I hurried back downstairs and discovered Charlie had set up a dining area in the garden. He'd found a string of fairy lights somewhere and strung them in the boughs of the oak tree, beneath which was a makeshift table made out of an upturned wooden box which the new tiles for the bathroom had come in. There was a citronella candle in the centre of the table and the places were set with the mishmash of second-hand cutlery we'd acquired. It was haphazard and messy and I loved it.

'Your table, madam,' he said bowing deeply and then escorting me to my seat. He stood behind the camping chair and pushed it in as I sat down, as if we were in a fancy restaurant.

'Dinner was meant to be my treat,' I protested, making to get up.

'You stay seated, I'll sort it out. I'm very good at following direction,' he said.

'I hadn't noticed,' I said. He responded with a grin. 'Fair enough, if you insist. The risotto should be nicely cooked by now, so all you need to do is serve it.'

'Delicious,' said Charlie as he ladled the portions onto the plates. Ted sidled into view and plonked himself down at our feet, never one to let a potential opportunity for scraps pass him by.

We took our time, talking and laughing throughout the meal. And afterwards we settled down on the second-hand sofa. Sitting together watching Netflix on Charlie's propped up iPad while Ted snuggled on our laps felt properly wonderful, the way things should be. Once again I felt that burgeoning longing for something more. But a casual remark from Charlie, speculating how much value the new kitchen would add to the house, soon brought me back to my senses, and reminded me to stop letting flights of fancy interfere with our very sensible plan to sell up and move on.

Chapter Twenty-Three

As the kitchen started to bear some resemblance to a place where you'd actually feel comfortable preparing food, I got the news I'd been waiting for. Granddad Arthur was finally going to be discharged from hospital. Unfortunately, that didn't mean he was well enough to return straight home, but instead he would be going into a care home where he would get intensive physiotherapy with the aim of giving him his independence back. Despite the fact that he was leaving hospital, Granddad had not taken the news about the care home well.

'Care homes are full of old people,' he'd complained, failing to accept that he would probably be one of the oldest residents there. I understood the sentiment behind his words, that he was scared that once he went into a home, there would be no return. I knew it was his idea of hell to be trapped in a place where there was enforced jollity and everyone treated him like an idiot. Mum reassured me that they'd managed to find somewhere really special for him where there would be no such patronising behaviour, but when I rang them up to arrange my first visit, I didn't have a good feeling.

The woman at the other end of the line had a very no-nonsense manner of speaking.

'Visiting hours are between twelve and three, and you must sign in on arrival. It's for security reasons.'

'Fair enough,' I said, although I really didn't like the idea of visiting being a restricted thing only allowed between certain hours. 'And can we bring Granddad's dog to see him?'

There was a sharp intake of breath. 'A dog? Categorically no,' she said, in a tone of voice that made it sound like I'd suggested smuggling illegal drugs into the home.

'Can I ask why that is? Is it for health reasons?' I said, determined to push the issue, for Granddad's sake.

'They are disruptive to the residents and get in the way,' she retorted. There was clearly nothing more to discuss.

I rang off and turned to Charlie, a disappointed expression on my face. 'They've said no to bringing Ted. Granddad is going to be gutted.'

'It's not because there's someone in the home who's really allergic?'

'No, I got the impression that the woman on reception doesn't like dogs. Probably too much fun for the residents.

That's such a shame. Granddad will be so sad, and I promised Ted a visit too.'

'Perhaps it's time we reviewed our "Terrible Twosome" credentials. We can't be disappointing Arthur and Ted, after all.'

'I'm not sure what we can do about it. We don't want to get Granddad into trouble.'

'Rediscover your sense of adventure, Freya. What's the worst that they can do? Don't worry, I have a plan,' said Charlie.

The plan involved smuggling Ted into the home in a giant Ikea bag. Simple, but hopefully effective, although I had my doubts. Charlie parked around the corner, and then we coaxed Ted into the bag.

'Are you sure he's going to be all right in this?' I said, already envisaging the countless things that could go wrong, many of which involved us getting Granddad evicted from the home for breaking the rules.

'He'll be absolutely fine, won't you, Ted? It's nice and open at the top so he'll get plenty of air, and as long as he stays still, the bossy person on reception will be none the wiser. We'll say we're bringing some extra clothes in for Arthur.'

'Hmm, it's the staying still bit I'm worried about. I can't recall Ted ever staying still, not even after he cut his paw open on some glass when he was a puppy.'

Ted peered up at me with his big brown eyes and I swear he winked.

Charlie gently lifted the bag up on his shoulder and

stood there, trying to look nonchalant as the contents wriggled.

'You couldn't look more suspicious if you tried,' I said.

'We'll go for distraction techniques,' said Charlie, seizing my hand and striding forward so confidently that I had little choice but to go along with him.

'Why are we holding hands?' I hissed as we walked up the front steps and into the reception.

'Trust me' was all he said.

There was a queue of people waiting to sign in, and from the growing rustling from the bag, I could tell that Ted was getting rather restless.

When we finally got to the front of the queue, Charlie suddenly kissed the back of my hand.

'Why don't you sign us in, babe?' he said. 'My fiancée is ever the practical one, and that's why I love her,' he explained confidently to the woman behind the desk, drawing her closer in a charming manner, the very picture of the besotted partner. Meanwhile he surreptitiously offloaded the bag onto my shoulder, I'm assuming so I could tuck it out of the woman's sight. But the sudden weight of Ted nearly made me stagger, which of course drew her attention straight back to where we didn't want it.

Charlie bent his head and briefly kissed me before turning back to the woman. 'She's overcome by my presence,' he said, still Mr Charm personified.

The woman actually giggled. As she turned away to check Granddad's room number, I rolled my eyes at Charlie and mouthed, 'What was that in aid of?' at him, my heart still pounding at the sudden delightful shock of feeling his lips against mine. He grinned.

'Means must,' he whispered. 'While she's focusing on love's young dream, she won't notice that Ted's about to climb out of that bag. Quick, make a run for it.'

I hadn't noticed either. I glanced down and spotted Ted's furry head poking up out of the bag. I gently shoved it down and then strode off down the corridor, hoping that if I looked like I was meant to be there, nobody would question my presence.

Fortunately, I heard Granddad's distinctive laugh in the distance, so I knew I was going in the right direction. I rounded the corner and nearly got taken out by a cheerful man in a wheelchair who was apparently involved in a race against my granddad. He reached the end of the corridor and slapped his hand against the wall, then punched the air in delight.

'Well done, Sjaak,' said Granddad as he reached the finishing post a mere second or two later. 'Freya love, it's great to see you.'

At the sound of Granddad's voice, Ted's head made a reappearance.

'Eh, Ted lad, let me introduce you to my good friend Sjaak. I think you two would get on like a house on fire, same sense of mischief the pair of you.'

I heard Charlie's voice drifting down the corridor, asking a question of someone in an overly loud manner.

'Watch out, the introductions are going to have to keep, I'm afraid. I think we might be about to get found out. Is there somewhere we can escape to?' I asked.

'Follow me,' said Sjaak. 'I've been here a few days longer than your granddad, so I know all the Colditz escape routes.'

He led us out of a fire escape, across a courtyard and then into a wing at the back of the building.

'Use my room for your visitors, Arthur, I'll go and keep watch,' said Sjaak, giving a cheery wave before he whizzed back out to run interference. I was glad Granddad had found a friend here, someone with the same bright outlook on life. Hopefully it would make all the difference to him settling into his new surroundings and making a speedy recovery.

A few seconds later Charlie slipped into the room, then we shut the door and let Ted out to greet Granddad properly. I don't mind confessing that their happy reunion brought tears to my eyes, while Charlie was also openly sniffing at the sight of Ted's tail wagging so hard it was shaking the rest of his body too. He picked Ted up and put him on Granddad's lap, whereupon Ted started fiercely licking Granddad's ears.

'Enough of that, lad,' said Granddad, although his voice was gruff as if he was also only just holding back the emotion. Ted settled down, nuzzled up against his master and started quietly snoring as Granddad stroked his head. 'Tell me how the house is doing. Have you fixed it up yet?'

'We're getting there,' said Charlie.

'I'd say we're quite a long way off,' I said at the same time.

Granddad looked between us, an amused expression on his face.

'Sounds intriguing,' he said. 'I can't wait until they let me out of this place so I can come and inspect your handiwork – especially yours, Charlie old boy. How is the…?'

'It's a joint effort, Arthur sir, as well you know,' said Charlie cutting him off partway through his sentence. I couldn't for the life of me work out what unspoken conversation was being held.

'Yes, of course,' said Granddad. 'Judging by the specks still in Freya's hair, you've been painting? A nice fresh colour that. I shall look forward to seeing it in situ.'

'We thought we might as well focus on the kitchen as the other rooms are going to need re-plastering,' I said. 'I'm yet to brave the tutorial videos about how to do that, and judging by my painting inabilities, I have a horrible feeling that plastering isn't going to be in my skillset either.'

'I think I might be quite good at getting plastered,' said Charlie with a grin. 'In fact, when you go back to school next week, I was going to take a go at it.'

I experienced a clutch of nerves, both at the thought of having to go back to work and at the idea of Charlie solo plastering.

'Are you sure we shouldn't wait until we can stretch the budget enough to find a professional to do it?' I said.

'But it could be months before we've saved up enough,'

responded Charlie. 'And until we've done the plastering, the rest of the work will have to wait too. It could set your timetable back ages.'

To be honest, the idea of delaying the timetable seemed appealing, as I was dreading the moment when the work was completed and Charlie and I went our separate ways. But it was clear that Charlie was not of the same mindset.

'I'm still not sure about it,' I said.

'Trust me, Freya,' said Charlie, sounding confident.

Granddad chuckled. 'Have a bit of faith in the lad. Anyway, it's exactly like decorating a cake. And he'll have expert guidance.'

'What do you mean?' I said.

'Arthur means that he'll be on standby on FaceTime to point out where I'm going wrong, don't you?' said Charlie.

'You mustn't push yourself too much,' I said.

'Don't worry, I am stronger than I look,' said Charlie with a twinkle.

'I was talking to Granddad, as well you know.'

Our conversation was interrupted by someone knocking on the door. Ted let out a whuffling bark in response and stood up on Granddad's lap, looking ready to defend him from whatever interloper might dare enter.

'Shh, Ted,' I hissed, looking desperately around for a hiding place and finding nowhere suitable. 'What are we going to do with him?'

'I'll distract them, you take him out of the window,' said Charlie.

'Why am I the one climbing out the window?'

Charlie gave a fake cough which sounded remarkably like Ted's bark. 'Because I can do this, plus, as you keep on telling me, I've got the gift of the gab, and you're far too much of a goody two shoes not to give us away by looking guilty.'

And that's how I found myself with Ted squirming in my arms as I clambered out of the window, which thankfully was a ground-floor one, and then running across the care home garden like a burglar caught in the act.

'You have a lot to answer for, matey,' I said to Ted, tickling his nose affectionately as we hid behind Charlie's car. 'What's taking him so long? I'm sure he and Granddad are up to something. What do you think?' Ted's response was to fall asleep in my arms, which meant that I was stuck in an extremely uncomfortable half squatting position, not daring to move in case I disturbed him.

'What's going on here then?' an authoritative voice boomed from above. I jumped, making Ted wake up and emit a sleepy groan of protest.

I was about to launch into an obsequious apology for breaking care home rules when I realised that it was only Charlie messing about.

'Thanks for nearly giving me a heart attack,' I said. 'You took your time. And you've broken the cardinal rule of dog care – never disturb a snoozing pooch. Ted's worn out with all the excitement.'

'Sorry about that. Ser…someone rang while I was on my way out,' said Charlie. 'I've got to pop out this evening by the way,' he added casually. Too casually.

'Sure, no problem. You don't have to ask my permission,' I said carefully, hoping that I was managing to keep my disappointment to myself. Since Granddad's accident, Charlie had been sticking at my side like the supportive friend he was. Now that Granddad was recovering and I was in a better place, it seemed only fair for him to take a bit of time to meet up with Serena, which was obviously what he was doing.

'How about you? What have you got planned for this evening?' he asked.

'Leila mentioned her roller derby team are having an open training session tonight. I thought I'd give it go,' I said, plucking something, anything out of thin air that sounded a bit more interesting than my original inclination, which had been to stay in preparing for the start of the new term. I blamed the spectre of Serena for making me say it.

'Like that film *Whip It*? Fast-paced, hold nothing back and take no prisoners. Now that sounds like great fun,' said Charlie. 'Good for you. I'll give you a lift there if you like. Isn't roller derby a sport where everyone comes up with cool alternative names for themselves? You should go for "Hellraiser Hutch" or something like that. That would terrify the opposition.'

'Not sure I'm much of a hellraiser. And I wouldn't want to put you out, I'll get the bus,' I said, plotting how I could pretend to go for the bus and then return to the house when the coast was clear. I'd only said it to try to make myself sound less lame. I wasn't sure I was brave enough to follow through on my rash declaration.

'Don't do yourself down. You can raise hell when you choose to, and that's what matters. And it's no bother for me to give you a lift,' said Charlie with a smile which told me he'd probably seen through my plan.

True to his word, that evening he drove me to the door of the sports hall where the session was going to take place and waited, waving cheerily, until I'd walked through the doors and been scooped up by the team member in charge of welcoming newbies. Which is how I found myself tying the laces on a pair of borrowed roller skates while Leila did up my helmet and strapped pads around my knees and elbows.

'The amount of protective equipment is making me seriously worried,' I said, the nerves jangling in my stomach. 'I haven't worn this much kit since Year Ten hockey, which ended up with me getting a seriously bruised ankle and having to hobble around for most of the term.'

'Which would you prefer, staying here and maybe falling on your bum a few times, or waiting around at home for Charlie to return from his date, or perhaps even stay out overnight, while your heart breaks a little more?' Leila fixed me with her best no-nonsense expression.

'That's not what I'd be doing at all,' I said, although she'd hit far too close to the truth for my liking. 'You make me sound pathetic.'

'You're anything but, Freya. But if you won't woman up enough to tell him how you feel, then you can't get away with being sad when he goes off with the lovely Serena for the evening.'

'Fine, I admit it. Despite my best intentions, yes, I have fallen for him. But it's not a simple situation. You make telling him sound easy, but it's really, really not. There's a lot to consider. There's so much at stake if I say something and he's not in the same place, which I really don't think he is,' I protested. 'We share a house. We're financially tied to each other. If I go and make things all awkward between us by declaring undying love while he's very much friend-zoned me, it's going to mess everything up. We'll have to carry on living together, all the while knowing that there's this great big uncomfortable elephant of a declaration sharing the house with us. I can't bear to imagine the sad but kind look he'll give me when he has to gently let me down. I know he'll be super nice about it, but that'll be even worse. Things will never be the same again. Can you imagine how humiliating it would be? I don't think I'm brave enough to put myself out there like that.'

'But it might not happen. Because you won't know for sure until you say something. But we've had this conversation before, Freya. If you're not ready to be brave yet, that's okay. The one thing I would advise is not to leave it too late. You don't want to regret it. Sometimes you've got to take a chance, and trust that things will work out for the best. That's what I did with Nim. And in the meantime, my other piece of advice for you is to channel your powers of confidence tonight towards staying upright. The girls aren't going to let you go until you've whizzed around the track at least once.'

She gestured at the circuit that had been marked out on

the very solid-looking floor. Members of the Screaming Sisters roller derby team were warming up, streaking around the room at lightning-fast pace, weaving their way in and out of each other with only centimetres to spare. It looked utterly terrifying, and I would have run away if I hadn't been wearing roller skates. Suddenly the prospect of speaking to Charlie felt like a doddle in comparison.

I'd expected to hate every minute of the training session. After all, it played on all my weaknesses – my fear of getting hurt, my inability to loosen up and go with the flow, and of course my lack of confidence in shouting up and saying what I wanted. But Leila and her teammates proved to be a supportive bunch, cheering everyone on, and making all us newbies feel like we were making good progress as we tried out the various skating exercises designed to help boost our confidence and develop our skills. Towards the end of the evening, I even dared let go of Leila to do a tentative, extremely slow lap of the track, and was greeted on my return by cheers as loud as if I'd won the league for them. I wouldn't be making the team any time soon, but to my surprise I found I'd thoroughly enjoyed the evening, pushing myself out of my comfort zone and making some new friends along the way. It had been so long since I'd been part of an activity group, I'd forgotten how much fun it could be. I was fired up with enough enthusiasm to sign up for their beginners' classes, which would be running up until Christmas.

'Proud of you,' said Leila, giving me a hug after the session finished.

'What, for staying on my feet? I was the slowest by far,' I said. 'And I must have fallen over more times than everyone else combined. I swear my skin is going to be black and blue in the morning.'

'But you kept at it, even though you were terrified. Sometimes the things that scare us the most give us the biggest return,' she said.

'Ha ha, I know exactly what you're getting at,' I retorted.

'I promise I'll stop going on about it. But regardless of what happens with you and Charlie, you're still growing as a person, my lovely friend. The Freya of the beginning of the year would never have let loose and allowed herself to have fun like this.'

'That's because the Freya of the beginning of the year was still saving for her house deposit,' I pointed out.

'Nice try, but you've told me enough times that you're still as poor as a church mouse, which if you don't mind me saying is a very weird phrase. Maybe there are some rich church mice. But that's beside the point. I think you used saving for the house as an excuse not to push yourself to do things that made you worried. Now you're feeling the fear, and doing it anyway. Well, in most areas of life.'

'I get the message, thanks, Leila. That promise to stop going on about it didn't last long, did it? The crux of what you've been saying is that I am now a person who knows her own mind and does what she wants. In the spirit of that, perhaps you'll leave me to make my own decision about the Charlie situation and act accordingly?'

Chapter Twenty-Four

The weekend before term started, Charlie and I decided to make one final push and complete the kitchen so it was one less thing hanging over me when I was back at work.

'We might as well have one completely civilised room to enjoy as the nights draw in,' said Charlie. 'Much better to be able to prepare food in a safe environment and all that, rather than having to cook under the stars.'

I experienced a pang of nostalgia as I thought about that wonderful night where we'd eaten mushroom risotto under the fairy lights in the oak tree. I was going to miss romantic evenings like that, even though I suspected the romance had been very much one-sided. Charlie's next comment confirmed my fears.

'Besides, with a finished kitchen we could start getting valuations, if you like,' he added.

'Sure, if that's what you want,' I agreed, although the thought of selling the house and moving on was far from the enticement it used to be. My dream of a home of my own had evolved a lot over the past few months. The practicalities of living alone didn't concern me, but the idea of existing without Charlie by my side did.

To help eke out our ever-depleting budget, we'd ordered a flatpack kitchen that we were going to put together ourselves. I'd spent several hours poring over the instructions, but they might as well have been written in Greek for all the sense they made. Charlie, on the other hand, had done his usual trick of barely glancing at the pictures before he set to, laying out the component parts.

'It looks like a jigsaw puzzle, and I can't even pick out the edges to make it easier,' I said.

'A 3D jigsaw puzzle, no less,' said Charlie in a gleeful tone. If I wasn't very much mistaken, he was enjoying himself.

I braced myself for the ensuing chaos. But while I religiously followed the step-by-step guide and made very little progress, Charlie was soaring ahead. In no time at all, he'd constructed an actual cupboard with seemingly no wasted effort, and was ready to slide it into position next to the windows underneath which the plumber was going to install the sink.

'I'm impressed,' I said. 'Have you been secretly studying or something?'

'What makes you say that?' said Charlie. 'Maybe I'm

turning into a hugely talented carpenter. The instructions aren't the be-all and end-all, you know.'

Using a pencil, he marked the cupboard's position on the floor, then moved it back into the centre of the room.

'Look at this,' he said, pointing at the floor where the cupboard was going to stand.

I knelt down beside him.

'One of Ted's painted paw prints. The outline is so clear, it's like he did it deliberately,' I said. 'Perhaps it was his way of making his mark on the room.'

'Better than his usual cocking his leg method,' said Charlie, smiling. 'I think we should follow suit.'

'I'm assuming you're referring to paint rather than leg cocking?'

Charlie laughed. 'Not sure that kind of territory marking would help the resale value. No, what I was going to suggest is that we sign our names next to Ted's paw print. Adding our signatures for posterity. Think of all the people who've lived in this place over the years, and the traces of them that we've seen as we've stripped their decorations.'

'People who were sadly lacking in taste,' I joked.

'Or people whose decorative standards were very much of their time,' suggested Charlie.

'You're right. Maybe in fifty years' time another couple, or friends,' I hastily corrected myself, 'will be looking at our decorations and wondering what on earth we were thinking.'

I thought Charlie was about to say something, but whatever it was, he changed his mind about it.

'So, how do we make our mark?' I prompted, feeling like I'd missed another opportunity.

'Do you happen to have any marker pens in your school bag? If we scrawl our signatures and the date next to Ted's paw print, they'll be hidden underneath the cupboard. Once the skirting board is on, nobody will be any the wiser.'

I hurried upstairs to my room and rummaged through my bag until I found my pencil case.

'Here you go,' I said, offering Charlie his choice of colours.

'Ladies first,' he replied.

I selected a blue pen and carefully signed my name underneath Ted's paw print, then passed the pen over to Charlie. He added his signature, then looked across the room.

'I think someone wants to go out in the garden,' he said. Ted was standing staring pointedly at the back door.

'I'll let him out.'

I escorted Ted to his now just about tolerated dog run, and left him there to stretch his legs. When I returned to the kitchen, Charlie was finishing putting the cupboard back into its proper position.

'That's a shame. I was going to take a photo of our names there. Can we move it out again?'

Charlie leaned against the cupboard, blocking my access to it. 'Erm, sorry, Freya, but it's fixed now. I don't think it would be a good idea to keep moving it. It might make it wobbly. Right, onto the next cupboard. No rest for the wicked.'

'I guess so,' I said, still disappointed.

Charlie whizzed through constructing another two cabinets before I finally admitted defeat with the instructions and asked for his assistance.

'Freya Hutchinson, Miss Do-It-By-The-Book, asking for my help, the King of Winging It? What is the world coming to?' said Charlie, pretending to swoon at the very idea.

'All right, no need to gloat. I'll admit that I'm not right all the time. In fact, a lot of the time, I don't have a clue what I'm doing. But being a teacher, I have to maintain an air of confidence and self-belief.'

'Even if you're a quivering wreck inside?' said Charlie.

'Especially then. So come on then, give up the secret to your success.'

Charlie put his head on one side and considered me closely. 'Maybe not quite yet. But I will help you work out where you've been going wrong with the cabinet you've been trying and failing to construct all day.'

'Tell me, o wise one.'

'Let me savour this moment of Freya calling me wise,' said Charlie, clutching his hand to his chest and closing his eyes.

'Keep that up and I'll leave you to do the whole thing by yourself,' I said, nudging my hip against his.

Charlie looked pained. 'What happened to "Team work makes the dream work"?'

'I'm definitely going to be seeing these cabinets in my nightmares, let me tell you.'

'It's quite simple, once you've got the hang of it,' said

Charlie. And then he settled in to helping me, showing great restraint by not laughing at me when we realised that I'd been trying to hang the cupboard doors upside down.

Just before midnight on Sunday, we finally downed tools and stood back to admire our hard work. Admittedly we'd had to sacrifice putting down the new flooring, realising that my plan of work had been way too over-optimistic in trying to incorporate that as well in the space of just forty-eight hours. But apart from the bare floorboards, the room was pretty much there. The 'Grecian Skies' walls made it bright and welcoming, while the scrubbed pine cabinets and dark green granite worktop created the perfect country kitchen atmosphere, cosy and homely, while also being smart and practical. The butler's sink was in position, the bottle-green and cream splashback tiles lending a sophisticated air to the room. Nobody would be able to tell that the sink still needed to be plumbed in, which would hopefully be happening tomorrow. And best of all, there was a cooker that actually worked at the flick of a switch. No more balancing huge pans over a tiny camping stove for us.

I massaged my neck as the effect of a whole weekend of manual labour started to kick in.

'Let me,' said Charlie, reaching across and kneading my shoulders in a way that made me want to groan out loud. I closed my eyes and enjoyed the moment.

'Perfect, don't you think?' said Charlie. I'm pretty sure he was referring to the kitchen, but my response was about something else altogether.

'Yes, it is.'

I took a deep breath. Perhaps this was it. The moment I should finally come out and say what had been playing on my mind for most of the summer. How would I say it? 'Charlie, will you be my boyfriend?' That sounded like we were back in the playground and I was about to challenge him to a game of kiss chase. 'Charlie, I think I love you.' It sounded so inadequate, like it didn't really do justice to the depth of my emotions and the conflict they'd been causing me. 'Charlie, I...'

'Earth to Freya, are you still in there?'

I shook myself back to reality and realised that Charlie must have been trying to speak to me for the last few seconds.

'What was that?'

'Good, you're back with me. I was saying I think we need to hang a few decorations up to finish the room off, and then it'll be perfect. Now give me two seconds, I've got a surprise for you.'

Charlie disappeared to his room, then returned a moment later looking very pleased with himself.

'Close your eyes and hold out your hands,' he instructed.

'That sounds ominous,' I said.

'Please do it,' he said.

I did as instructed, but only after I'd rolled my eyes in response to his faux bossiness.

'Here you go,' said Charlie.

I'm not sure what I was expecting, but it certainly wasn't

what he placed in my hands. It felt like a large wooden frame – some kind of picture perhaps?

'Am I allowed to open my eyes now?'

'Go on,' said Charlie, his voice eager with excitement.

I looked down and saw The Rules now encased in a classic wooden frame, my scrawled writing preserved and protected behind a sheet of glass. On the back of the frame, a card was stuck on saying 'For Freya from Charlie' followed by the date. But the beauty of the frame didn't matter a jot to me compared to the potential significance of the gift. I turned it back around and started reading The Rules, the guidelines that I'd so naïvely compiled when the idea of buying a house with an old friend seemed simple and straightforward. One in particular immediately stood out to me, Rule 18c: 'No getting involved'. It was the rule I had dictated, and it was a rule I had been seriously considering breaking. But perhaps that was the reason Charlie had presented me with the frame. Was this his subtle way of acknowledging that he'd recognised my developing feelings and trying to warn me off before I said or did anything we'd both regret?

'That's lovely, Charlie, what a great idea,' I said, trying to inject as much jollity into my response as I could.

My acting abilities were obviously not up to scratch because I caught the expression of hurt that crossed his face before he carefully masked it.

'I thought we could display it in our almost-completed kitchen in pride of place,' he said. 'A reminder of where we've come from.'

'Sure thing, right where we can both see it every time we come and go,' I said. 'No chance of either of us forgetting The Rules.' Yes, that had to be the reason why he'd done it. Being Miss Rule Maker was turning round and punishing me now. It was typical Charlie, a thoughtful, sensitive way of gently letting me down so neither of us had to go through the trauma of rejection with words that could never be unsaid or forgotten.

Seeing that I wasn't about to move, Charlie took the picture frame out of my hands and started walking around the kitchen, trying it out in different spots.

'What do you think?' he said, holding it up to the right of the window. 'No chance of us not being able to see it here.'

'Anywhere's great,' I said, the effort of trying to keep a smile on my face making my eyes water. At least, that's what I told myself was the reason for the moisture threatening to spill over and drip down my face.

'Or how about here?' suggested Charlie, walking over to the wall next to the living room door. 'It stands out even more in this position, don't you agree?'

'Seriously, wherever you think's best,' I said.

'Are you all right, Freya?' asked Charlie, turning around and catching the pained expression on my face.

'Never better,' I replied in an overly enthusiastic manner. Then I pretended to check my watch and yawned. 'Goodness me, how is that the time? If you don't mind, I'll leave you to it. I'm due at a staff meeting in fewer hours than I care to think about. Night, sleep well.'

I hurried from the room, not even daring to take one final look at Charlie's face. I'd got his message loud and clear.

Chapter Twenty-Five

After a sleepless night, I got up extra early and fled, taking the very first bus out of the village so there was no danger of bumping into Charlie on my way out. But even as I dashed through the kitchen, a sleepy Ted only bothering to half-heartedly wag his tail at me, I noticed that the framed copy of The Rules had been propped up on the work surface. Charlie had obviously given up on his plan to hang them on the wall, but they were still prominently on display, and there was no escaping the message they delivered.

Normally I found the start of a new school year exciting, with the fun anticipation of meeting my classes, who were generally full of enthusiasm in return, the novelty factor of being in a new year group yet to wear off. But although I enjoyed greeting the pupils and catching up with the stories of their adventures over the summer break, I was reluctant to say much about what I had been up to during my holiday, the memory of The Rules framed in the kitchen setting my stomach churning with doubt and distress every time I thought about it.

I was also actively avoiding Leila as I knew she'd pick up on my low mood the second she saw me, and I wasn't ready to talk about it yet. To be honest, I wasn't sure I would ever be ready. Instead I was trailing around after Mr Rhys, a real form of self-punishment, listening to him running through his favourite complaints and grumbling about his workload, while I tried to persuade him to offload some of his tasks on me so I'd legitimately look busy if Leila came in search of me.

'I'm glad I've got you alone, Miss Hutchinson,' said Mr Rhys as we sat together over lunch, a phrase which would have sounded vaguely predatory if it hadn't been clear that any lustful thoughts he had were mostly directed at his dessert. 'I wanted to ask you if you've made your mind up.'

'About what?' I asked, buying myself some time, even though I knew exactly what he was getting at.

'I'm going to officially announce my retirement, which means that the advert for my replacement will soon be going live. What are your thoughts?'

I was relieved that he didn't repeat his earlier speech about how good value I'd be for the role. And although he didn't seem to be about to offer any other kind of endorsement, I realised that it didn't matter to me. Whether I went for the Head of Department job was my decision, and my decision alone. The important question was whether I was ready for the greater responsibility, whether I believed in myself enough to apply and make that bold statement that I had the talent and the ability to make a success of the role, and to be the Head of History that the pupils and staff needed.

I took a deep breath. 'I'm very keen to apply. I'm looking forward to proving that I'm the right person for the job.'

I was adding a whole extra layer of stress to my already very pressured life, but as I said the words out loud, I knew they were true. It was time for me to be brave, and back myself for a change, at least in my professional life. It felt good.

Mr Rhys nodded. In fact, he opened his mouth in what I think was meant to be a smile, treating me to the sight of the rice pudding sloshing around in there.

'If you'd like a second pair of eyes to look over your application, I might be able to find some time to oblige,' he said. 'Now I'll let you go. I believe one of the PE teachers is trying to attract your attention.'

I hardly had time to acknowledge his offer of help before Leila descended.

'Coffee time,' she said, scooping me up and thrusting a cup into my hands. She hustled me out of the dining room and down to the bike sheds, where we turfed out a couple of sixth formers who looked like they were about to become the first golden couple of the new school year.

'Off you go, you two. And hand over that chewing gum before you get yourselves into any more trouble,' said Leila, as the dishevelled pair slunk off to find another quiet corner.

'Love is in the air,' she said with a grin after they'd gone out of hearing range.

'Not everywhere,' I said, my mood dipping again.

'What, not you and Charlie?' she said, the surprise evident in her voice. 'You finally said something?'

'No, I didn't. And I'm not going to because Charlie has made it very clear that he is definitely not interested in me in that way.' I explained about how he'd presented me with a framed version of The Rules as Leila listened carefully and made sympathetic noises.

'If I were you, I wouldn't rush to conclusions,' she said. 'You don't know that warning you off was his reason for getting them framed.'

I turned to face her. 'It seems pretty clear to me. How else am I meant to interpret it? I set The Rules. I wrote in big, bold handwriting the words "Don't get involved". And he's gently reminding me to keep to that resolution. Because he's a thoroughly decent guy, and he doesn't want to hurt me, or see me suffering through the mortifyingly painful experience of being kindly let down by him. We made a practical business arrangement, and he's reminding me of that fact before I mess everything up. Clearly, I need to listen to the message he's giving me. And there's the small matter of Serena to consider too. There's so obviously something going on between them. I need to get my act together, and stop letting myself get carried away by imagining he would be likely to reciprocate my feelings. Time to concentrate on doing the house up, and getting my promotion.'

I quickly told her about the Head of Department job, feeling guilty that I hadn't confided in her before. But Leila wasn't one to bear grudges and she knew, without me having to explain, why I'd kept so quiet about it.

'You go, Freya. I'm so proud of you. You'll be ace at the job.'

'Funnily enough, that's exactly what Charlie said.'

'And Charlie's right. And sticking with the subject of Charlie, if you can have self-belief enough to go for this job, then why not apply that in other areas of your life?'

I pulled a face.

'No, hear me out,' said Leila. 'I think you've so convinced yourself that things couldn't possibly work out for you and Charlie that you're seeing problems where they don't exist. You need to have more faith in yourself, and not jump to conclusions when you haven't even dared to have the conversation with him. Trust what your heart is telling you, and trust that it's not an impossible idea that a great guy like Charlie would reciprocate your feelings. The best relationships are built on a solid friendship, after all. And if there's one thing about you guys, you have a really, really good friendship.'

I threw my hands up in exasperation. 'And clearly friendship is what I am going to have to resign myself to. It was foolish of me to hanker after something more. Anyway, I really don't want to discuss it any further. The subject is closed. I need to move on with my life, and stop allowing myself to get distracted by this whole sorry situation. It's time to focus on building a future for myself alone.'

'You can still be a strong and independent woman as part of a couple, if that's what you're afraid of,' said Leila, trying one final push.

'Or I can be a strong and independent woman who's happily single,' I retorted.

'Happily?' said Leila.

'Ecstatically so. Now if you'll excuse me, I have essays to mark.' I turned and started marching towards the staff room, keen to find safety in numbers so I wouldn't have to continue this painful conversation.

'It's the first day of term,' I heard her calling after me. 'Even you don't have essays to mark.'

I waved vaguely back at her, and went to bury myself in my work.

By the end of the day, I'd signed up for half a dozen extra duties and given my students a mountain of homework which had set them groaning. I meanwhile was positively relishing being able to keep myself busy. The less time I had for dwelling on my heartbreak, the better. I spent the journey home on the bus formulating a plan of action for future life at Oak Tree Cottage, and even got off a stop early so I could have some extra time walking to complete it. I needed to demonstrate to Charlie that his message had been received and understood, and to make it reassuringly clear for him that from now on, I was going to keep things business-like and normal between us, with absolutely no rule-breaking. By the time I got back to the cottage, rather later than intended, I felt confident I had a plan that would see us through until we had sold up and moved on.

I hesitated by the front door, remembering how we had unlocked it together for the first time back in April, with so much hope and excitement at what lay ahead of us. Despite my assertion that we should change the locks, I'd not pushed the matter, savouring the memory of both of us holding the old-fashioned key, Charlie's hand wrapped around mine as we turned it together and stepped over the threshold into our new future. I firmly told myself to get it together. If I was going to become sentimental every time I looked at the cottage, my plan was going to fall apart and I was never going to be able to move on with my life.

Mustering my confidence, I marched around the side of the building, where I encountered none other than Serena, who was checking her appearance in the wing mirror of her car prior to getting in and driving off. She looked rather tired, I thought, then I told myself off for being catty. It was probably best not to think about what had caused her to look fatigued.

'Hello, Freya, good first day back?' she asked, making it clear that I must have been the subject of discussion between her and Charlie at some point.

'Great, thank you,' I said, in a cheery manner, which sounded forced even to my own ears. 'Nice to see you again,' I added. 'You know you don't have to worry about me being in the way when you visit. I'm always happy to make myself scarce.' There was little doubt in my mind that Charlie would have talked over the situation with her, and told her what he had done to deal with it. The least I could do was reassure her that the message had been received and understood.

'Er, thank you,' said Serena. I couldn't tell if she was pleased or perhaps embarrassed by what I'd said. It must be awkward talking to the woman who has a huge crush on your boyfriend, after all. I held the gate open for her as she drove off, then carefully closed it behind her and made my way through the garden, my feet slowing down with every step. Now that the moment had come, I was dreading going into the house and having to pretend everything was normal.

Ted provided some welcome distraction, charging up to meet me when I got to the back door, going so fast that he skidded as he turned a corner and ended up bouncing off the wall.

'Careful, Teddy boy, you'll hurt yourself,' I said, bending down and patting him, checking him over for damage.

He wriggled in response, then bounded off back to Charlie, who was leaning against the living-room doorway looking like an advert for DIY. He was wearing a tatty old pair of jeans that were hanging off his hips, while his grubby T-shirt showed off muscles that seemed to have only grown firmer with all the hard manual labour of the summer. I swallowed. So much for my plan to get a grip and move on.

'Good day at work, dear?' he said, reprising his 1950s housewife imitation.

'Busy,' I said, forcing myself to smile as if everything was fine. 'Did you get much done? The accounts you look after were rather quiet today.' As soon as I said it, I kicked myself for revealing too much. Charlie knew that I didn't really do social media, so he'd be able to work out what I had been up to, which was surreptitiously logging onto Instagram on my computer at school between classes and trawling through the accounts I knew he managed, to see what he'd been up to, a vicarious way of feeling close to him. Now I realised it just made me look like a stalker. I hurried on, trying to gloss over my mistake.

'Serena's looking well.'

'What? Oh yes, I guess so,' said Charlie. 'Can I show you how I've been getting on with the building work whilst you've been out? You're right, I did skive from the business a bit today so I could make some house progress.'

I nodded. 'I wanted to talk to you about the house. I think we need to up the pace with the renovations. There's still a lot to be done, and according to my research, the best time to put the cottage on the market would be in the new year. People like to get Christmas out of the way without any big changes, then they start looking for new properties in January as part of their new year's resolutions. It would be foolish to miss an opportunity like that.'

Charlie frowned. 'I hadn't heard that. The estate agent I work for is normally pretty hot on such trends, if they exist.'

'There have been several articles about it in reputable publications,' I said, knowing I sounded prissy.

'I guess it must be true then,' said Charlie.

'Good. With that in mind, I think we should have a new approach to our renovation work. Divide and conquer.'

'Divide and conquer?'

'Yes, that's it. We take a room each, and focus all our individual attention on it, perhaps even set ourselves a deadline. That way we can double our efforts.'

'Or potentially halve them, given that we'll be halving the labour,' pointed out Charlie.

'I think this way is best,' I pushed, unable to bear the thought of having to spend my free time working alongside Charlie, and the pain this would cause me.

'Let's talk about it over dinner,' he said. 'I wondered if you fancied macaroni cheese tonight? You know it's my special.'

'I already ate my main meal at school,' I said hurriedly, knowing that I wasn't yet strong enough to eat with him and pretend that everything was back to normal. 'If I get hungry later, I might have a snack, but don't worry about waiting for me. In fact, you should feel free to eat when you like and not bother about me. Not that you need my permission to choose what you do, of course. I just thought it might make things easier as I'm going to be tied up with school a lot this term, and I know you've got your own life to lead.'

I knew this was the moment where I should tell him that I'd decided to go for the job, but it felt safer not to prolong the conversation. I needed to protect myself from further pain.

'Right,' said Charlie.

'Good. I'm glad that's all sorted. I'm going to change, and then I might get started on the dining room.'

'You might want to wait until the plaster has dried,' he called after me.

'What's that?'

'You didn't ask what work I'd been doing while you were at school. It was plastering. I've done the dining room. And with your permission, I'll take a look at your bedroom tomorrow.'

'No need,' I said. If this was his way of trying to make up for not returning my feelings, then he shouldn't bother. The last thing I wanted was to lie in bed at night and have the image of Charlie plastering the walls filling my head.

Charlie looked rather hurt. 'You haven't even looked at the dining room yet. I wouldn't reject my work out of hand.'

'I'm sure you've done a fine job, Charlie, but you plastering my bedroom is hardly following our new "Divide and conquer" tactic, is it? I'm sure I'll manage fine by myself. We've got to be pragmatic about this.'

And then I ran up the stairs and shut the door of my room behind me, so he couldn't see how much the speech had cost me.

Chapter Twenty-Six

Over the next few weeks, I spent every waking hour either working at school or flogging myself with renovation tasks, driving myself to the point of exhaustion. I was on edge all the time with the strain of trying to pretend that everything was okay, when it really wasn't. It was like just before Granddad's fall, when Charlie and I had been walking on eggshells around each other, only this time it was so much worse. Because every time I saw him, I pictured him holding up the framed copy of The Rules, and I felt mortified all over again, stumbling over my words, failing to respond to his attempts at banter with anything but awkwardness, and basically making a complete fool of myself. And so I made a point of arranging that I very rarely saw him.

But one day, he caught me when I was about to sneak off to work early, having signed up to supervise the breakfast club. I'd pretended to Leila that my sudden enthusiasm for helping with extra-curricular activities at school was down to my eagerness to get the promotion, but we both knew it was a convenient excuse for me to hide from my house partner, who I feared was also becoming wise to my scheme.

'Are you avoiding me again, Freya?' said Charlie, sitting on the worksurface in the kitchen, where he'd obviously been lying in wait for me.

'Don't sit on the worksurface. It could scratch it and it's not very hygienic,' I said to deflect his question, then hated myself for saying it.

He folded his arms casually. 'Nothing's going to destroy this granite, as you well know.'

'I still don't think you should do anything to damage the house value.'

A look of exasperation crossed Charlie's face. 'A home has to be lived in. It's only natural to expect it to have a few scratches and scrapes. They're signs of character. Anyway, you still haven't answered the question, Hutch.'

'It's Freya,' I snapped, suddenly unable to bear the nickname that reinforced my position as his mate and nothing more. He raised an eyebrow in response, but I pretended not to recognise the surprise in his expression. 'And why would you think I was avoiding you? Funnily enough, my life doesn't revolve around you and what you're doing. It doesn't even cross my mind half the time what you're up to. I'm very busy with school, and when I'm not there, I'm very busy making sure this cottage achieves its potential so that we can both get a return on the significant investment we made. We're restoring a house, not making a home here, as you've made very clear. I'm not quite sure what more you want from me.' I thought he was going to say something, but I ploughed on. 'Allow me to try to regain a bit of dignity in this situation. Now if you'll excuse me, I have a bus to catch. Some of us can't hang around chatting all morning.'

And with that, I stomped out, slamming the door with enough of a bang that I could hear Ted whimper in surprise inside. I was angry with myself for acting this way, so crotchety and over-sensitive, but it was an act of self-preservation. I'd thought that if Charlie couldn't be my partner, he could still at least remain my friend, but even that seemed to be sliding away from me. We couldn't pretend that everything was normal, that we could go back to how things were. I was beginning to accept that it was going to be far too painful to continue in this way, seeing the gradual destruction of everything that I'd held dear while all the time not being able to stop myself adding fuel to the fire.

I spent the day at school stewing over the early morning conversation. The situation couldn't carry on this way. It was making me miserable, and Charlie couldn't be much happier, stuck with a bad-tempered, resentful house partner who was struggling to get past her disappointment. Perhaps it would be better to cut our losses and move on, allowing us to escape from this increasingly difficult arrangement. The house was in a much better condition than it had been, and while it was still a long way off the finished article we'd spent so long talking about, it would surely have gained enough value to put both Charlie and me in a stronger financial position. And now we had at least six months of mortgage payments under our belts, we'd be seen as better prospects as individuals, much more likely to be able to succeed if we decided to go it alone. Maybe we'd be better off selling up now. If I could be certain that we'd added enough value to the house to benefit both of us, then that could be the ideal solution. It would set Charlie free, so he could have his own life and not feel obliged to the old schoolfriend who'd got in way over her head. And it would mean that I could move on too, put the intensity of the last few months behind me and start building my own future, whatever that might hold.

Before I could change my mind, I disappeared to the bike sheds to make a phone call in private. Trying to keep my voice steady, I rang up the estate agent who'd originally sold Oak Tree Cottage to Charlie and me, and arranged an appointment for him to revalue the house. He was surprised to hear from me so soon, but when I described the work we'd done so far, his voice grew more interested and he booked the meeting for the weekend, the earliest opportunity he could make. I'd hoped that when I ended the call I'd feel better, having taken a positive step forwards. But I just felt hollow inside.

As the week went by, I wrestled with whether or not to tell Charlie what I'd done. On the one hand, he had every right to know. It was his house too, after all. But on the other hand, wouldn't it be better to wait until the valuation had happened, then I could present him with the facts, rather than a theoretical situation?

After my outburst, Charlie was making an extra effort to be polite on the now rare occasions we encountered each other in the house, while I could only survive by pretending to myself that he was a distant acquaintance and treating him accordingly, which was making me feel worse. Even when we'd bumped into each other at the pub for the first time in years, things hadn't been this stilted and uncomfortable. I was basically living in my bedroom, working hard at its transformation, only sneaking out to get meals or to do a bit of painting in the living room when I was sure the coast was clear. It felt important to keep working on the house, but the joy had gone out of it, and I feared it was being reflected in the standard of my work.

The rooms Charlie had taken charge of meanwhile were looking far better than the ones I was doing in my 'Divide and conquer' plan. When I snuck a look at the dining room, I was astonished by the smoothness of the plastering, almost wondering if he'd secretly paid someone to come and do it for him. My own efforts in my bedroom were dire in comparison. Despite having studied the technique closely, my first attempt ended with the plaster literally falling off the wall, and I feared my second try was going to go the same way. I was too stubborn to ask for Charlie's help, and it irritated me that I was letting the side down. If the house valuation was lower than hoped for, I only had myself to blame.

The day of the valuation arrived, and despite it being a

Saturday, when Charlie would normally be heading off to his side hustle at the estate agent in Harrogate, he showed no sign of going.

I'd had a rare lie-in after spending most of the night awake worrying about whether I was doing the right thing, and wandered into the kitchen to fix myself a late breakfast, still feeling groggy and confused.

'Morning, Freya,' said Charlie, making me jump. 'I'm making veggie sausage sandwiches. I thought we could spend the day together.'

Ted beat his tail on the floor in approval of the plan.

While nothing would make me happier, I knew it would also be a form of exquisite torture. Why was he pushing this? I needed to harden my resolve.

I glanced at the clock on the oven, trying to avoid looking at The Rules, which were still propped up as a terrible reminder on the worksurface. Not long until the estate agent was due to arrive.

'Shouldn't you be at work?' I said, deciding it was better to get straight to the point.

'I've taken the day off. In fact, I was thinking about dropping the Saturday job altogether. I thought it might be nice to be able to spend a bit more time here, not be disappearing for half the weekend.'

'I wouldn't be too hasty about making the decision,' I said. It was a steady source of extra income for him, and I knew it would be useful when he was paying a mortgage solo.

'Oh.' He sounded disappointed. 'I thought you'd be pleased.'

'You're not obliged to do things to please me,' I said. 'What you choose to do with your life is your decision, and the same goes for me.'

Who was this ice-cold Freya? A quick glance at him told me that the apparent indifference in my tone had made its point. I decided to hammer it home. It would be much better to get him out of the house before the estate agent arrived. I'd had enough confrontation for one day.

'And don't bother with the breakfast. I thought I'd made it clear that we were looking out for ourselves now. To make things easier.'

'It's no bother,' insisted Charlie.

'Maybe I don't want you cooking for me, Charlie. I know you're trying to be kind and making it up to me, but I've got the message, and I'm trying to move on, as you want me to. But I can't do that if you insist on making things difficult by being so bloody nice all the time.'

Ted stood up at the distressed tone in my voice, and slunk to his bed, burying his nose in his paws and making himself as small as possible, as if by pretending to be invisible he could disappear from this situation. I could empathise with that feeling.

Charlie set the frying pan and wooden spoon carefully down on the worksurface and took a step towards me. I backed away, not able to bear the thought of him coming near me. It would be too painful when I knew I'd only want him to be closer still. It was that automatic reaction of flinching that seemed to cause him the most hurt.

'What are you talking about, Freya? Forgive me for apparently being unable to read between the lines, but I don't have a clue what you're going on about. What do you mean, you've got the message?'

I was actually crying now, and my weakness in showing the extent of my vulnerability to him made me even angrier.

'Stop pretending, Charlie. The situation is what it is, and you don't need to worry about me being a problem any longer, okay?'

Before he could answer, there was a knock at the door. Charlie looked like he wanted to finish the conversation off first, but good manners got the better of him. Although I knew who would be there, and that it might be better for me to run interference, instead I took the opportunity to quickly blow my nose and try to look more respectable, even though I knew my eyes would be red regardless.

'Good morning, good morning,' said the estate agent in what felt like an overly jolly manner. 'Great to see you both again. I must say you two have done a fine job. I would never have expected the place to look this good in so short a time. If I hadn't seen the sign for Oak Tree Cottage by the front door, I would have assumed I'd taken a wrong turning and gone to a different house.'

'Can I help you?' said Charlie, looking completely confused.

'I'm here for the valuation,' said the estate agent, before I could stop him.

'The valuation, right,' said Charlie, looking back across at me with an expression of such hurt on his face that I felt chilled to the bone. I shrugged my shoulders, feigning indifference. He might be cross for a short time because I hadn't consulted him about it, but longer term he'd come to see the sense in my idea. It would set him free, I told myself once again.

When I didn't say anything else, Charlie shook his head, as if he was disappointed with me. 'I don't know what to say. I guess this is my cue to leave,' he said. 'Don't wait up for me.'

And with that, he snatched up his car keys and strode out, the door slamming behind him. I strained my ears to hear the sound of the Land Rover's engine fading into the distance as meanwhile the estate agent kept up a torrent of meaningless conversation.

'Mrs Humphries, shall we start upstairs and work down? Mrs Humphries?' he repeated as he tried to get my attention.

'It's Miss Hutchinson, actually. And yes, take your time. I'll leave you to it.' I couldn't bear the thought of seeing his face as he translated our hard work into a price. However high it was, it would never truly reflect the value of what this place had given me – and what it had taken away.

I sat down on one of the camping chairs while I waited for him to do his job, and experienced yet another pang of nostalgia. What would happen next? Where would I go from here? I couldn't imagine living in a new place without Charlie at my side. My dream of home ownership had changed. I knew I'd find the strength from somewhere to carry on, and maybe one day put this behind me, but equally I knew that it would be like living life in monochrome.

'It's the right thing to do,' I said to Ted, who merely blinked at me. 'Honestly, it is,' I insisted. 'Before you know it, you'll be back with Granddad, Charlie will be happily moving on and probably shacking up with Serena, and I'll...I'll be back at square one. No, that's not right, I'll be Head of History and rising in the ranks of the professional world. I'll find my own place one day.'

But it wouldn't be Oak Tree Cottage, a home where every inch of floorboard, every lick of paint held memories of Charlie and me.

The estate agent eventually left, whistling happily. As expected, we wouldn't make as much profit as we would have if the place was finished and pristine, but we'd certainly have enough to give us a modest deposit apiece. Financially I would be in a better position than before. Emotionally was a different matter.

I spent the rest of the day burying myself in schoolwork, putting on a hoody and then pulling a blanket over me on the sofa as the wind got up and the rain started lashing down. The cottage was certainly less draughty than it had been, thanks to our new windows, but we were definitely going to have to look at fixing the central heating before winter set in, I thought. And then I reminded myself that there was no guarantee that we would still be living here by then.

The hours slipped by, and still there was no sign of Charlie. Maybe he'd gone to work after all. I fed Ted, and forced myself to have something to eat as well, but I got no enjoyment out of the meal, remembering Charlie's cheerful offer to make me breakfast this morning and my cruel rejection of his kindness. I considered his actions more carefully, replaying our discussion. It was like picking at a wound, but the more I thought about what he'd said, and the way he'd said it, the more I started to wonder about the confusion in his manner. When I had said I'd got his message, he'd seemed not to know what I was talking about. Could it be that I was the one who'd got the wrong end of the stick, who'd jumped to a conclusion? All he'd done was hand over the framed copy of The Rules, from which I'd drawn a whole heap of assumptions. And didn't a part of me wonder if I'd jumped on that interpretation of his actions because it gave me a convenient excuse? All along I'd been finding reasons to justify not telling him how I felt, from not wanting to risk our mortgage, to the presence of Serena in his life. Because to confess my true feelings to Charlie would be to make myself completely vulnerable, to expose myself to the risk of his rejection. In deciding that he was sending me an oh-so-subtle message with The Rules, I'd saved myself from that vulnerability. And yes, it had caused great pain in other ways, but it was an expected pain, one that I could handle. Because hearing Charlie spelling out a rejection in actual words would be a very different thing.

But how long could I or should I carry on giving myself

excuses? I was beginning to acknowledge that I spent far too much of my life taking refuge in rules and guidelines, keeping myself safe, not daring to take risks. But if I continued in that safety zone, would I ever be able to say that I was truly living my life to its fullest? I had taken a leap of faith buying a house with Charlie, the most daring thing I'd ever done. I was putting myself out there by applying for the Head of Department job. Maybe it was time to take another risk, allow myself to be vulnerable and open up to Charlie. Perhaps when he returned, I should be brave, and tell him how I felt. Because if I didn't take that chance, and follow my heart for once, wouldn't I always regret it? But I knew it was easy to decide that when he wasn't around. It would take all my courage to follow through on my promise to myself once he was actually back.

I checked my watch, wondering when that would be. It was getting on into the evening, and it wasn't like him not to have let me know he was planning to be late. But then again, one of the last things I'd said to him was to emphasise that we were leading separate lives and weren't answerable to each other. Why should he tell me what he was doing? I decided to try to distract myself in the meantime.

'Do you want to go for a walk, Ted?' I hauled myself off the sofa, and into the kitchen, opening the back door into the garden. The wind sent a flurry of leaves into the room and the heavy rain started to form a puddle on the threshold within seconds. Although Ted had followed me into the kitchen, probably in the hope of getting a snack, when he saw the conditions outside, he looked at me as if I was deranged.

'You're going to have to go out. I know you've got a bladder like a barrage balloon, but it's not good for you to be crossing your legs.'

Of course, the manipulative pooch managed to persuade me to go out with him by gazing up at me with sad eyes. I pulled on my wellington boots and a raincoat, then ended up standing over him in the garden with an umbrella so he didn't get wet while I bore the brunt of the shower. The rain was lashing down, pouring in torrents and collecting in deep puddles on the uneven ground. The foliage was rustling, while the branches of the oak tree were creaking as the wind shook it to the very roots.

'I hope your dad's all right,' I said to Ted, as we stumbled back into the kitchen after his quickest pee break ever, both of us dripping wet. I left my wet weather gear to dry in the sink. Maybe in the future we could build a porch area around the back door to make this kind of situation easier, I thought idly. If I spoke to Charlie and it turned out I'd got the wrong end of the stick and that actually he did reciprocate my feelings, we could stay here and continue to build our happy ever after, complete with back door porch. But it was a big if. 'The weather's getting really nasty, and the wiper blades on the Land Rover are a bit dodgy. I meant Charlie, by the way,' I added, realising my slip. It was comforting to think of Charlie, Ted and me as some kind of family unit, though, as I reminded myself, even Ted was only here on loan while Granddad recuperated from his accident. 'Should I text him, do you think? Make sure he's okay?' Ted seemed unbothered by the internal drama I was going through, returning to his bed and lying down with a contented sigh. Before long his legs were twitching as he relaxed into a puppy dream. 'Perhaps you're right. I did make a big point to him of saying we didn't have to tell each other what we were up to.'

As the noise of the storm outside grew louder still, I decided to distract myself from wondering where Charlie was by putting up some shelves in the upstairs hall. After all, there was no reason to think that he'd be out and about in this weather, getting drenched by the driving rain or struggling to keep the car going straight in the wind. He was probably visiting his parents, or out with friends. Or maybe he was with Serena in a swish restaurant, laughing as they fed each other dessert, or settling down on the sofa at her place to watch whatever TV series they were bingeing as a couple. Stop it, Freya, best not to go there, I told myself.

I forced myself back to thoughts of shelving. The estate agent's parting gambit had been to advise me to add a few more decorative touches and maximise the storage possibilities before we put the house on the market, so potential buyers could get a sense of the best use of the space the cottage offered. Bookshelves on the landing could only be a good thing, whether we stayed or left.

'Do you want to come and join me, Ted?' I invited, in need of his company, but he merely stood up and stretched, then turned his back on me and flumped back down on his bed with a big huff.

'*Et tu*, Teddy?' I said, feeling more alone than ever. 'I'll be upstairs if you want me.'

It still felt somewhat of a novelty to be able to turn the lights on to see what I was doing. I laid out the pieces for the shelves, then used my phone to scan the QR code that was meant to lead me to the instructions. Unfortunately, it came up with a 'Page not recognised' error, and when I tried to Google the manufacturer's website to see if there were instructions on there, nothing appeared. Then my phone stopped connecting to any website at all. Perhaps the storm had got to the broadband.

I could hear Charlie's voice urging me to go with the flow and have a try anyway. I knew he'd say something like, 'What's the worst that could happen? Trust yourself.'

Maybe he was right.

I measured the space, picked up the spirit level and made some pencil marks so I knew exactly where the first shelf would go. Then I decided to get a couple of books to make sure that I left enough of a gap between the next shelf. As the shelves were going to be slightly closer to Charlie's room than mine, I went in there for the books – a lame reason, which I knew wouldn't stand up to closer scrutiny. I'd not set foot in his room since we'd set up the double bed in there, deeming it better for my sanity to try to avoid that particular temptation. As I stepped over the threshold I saw how much of a change he'd made, every bit of the room reflecting his personality. The new plastering was even more smoothly done than in the dining room, and I recognised the tint on his walls as the left over 'Grecian Skies' paint from the kitchen. I noticed that his collection of pictures had finally gone up on display too. Only this time there was a new one there. Telling myself that I'd only take the briefest of looks, I stepped closer and peered at the photo. It was a selfie we'd taken to send to Granddad on the day that Ted had moved in. Charlie was holding Ted up to the camera between us, complaining that the little dog weighed a ton, all the while unable to stop himself grinning at his antics. I'd been in charge of taking the picture, I remembered, and Ted had wriggled so much that he'd nearly squirmed out of Charlie's arms. The picture captured the moment where we were both laughing, our heads bent towards each other, our happiness evident. And then I looked more closely, and saw that Charlie wasn't looking towards the lens. Instead, his gaze was fixed on me. Was that the expression Leila had meant when she said I didn't know how he looked at me when I wasn't aware of it? Because I thought I could recognise something there, the deep desire and longing that I felt must appear on my own face when I looked at Charlie. I could be mistaken, I firmly told myself. It was easy to look at a picture and see what I wanted to see. Photographs didn't always tell the truth, they only reflected a moment in time. A chance expression captured in the briefest of flashes didn't mean anything.

But why did he have this picture in his bedroom, displayed on the wall where it would be one of the first things he saw when he woke up and the last when he went to sleep? the little voice of desperate hope at the back of my head pressed.

I stamped down on it, hard. It was only a picture. It didn't mean anything, and neither did the lack of a picture of Serena on the wall. For all I knew, she was the background image on his phone screen, somewhere where she could be seen and admired throughout the day. I had done enough speculating and second-guessing. The only way I could get answers was by talking to him, laying bare my feelings and accepting whatever his response might be. I forced myself to turn around and go back into the hall, all thoughts of picking up a book to help with building the shelves forgotten. I'd carry on without one.

'Sod it, what's the worst that can happen?' I muttered as I picked up the power tool and started drilling into the wall.

And that's when all the lights went out.

Chapter Twenty-Seven

My first thought was that I had gone through a power cable. I dropped the drill, panicking that it might be about to send an electric shock through me. But instead of that, it landed heavily on my toe, the pain of the impact completely knocking the wind out of me. I hopped around in the dark, swearing loudly, torn between relief that no one was here to see my incompetence, and disappointment that there wasn't anyone who could show me some sympathy. If I hadn't broken the toe, it would be a miracle. But as I got my breath back, I acknowledged that I cared less about the damage to myself than the damage to the house. If I had gone through a power cable, it would be a massive faff to sort out at best, and potentially very dangerous at worst.

Slowly, cautiously I hobbled my way to Charlie's room once again, so I could open his door and get some light into the pitch-dark hallway. It didn't make much difference. The village didn't have street lights and any brightness from the moon was blotted out by the driving rain. I limped back along the hall and felt for the drill. It wouldn't do to cause myself more injury by treading on it. Once it was safely out of the way, I scrabbled around feeling for the screws that I'd so carefully set out. Halfway through the task, my good sense returned and I took my phone out so I could use the torch.

I gingerly stood back up and then shone the beam of light on the hole I'd drilled into the wall. I didn't want to get too close to it, but then again, it would be helpful to know if there was a live wire sticking out which could cause me further problems. I couldn't see anything, but that didn't mean it wasn't there. The other place to check was the fusebox, but I was rather nervous of trying to make it down the stairs with my current injury.

I quickly concluded that this was not a one-person job, and that I was going to have to call for help, loath as I was to admit it. After wrestling with my head and my heart, I tried Charlie first. But it went straight to voicemail without even ringing. Granddad was next on my list, although I knew his assistance would have to be provided over the phone. Thankfully he picked up on the first ring.

'Hello, and how is my favourite granddaughter?' he said. 'Funny you should call, I was just thinking about you and your young man.'

'He's not my young man, Granddad.' *Unfortunately*, I silently added as I patiently corrected him.

'Yes, yes,' he replied. 'How is he?'

'Charlie's absolutely fine as far as I'm aware, as is Ted.'

'But you're not. I can hear it in your voice, love.'

He didn't miss a trick, even though the line was crackly because of the weather.

'I'm having a bit of an issue, Granddad. I think I might have drilled through an electricity cable.' I tried to say it in as understated a way as possible so I didn't worry him.

'Oh dear. It's easily done,' he said in his usual comforting manner. 'I remember doing that on a job once, ended up shorting the whole house. After that mistake, I bought myself one of those little devices which check what's in the wall before you hammer anything in. It made the world of difference.'

I felt a bit better knowing that even my granddad, builder extraordinaire, had made mistakes.

'I wish I'd known about that handy device before I did it. I think I was a bit too gung ho.'

'No harm done. You're here talking to me, after all. If you'd done any serious damage, it would be the emergency services you'd be on the phone to right now.'

I decided not to tell him about the pounding pain in my foot, not wanting to worry him any further.

'That is very true. Anyway, I was wondering if you had any advice about what I should do next? I was thinking the fusebox might be a good place to start.'

'A very sensible idea. If you're not sure what you've hit, it might be best to turn the mains off until the morning when you can get a proper look in the daylight. And if you discover you have gone through a wire, then definitely leave it to the professionals to sort out.'

'Don't worry, I will.'

'The other thing to consider is that it might be a big coincidence and that it could be a power cut because of the storm. If the wind is raging there anything like it is here, it wouldn't be surprising if it's brought down a few wires. Sjaak was telling me a real humdinger is forecast.'

'You make a very good point, Granddad. That could be what's happened, as the internet went down shortly beforehand. I guess coincidences do happen sometimes, even though the timing does seem rather iffy. Thanks for the help.'

'That's what grandfathers are for. And when can I next expect a visit from you, Charlie and Ted?'

'As soon as you like. Although I can't promise for Charlie, of course. He's got a lot on at the moment.' I was skirting around the truth.

'That's a shame. There was something I was hoping to discuss with you both.'

'Oh?' I said. 'Do you want to talk about it now?'

Somewhere in the background I could hear laughter, and then the sound of a song being played on a piano.

'Sorry, love, but I've got to go. It's dance night here, and my physiotherapist has ordered me to join in.' He sounded like it wasn't going to be a huge hardship. I was pleased that he seemed to be settling into his new surroundings. 'Besides, I think it's something that would be better discussed in person. See you soon, Freya.'

'Bye, Granddad, love you. Ted sends his love too.'

I felt even more alone when I hung up the phone. On impulse, I scrolled back to my favourites and dialled Charlie again.

This time the call was answered on the third ring.

'Hello, Charlie's phone,' said Serena in her Scottish burr.

'Oh,' I said, surprised, although I shouldn't have been. I wished the connection was better so I could hear the background noise and try to work out where they were.

'Charlie's popped to the loo. Can I take a message, or get him to call you back, Freya?' she offered.

'No, no, it's fine. Sorry to disturb your evening,' I said, suddenly desperate to get off the phone. Her politeness was making me feel worse.

'It's not a problem. Are you all right?'

I'd either given myself away with the catch in my voice or this was a loaded question, asking so much more than if I was okay at the moment.

'I'm grand, thanks,' I said, forcing a smile so it reflected in my tone. 'I'll leave you to it.'

'Hold on a sec, I can hear Charlie coming down the corridor. I'll wave at him to hurry up.'

'No, really, it's fine. You don't even need to tell him I called. Everything's under control. Bye, Serena, lovely to talk to you.' And with that, I quickly hung up.

I allowed myself thirty seconds of wallowing in misery in the dark hallway, and then I forced myself to get a grip. Just because I knew for a fact now that Charlie was spending the evening with Serena, it didn't change anything materially. And it was hardly the most important thing to consider given that I was sitting here in a blackout with a potentially broken toe throbbing painfully. At least things couldn't get any worse.

I shouldn't have tempted fate.

Chapter Twenty-Eight

Knowing that the steep staircase was dodgy at the best of times, let alone in the dark with an injury to contend with, I decided to make my way down to the fusebox on my backside, carefully lowering myself onto each step, illuminating my route with my phone in one hand while trying to hold onto the banister with the other.

Outside the wind had grown stronger still, and I could hear it whistling through the eaves of the house, setting the slates on the roof rattling. I only hoped the builders' work to repair the chimney stack was up to weathering these conditions. Thank goodness we'd managed to get it fixed before this storm came along. I flinched as something clattered down the roof and went crashing to the ground. I told myself that the house had stood firm for several hundred years. A few tiles coming loose were neither here nor there in the scale of things.

I was about halfway down when there was a thudding gust that felt different, more sinister in its intent. The whole house shook with the impact, and the silence that followed was somehow worse than the noise. It stretched out, seemingly endlessly, building my feeling of tension, making me brace every muscle in my body in dread at what was to come. Just when I finally dared to let go of the breath that I hadn't consciously started holding, a new sound interrupted, a shrieking, twisting din that I didn't have much time to interpret before something smashed its way into the house. I instinctively put my head in my hands, trying to protect myself from the impact that I knew must be about to follow. My breathing accelerated, and adrenalin surged around my body, as I braced myself in fearful anticipation. Now I could feel the wind whistling through the house as well as around it, the cold air dancing gleefully around the rooms we'd worked so hard to bring back to life.

Slowly, carefully, I looked up, flashing the light of my phone around me so I could check what the damage was. The stairwell appeared the same as it had been a few minutes ago. But over the sound of the storm, I could hear another noise, a terrified whining. For a moment, I told myself that it couldn't be possible, that Ted would never make such an unearthly sound as that. And then sheer terror set me on my feet, fear anaesthetising my damaged foot as I ran down the rest of the stairs, full of dread at what I might be about to discover.

I got to the bottom of the steps and collided with a furry cannonball.

'Oh, Ted,' I said, scooping him up and holding him close. I could feel his heart racing against his ribs as he trembled in my arms. 'It's okay, boy, you're safe now.' I crooned comforting nothings into his ears, speaking softly and tenderly, trying to reassure him that everything was all right, without really knowing whether I was telling the truth. I wanted to check him over for injuries, but every time I tried to move, he buried his head still deeper into my armpit. Eventually he consented to let me sit down on the bottom step, and I held him close, gently stroking him, running my hands over his fur, as I reassured myself that he wasn't hurt and it was fear, not pain, that was causing him to act in this way. Only when I was satisfied that he was unharmed did I dare look further into the kitchen.

'Oh my goodness,' I breathed, unable to comprehend what was in front of me. The room was like a surreal piece of artwork, where the artist had played with the audience's expectations by bringing the outside world indoors. Because the oak tree after which our cottage was named was now leaning drunkenly against the house, and some of its heavy branches had smashed their way in through the kitchen walls. The scrubbed pine cabinets that we had so lovingly constructed and installed were broken up like firewood, and the heavy granite worktop had slid to the ground, the gouge in the floorboards showing its path of destruction. Rain was dripping down the 'Grecian Skies' walls following the path the branches had forged, mixing with the moss and soil from the tree to leave an ugly trail. And yet in amongst this scene of devastation, the framed copy of The Rules remained untouched. It was the unfairness of this that hit me hardest. The damage was almost too big to contemplate, and so instead I wept in anger that fate had seen fit to preserve The Rules while destroying everything else.

As my tears fell into Ted's soft fur, they seemed to bring him back to his senses, reigniting his protective instincts. He licked the salty tears from my cheeks and wagged his tail a couple of times, as if trying to reassure me that everything would be okay.

'I'm not sure how, my friend,' I whispered, scared to raise my voice. As I slowly assessed the state of the room from my position of relative safety, I started to realise that it couldn't be the only part of the house that had fallen victim to the impact of the tree. Charlie's room above the kitchen must be in an even worse state, and who knew what condition the roof would be in. Given how big the trunk had been and the force it had fallen with, I was amazed Oak Tree Cottage was still standing. As if in answer, the foundations of the house seemed to groan. The storm wasn't over yet and I needed to get Ted to safety, in case anything else happened. But I couldn't go out there into the elements without shoes and some form of waterproof; it would be dangerous in these conditions. But mine were in the kitchen, probably pinned underneath the fallen tree. However, I could still grab some trainers and another layer from upstairs. I knew it was going to be painful trying to put shoes on over my wounded foot, but it was more sensible to do that than run the risk of walking over the debris and adding cuts to my problems. And of course there was important paperwork to be rescued, documents I couldn't leave to the mercy of the rain. Dare I leave Ted down here while I tried to get back upstairs to pack the essentials?

As soon as he realised what I was going to do, Ted let out another pitiful whimper that made me relent at once.

'Don't worry, boy, I won't leave you behind.'

It took me twice as long to gingerly lever my way back up the stairs, now with the added hazard of a scared dog in my arms, although for once at least he wasn't wriggling around. When I finally reached the landing, I wished I hadn't forced myself to make the effort. Charlie's bedroom door was smashed through, a branch protruding from the gap. It was like the tree was a creature from the underworld, reaching out to grab any unfortunate victim in its path. Although I wanted to, I decided it was more sensible not to investigate further. Who knew what structural damage had been wrought, and Ted and I were in a precarious enough position as it was.

My bedroom, on the other hand, looked like it wasn't even in the same building, untouched by the ravages of the tree's invasion. I finally set Ted down on the floor as I quickly packed a bag with the bare essentials. My room might look unscathed, but there could be all kinds of invisible damage to the house, making it imperative that Ted and I get out of there as soon as possible. He trailed around by my ankles, sticking to me like a furry shadow. Somehow in the dark I managed to find the ring binder with all the documents for the house. Once I'd got us to safety, my first port of call was definitely going to be the insurance company. I had to find some way of regaining control in this terrifying situation.

Chapter Twenty-Nine

Sheila and Frank were kind enough to take Ted and I in, fussing over the pair of us as they exclaimed over the impact of the storm. I soon realised that the cause of the blackout at Oak Tree Cottage hadn't been my drilling after all, but was an area-wide power cut. It was a small comfort, the problem meaningless in the face of the much wider damage to the house. They hustled us into a guest room, not even trying to separate Ted from my side, handed me some clean towels and urged me to sleep for as long as I needed to. I opened my mouth to protest that I was far from tired, but a yawn came out instead. Delayed reaction had caught up with me, making my limbs heavy and protecting my mind from thinking too much by making me focus on how much I needed to rest my head on that soft pillow.

I lay down, still fully clothed, Ted curled up at my side, both of us acknowledging that this was a situation where the normal rules about him not sleeping on the bed did not apply. My last waking thought was that I must let everyone know that I was safe, but before I could reach out for my phone, I had dropped off, worn out by sheer exhaustion.

The next morning, I woke to the sound of the birds singing, and light pouring through the open curtains. There was no moment of confusion, no questioning where I was, but as I sat up and looked out of the window, the peaceful tranquillity almost made me wonder whether last night's events were real or a horrible dream. But there was no denying the fact that I was in our neighbours' spare room, and that my toe had swollen to nearly twice its normal size and was throbbing painfully.

I checked my phone for messages, but it had run out of battery. I rummaged in the bag of random stuff I'd managed to rescue from the house and eventually found the charger at the bottom. As I plugged the phone in and waited for it to come back to life, I decided to search through the paperwork folder to find our insurance details. Oak Tree Cottage wouldn't have been the only casualty from last night's storm and it would probably be a good idea to start the process of getting the insurance assessors out and making a claim as soon as possible. The ramifications of what had happened were too big to think about, and I needed to focus on the practicalities to try to regain some sense of control.

My phone was still taking its time to revive, so I

carefully made my way downstairs and begged another favour from our kindly neighbours who were only too happy to oblige. They'd seen the damage wrought to Oak Tree Cottage on an early morning walk, and were marvelling at their own lucky escape.

'We only lost a few tiles, love,' said Sheila. 'But the state of your place. It looks worse than it did when you first moved in.'

Frank cleared his throat.

'Yes, well, what's done is done. And that's what insurance is for, isn't it love?' she added hastily, before pressing a steaming mug of coffee into my hands and backing out of the room to leave me to my phone call.

I checked the number on the printout and dialled, scanning through the document in vain to try to find the policy number. My head was still all over the place and I was struggling to make sense of the paperwork. After a long time waiting in a queue during which I was repeatedly told by an electronic voice that my call was important to them, an actual human being finally picked up.

'Hello, my name is Craig, just to warn you, your call may be recorded for training purposes. Can I take your name and your policy number?'

I gave my name, but explained that I'd failed to find one.

'I'm sorry,' I apologised. 'I can't seem to think straight today. The storm was so unsettling. I can't believe that a bit of wind managed to inflict so much damage.'

Craig gave a grunt, which I chose to interpret as

sympathetic. The poor man probably had to deal with this kind of shell-shocked chatter every day.

I scanned through the paperwork again. 'I'm really sorry. This is so embarrassing, but I still can't find it.'

Craig gave a heavy sigh. 'Let me run you through some other security checks, and I'll see if we can find you that way,' he offered eventually.

After he'd extracted a huge amount of personal information from me, his voice changed.

'O-kay.' He paused and I could hear the sound of him tapping on his keyboard again. 'Let me put you on hold while I check something. Two minutes,' he said, not giving me a chance to respond before a tinny version of the James Bond theme tune started playing from the receiver. I drummed my fingers on the desk, wishing I'd brought my phone downstairs with me to charge. I still hadn't managed to get in touch with Charlie to warn him about what had happened. And the fact that I hadn't heard from him yet was making me worried for his safety too, although the obvious explanation, which caused me a different kind of angst, was that he'd stayed at Serena's overnight. But if he returned this morning and saw the state of the house, he'd be in for a shock. I needed to let him know that I was okay, even if the house wasn't.

'Miss Hutchinson, are you still there?' Craig's voice had changed to one of sympathetic patience. 'I'm sorry to have to tell you, but you don't have an insurance policy with us.'

The words made no sense.

'I'm sorry, can you repeat that?'

He spoke the same phrase back at me, but I still couldn't figure out what he meant.

'But of course we have a policy. I have the details here. I'm really meticulous when it comes to paperwork, and there's no way we would have moved in without getting the appropriate insurance. Could it be with a sister company instead, perhaps? I'm reading this piece of paper here, and it says 'Quotation for building and contents insurance'.'

Speaking slowly and carefully, he explained exactly what had happened. 'You approached us for a quotation, which we provided, then we sent you the paperwork to complete. But it was never returned to us. Cover is only in place once the forms have been filled out and the money has been paid.'

'There must be some mistake, I'll call you back.'

I hobbled upstairs as fast as I could manage and rescued my phone, ignoring the half a dozen messages and missed calls that had landed since it started charging, and scrolled through the neatly labelled folders in my email inbox to the one called 'Insurance'. There were copies of the life insurance we'd had to take out as a condition of getting the mortgage, and the insurance for Charlie's car after he'd insisted on adding me to his policy as a named driver, even though I was yet to take him up on his offer to lend the vehicle. Also in the folder was the paperwork for the house insurance, ready to be filled out. But when I searched my sent items for the completed forms, there was nothing there. Finally, with growing horror, I went into my drafts folder and scrolled through the dozen or so incomplete emails lurking there, forgotten about. And I found it. The paperwork, all filled out, but never actually sent off.

I felt physically sick. I stared at the draft email, willing it to be a figment of my imagination. And then I searched back through my emails again, in case I was mistaken. Finally, I checked my banking apps, hoping that I'd see regular payments to the insurers from either my personal account or the joint one that Charlie and I had set up to deal with house issues. But there was nothing in either. How had I been so stupid as to let this happen? Why hadn't I noticed that the email hadn't been sent, or that we were slightly better off at the end of each month than we should have been because the insurance direct debit wasn't being taken out of the account? How had I let this nightmare happen?

There was a light tap on the door, and Sheila stuck her head around it. Before she could speak, Ted had scurried through the gap, his claws clicking as he ran downstairs.

'Aw, your little dog knows Charlie's in the kitchen, love,' she said. 'I don't mind telling you that he was in a bit of a state when my husband found him. We were looking out for his car, you see. He thought you were trapped in the house because he couldn't get through to you, and was about to call the fire brigade, only Frank told him you were here first. I can't tell you how relieved he looked.'

His relief would be short-lived when he realised what I had done, or rather failed to do. I nodded numbly. 'Thanks, Sheila. I'll be down in a minute. I'll just gather my stuff together.'

'No rush. I suggest he takes you to the hospital to get that foot of yours looked at. It looks very painful. Do you want me to send him up to help you? I would offer myself but I'm not as strong as I look, I'm afraid.'

'I'll manage,' I insisted. I wanted to postpone the inevitable horror of the reunion with Charlie for as long as I could. I was so ashamed of myself. I couldn't bear the thought of how much pain I was about to inflict upon him. Because by failing to insure our cottage, I'd single-handedly destroyed both our futures. There would be no chance now of us selling up with a modest profit and moving on. And even being able to stay put seemed unlikely. We'd be lucky if the destruction from the storm hadn't condemned the building, as well as wiping most of the value off the house. All the money, all the hard work, all the love we had poured into Oak Tree Cottage over the last few months, it was all meaningless. Because we were now back to where we started. No, we weren't even at that place because the house had a dirty great big tree through half of it, destruction where the kitchen was meant to be, and devastation instead of the second bedroom. And we'd still have a mortgage to pay on it, regardless of its state.

I was fixating on the money side of things because it was a tangible concept. But there was so much more to it than that. Despite the current condition of our relationship, Charlie and I had had some very happy times in that house. We'd rekindled a friendship, and I'd found something so much more. In Charlie I had found the perfect foil. He was calm where I was stressed, he was brave where I sometimes would hold back. But during the months that we'd spent together, I liked to think I'd grown as a person. He helped to bring out the best in me, not by making me dependent on him, but by allowing me the space to see certain qualities in myself, and feel confident enough to bring them to the fore. We'd bought a house, but together we'd made it a home. Until I'd gone and messed it all up.

There was no point in dawdling and putting off the dreaded moment any longer. Steeling myself for what was about to happen, I slowly and steadily made my way down the stairs to where Charlie was waiting for me in the kitchen.

'Freya, thank goodness you're all right,' he said, rushing towards me, then stopping halfway across the room when he saw the awkwardness of my movements.

'What happened to your foot? Did you get trapped? Why didn't you call me as soon as the storm hit?

'Too many questions,' I said, as he wrapped me in a big bear hug, holding me tight, as if wanting to reassure himself that I was really there.

I held myself tense, not daring to allow myself to relax into his arms. He wouldn't be hugging me like this if he knew what had happened.

'I think we should go back to the cottage now,' I said eventually, knowing that I couldn't put off the dreaded moment any longer.

After what felt like forever, but also didn't feel long enough, he loosened his grip, although he then looped his arm through mine.

'Let me help you, lovely,' he said, the affectionate term feeling so undeserved.

'You're both welcome to stay here if it helps,' offered Sheila. 'It's nice having some young people around the place. We've been saying how good it has been to have you in the village, neighbours who care so much about the place. We always thought it was such a shame that Oak Tree Cottage was allowed to get into the state it did. All it needed was a little love in the place.'

'Thank you, but you've been more than kind already,' I said, before Charlie could say any different. 'We'll be okay.' I was fairly sure that was a lie.

We made our way slowly down the lane, Ted sticking closely to our heels, not wanting to be left behind. When we got back to Oak Tree Cottage, we both stood in stunned silence, surveying the damage. The front and right-hand side of the house looked pretty much as normal, but the back left-hand side of the building was a different story, the house's innards exposed to full view thanks to the tree-shaped hole in its fabric. The curtains in Charlie's room were gently flapping in the breeze, but the window they normally surrounded was smashed straight through. Vaguely I wondered if the fact that the tree had missed the corner of the house was a good thing, some distant memory from school physics classes about structural integrity striking a chord. That would be one of many things we'd have to investigate. If we could afford to.

'You should have rung me,' repeated Charlie. 'I know

we'd had words in the morning, but I hope you know that I'll always be there for you in a crisis, Freya.'

He might change his mind when he'd heard my confession.

'I did try to call you,' I said, 'but it was earlier in the evening, and Serena picked up instead. When everything kicked off, it was all I could do to get Ted and I out of there safely. By the time we'd made it up the road, I was so exhausted, I virtually collapsed into bed. But it's no excuse. I should have rung you then. I'm sorry I didn't.'

'That's okay. It's understandable. But I wonder why Serena didn't mention your call.'

'Because I asked her not to. I had a pang of conscience that I was ruining your date night.'

Charlie laughed, a strange sound to hear given the scene in front of us. 'It wasn't a date night.'

While my heart wanted to explore that answer further and its ramifications, my head told me that I needed to focus on the task in hand, confessing to Charlie.

'That's beside the point. What I really needed to say was—'

'Why do you think I'm dating Serena?' he asked, not letting me even get started.

'Charlie, now really isn't the time. It's not important.'

He fixed me with that penetrating gaze of his, seeming to look right into my soul, seeing all the confusion and doubt and pain lurking in there.

'It's pretty important to me. And I'd like to hope it's important to you too. It feels like something we should clear up,' he continued. 'I didn't spend the night with Serena. After my—'

'Charlie, I didn't sort the insurance out properly so we're royally screwed,' I interrupted him, coming out with it quickly so I could get the dreaded moment over and done with. Unfortunately, I said it so quickly that judging by the look of confusion on my face, he didn't take in a word of what I'd said.

I took a deep breath and explained the situation in full to him and how it was my lack of attention to detail that had caused it.

'But I've thought of a solution,' I concluded. 'I've got a plan to sort this out.'

The idea had come to me as we were walking down the lane, a way of making things better for Charlie. It didn't matter about the price that I would pay. This was about doing what was right.

'And what plan might that be?' asked Charlie. I couldn't work out from his tone how he was feeling about the situation. If he was angry with me, he was doing a very good job of keeping it contained.

'As you know, yesterday I had the house valued. Obviously, in light of what happened overnight, that valuation is going to be meaningless. But I am sure the estate agent can give me a fresh figure. We'll sell the house as a fixer upper, just like when we bought it, and then whatever it makes, you can take. All of it. I don't want a penny. And if it ends up that we still owe the bank money after it's sold, I will take responsibility for making sure that that money is paid off.'

'But we bought it fifty-fifty,' said Charlie. 'Both our names are on the mortgage, and both of us are responsible for paying it.'

'I know that. But I was the one who took responsibility for sorting out the insurance, and I was the one who failed to arrange it. It's my fault that this has happened, my fault that we're in this mess. You shouldn't have to pay the price for my mistake. I'm not going to let that happen.'

It was an offer that would destroy my dreams of house ownership, potentially for ever, condemning me to going back to where I had been, or perhaps to somewhere even worse. Being able to afford to live in a dodgy place with a landlord like Evil Stevil would probably seem like a distant dream. But I didn't care about the consequences. What mattered most to me was looking out for Charlie, making sure that he was going to be all right, that he didn't have to pay the price for my wrongs.

Charlie scratched his head slowly. 'Always the one with the plan, eh, Freya. But if you ask me, this plan is of the same calibre as The Rules, so if it's all the same to you, I'm going to turn it down.'

I blinked in astonishment. 'What are you saying? I'm offering you the house, Charlie. It's yours.'

'I don't want it if you're not going to be there too,' he said, his body language plainly telling me that he would not be moved on this point.

I shook my head, trying to get it clear. I was full of hope, but also terrified in case I had misunderstood what he was getting at. And so I fixed on perhaps the least important part of what he'd just said.

'I thought you liked The Rules?' I said tentatively.

Charlie laughed. 'I only ever saw them as a bit of fun, Freya. They only mattered to me to the extent that they mattered to you. I notionally agreed to them because it seemed important to you, but the reality is that I don't need a bit of paper to tell me how to act towards you or how to feel about you.'

My heart started beating faster as the hope built in my chest. 'But the frame? You had them framed. Why, if they were so meaningless?'

'Because I am at heart a sentimental beast, and I wanted to preserve them for posterity as they had played such a key part in bringing us back together again. They're meaningless in terms of the contents, but they mean everything as a symbol of the journey we've embarked on together. It's a bit like saving that empty champagne bottle from the first night we moved in. Ultimately, it's an empty bottle, but seeing it reminds me of us laughing together as we drank from it, stumbling around in the dark as we tried to settle ourselves into our new adventure, wondering what on earth we'd let ourselves in for.'

'But I thought you were making a point, that you feared I was going to break The Rules, or rather one of them, and wanted to warn me off before it was too late,' I said.

'If there's one thing that has become clear while living

with you, Freya, it's that you're not one for rule-breaking,' said Charlie, a note of disappointment in his voice.

I stared up at the broken house and thought of my earlier resolve to speak up. Was I wrong to even be considering still going through with it now? But on the other hand, what did I have to lose? For weeks I'd been holding back, not daring to say what was on my mind, making myself miserable, allowing it to destroy our friendship. I'd experienced the agony of rejection over and over again, not because it had actually happened, but because I'd let fear get the better of me, because I'd listened too closely to that nasty voice in the back of my head telling me that I wasn't worthy of being loved.

But it was time to stop letting that voice dictate my behaviour for the rest of my life. If Charlie rejected me, I would be devastated. But if I carried on not knowing, then that would be a torture more painfully slow and more destructive. I had to try, then at least I wouldn't have to go through the rest of my life wondering 'what if'.

'I've always been brought up to follow the rules and do the right thing. But I'm starting to realise that they're two separate beasts,' I said slowly. 'Because not long after we moved into the house I knew I was in definite danger of breaking The Rules, or rather one rule in particular.'

Charlie's expression remained hard to read, but he did at least give me a prompt.

'Which rule was that?' he asked.

'Rule 18c.'

'You'll have to remind me which one that is,' he said, to

my surprise. I'd still half believed that that particular rule was the reason he'd had them framed.

'Rule 18c. "No getting involved",' I said.

'You're going to have to spell it out for me,' said Charlie. 'Tell me what you really mean, Freya.' He wasn't going to make the rest of this easy for me.

Summoning up all my courage, I said, 'I got involved. Your friendship means everything to me, Charlie, and since we've rekindled it, it has brought me such joy. You are the person who knows me best in all the world. You've seen me at my worst and best moments, and you've still given me your friendship.' I took a deep breath. 'But now I'm hoping for more. You are my best friend, but I've also fallen in love with you. I couldn't feel more involved if I tried. When we were kids, the grown-ups always used to say we were partners in crime. What I'm trying to say is that now we are adults ourselves, I would love it if we could become partners in life.'

My heart was racing, my mouth was dry. I had made myself vulnerable, made that move from which there would be no going back. But now that I had said it, I also felt strangely calm. The words were out there. I had said my piece. It was up to Charlie now. Whatever his reply, I knew with certainty that I wouldn't regret what I'd done, and I was proud of myself for doing it.

Charlie took a step closer towards me, and suddenly I knew his answer before he even opened his mouth to say it.

'I thought you'd never ask, Freya,' he said softly.

Chapter Thirty

Of course, it was never going to be as easy as admitting our feelings for each other and then skipping off into the sunset for our happy ever after. For a start, as I pulled Charlie towards me, my senses zinging with anticipation at finally being able to kiss him properly, Ted decided that he was sick of hanging around in the lane and went for a wild run, zipping around the house and aiming for the hole in the side of the kitchen, judging it to be the shortest route back to his bed.

'Ted, no, come back.'

We set off after him, initially still holding hands, but quickly separating when we accepted that it wasn't the most practical way of capturing a rampaging dog, especially given my slow pace due to my injured foot. Thankfully we managed to stop him before he went back into the house and Charlie deposited him in his run.

'I can't help feel rather smug that it survived the storm,' he said.

'I don't think Ted would agree with you,' I replied, as Ted turned around three times on the spot and then flung himself onto the ground, his back pointedly facing towards us.

Now that we were in the garden, we had an even clearer view of the challenge facing us.

'I know we used to joke about living in the house being like camping. But now we probably really are going to have to camp in the garden. Where are we going to start with trying to solve all this?' I said, as Charlie took my hand once again and we picked our way through the debris.

'The roof and walls,' he said casually, as if it was going to be the easiest task in the world.

'Oh well, that's sorted then. Nice and simple, just a couple of little minor tasks,' I said with a laugh, wishing that my words were true.

Charlie fixed me with a steady look. 'But the foundations are still good. And as long as the foundations are strong, everything else will fall into place.'

'We don't know that for sure.'

'I think we do,' he replied.

I figured he wasn't just speaking about the house. We leaned towards each other, and then our lips touched at last. I could feel the smile on his mouth as finally we kissed, softly at first, then with growing urgency, our bodies pressed against each other. I couldn't be close enough to him.

'There is one slight problem, Hutch,' Charlie breathed against my lips some time later.

'I can't think of anything that would cause us a problem,' I replied as I trailed a row of kisses along his jawline and then proceeded to explore his neck in greater detail.

'We only have one double bed, and it was in my room,' he murmured.

'Then I guess we're back to sharing the single,' I whispered against his ear. By that point, I think both of us were prepared to cast aside any health and safety concerns and go inside the house anyway so we could continue in more comfort. But the jarring sound of yet another slate sliding off the roof and smashing to the ground forced us back to our senses.

'Perhaps we should get a professional out to assess the damage before we risk anything else. While I'd love to hear you say the earth moved for you,' said Charlie, his eyes sparkling with mischief, 'I'd prefer it to be in the heat of passion, rather than because the house was literally falling down around us.' The expression on his face turned my insides molten.

I rested my forehead against his. 'I suppose that would be for the best.'

'I'll give Serena a call,' he said. 'Have you figured out who she is yet?' He looked amused.

'Well, apparently she's not your date.'

'Serena's far too sensible to want to get involved with me,' said Charlie. I pretended to swipe at him, which made him laugh. 'She's the builder granddaughter of Arthur's friend. She runs the firm that supplies us with skips. And she graciously allowed me to attend some of the classes she runs at the building college, giving me some extra tuition so that I could hold my own on the DIY front. Last night I was at a workshop on woodwork, then ended up staying on a mate's sofa because the weather was so bad. Arthur suggested I take some lessons when I was chatting with him one day, and confessing that however hard I tried, I couldn't seem to keep up with your fix-it skills.'

'Hence your sudden talent for plastering and for putting kitchen cupboards together,' I said with a smile. It was all starting to make sense now.

'I can't deny it. You always seemed to be so in control and to know exactly what you were doing. I didn't want to let you down.'

'You couldn't let me down if you tried. And I'm a slave to the instructions, as well you know. But why didn't you say something?'

'Because I didn't want to lose face in front of the woman I was falling in love with,' admitted Charlie. 'I might as well confess now that when we were kids I had the hugest crush on you. And as I got to know you better as an adult, that affection grew stronger, until I realised I was completely in love with the woman you've become. And I wanted to impress you. It sounds so childish when I put it like that.'

'You didn't have to become an overnight success at building to impress me, Charlie. Your kindness, your support, and the way you can always make me laugh did that for you. I wish we'd both said something sooner.'

'It's always easier in hindsight. Besides, I was hoping you'd find your own way to overturning The Rules.'

'I was desperate to, but I was scared at the same time. It felt like there was so much at stake. But I should have known better, and talked to you about it.'

'Communication is key,' said Charlie lightly. 'I'm pretty sure that's mentioned several times in The Rules.'

'Damn The Rules,' I said, before I kissed him to soften the harshness of my words. 'We don't need guidelines telling us how to be with each other.'

'I couldn't agree more,' he said.

***

Serena's professional assessment of Oak Tree Cottage was thankfully that it was not in imminent danger of falling down. She did however advise the addition of some scaffolding to support the walls and heavy-duty tarpaulin to cover the holes in the roof before we moved back in again. And she warned us that we were going to have to come up with a better solution before the winter really set in. Thanks to her connections in the trade, she managed to get contractors out on the same day to chop up our beloved oak tree and remove the parts of it that were inside the house. She went away to compile an estimate of how much the new building work was going to cost, but judging by the expression on her face when she'd seen the damage, it was going to be a fair sum.

Once Oak Tree Cottage had been declared safe to re-enter, Charlie and I picked our way through the wreckage of our kitchen, our feet crunching on the new floor covering of leaves, twigs and sawdust.

'I think we're going to need more than a fresh coat of paint to make this look good again,' he said.

When I didn't reply, he turned to see what I was looking at.

'You wrote this when we were decorating,' I said. I pointed at the inscription on the floor, which had been exposed because the cabinet above it had been knocked out of place by the tree. Either side of Ted's paw print were our signatures, but I noticed that an additional word had been added between them so it now read, 'Charlie Humphries loves Freya Hutchinson.'

Charlie blushed. 'It seemed like too good an opportunity to miss,' he admitted.

'So that's why you put the cupboard in place so quickly while I was letting Ted out into the garden. I wish I'd seen it then, it would have saved a lot of heartache. You're a sentimental soul, Charlie Humphries.' I stood up and gave him a hug, pulling him tight to me so he could hear the next words I whispered. 'It's one of the many reasons I love you.'

'I should graffiti the kitchen floor more often,' he murmured in response.

I brushed some broken twigs away so I could see it more clearly.

'I know the tree has caused us major issues, but I'm also sad that it's no longer standing. It was so majestic. The place isn't the same without it. Oak Tree Cottage without the oak tree.' I shook my head. 'It seems wrong.'

'Ah, but you don't have to worry about that,' said Charlie. 'Let me show you something.'

He led me across the garden to a patch of earth just beyond Ted's run.

'When I was clearing space for the hound and making the garden doggy-proof, I found a tiny tree which must have sprouted naturally from a fallen acorn. Look.' He pointed out a small sapling, which was only about a foot high.

'I'm amazed it's managed to survive given the state of the garden and Ted's love of sticks,' I said.

'I think it's a determined thing, like the cottage and its owners. It's got a long way to grow until it reaches the height of its parent tree, but the continuity is there.'

'Oak Tree Cottage still has an oak tree.' I nodded. It was a strange source of reassurance, but it made me feel that somehow everything would work out all right.

Our first night as a couple mirrored our first night in Oak Tree Cottage in that we ordered a takeaway and lay down listening to the sound of the cold wind creeping its way into the house. Ted's normal sleeping spot in the kitchen was not an option for obvious reasons. Fortunately, he seemed content to curl up on the bathroom mats, snoring almost pointedly as we quietly shut the door behind him so we could enjoy our first night together without a doggy audience.

We lay entwined together under the duvet, Charlie stroking my hair while I rested my head on his chest.

'Penny for 'em,' said Charlie.

I propped myself up on my elbow so I could see his face in the moonlight.

'I still feel bad about the insurance situation,' I said.

'Don't,' he said simply.

'Easier said than done.'

'Freya, we all make mistakes. There was no malice behind it. It was a simple oversight. Much like when I forgot to pick up an order from the DIY shop, or gave Ted his dinner even though you'd already fed him.'

'But neither of those things had such huge implications.'

'Ted would argue otherwise. We'll get past this challenge, just as we got past all the others that presented themselves during the renovation. And you're forgetting the insurance situation finally led you to declaring your feelings for me. I shall be eternally grateful to it, because now I know the full extent of your utter devotion.'

'Utter devotion? You think very highly of yourself, Charlie Humphries.' I lowered my head and kissed him deeply. 'But you're right to. Camping in a building site with you is better than living in luxury with anyone else. You'll have to remind me of that when we're shivering in the height of winter as another gale blows through the house.'

'I'm sure we'll find a way of keeping each other warm,' said Charlie, with a laugh. 'Seriously though, the work ahead is going to take a toll on us and our bank balances, but we'll find a way to cope. As long as we've got each other, that's what matters. The rest is merely detail, which will find a way of working itself out.'

And true to Charlie's optimistic faith in fate, things slowly began to fall into place. When Serena's quotation first came back, I feared we were going to have to sell a kidney apiece to make it work. But we managed to get the price down a bit by agreeing to do some of the work ourselves. My YouTube playlist was going to be spectacularly long by the time we finished this project. And after some seriously hard negotiations by our mortgage broker, he managed to squeeze some extra money out of the bank to cover the rest of the major structural stuff. The icing on the cake was when I found out I'd got the Head of History job. By my calculations it would only give me approximately a pound extra in income per week, but hey, every penny helped.

But best of all, away from Oak Tree Cottage, we had good news about Granddad, who of course had spotted the change in Charlie and me as soon as we set foot in his room in the care home on our first visit after we got together.

'Ah, so you've finally said something then,' he said, not making it clear to which of us the comment was directed. 'You two were meant for each other. I knew it would happen one day. I'm never wrong about these things. That makes this a day of double celebration.'

'What are you celebrating, Granddad?' I said, somehow

not surprised that he'd spotted something it had taken me so long to work out for myself.

'I've been given the all clear to leave the care home,' he said.

'Does that mean you'll be moving back to your cottage?' I said. 'That's not good news, it's great news.'

'Not exactly,' he said. 'Your mother has been going on at me to speak to my landlord about adaptations to the house. You know the kind of thing – a stairlift, bath hoist, grab handles, stuff that old people use. But I've come up with a much better solution, which by some miracle she also thinks is a great idea. And funnily enough, it was you two that inspired me.'

'Are you getting yourself a fixer upper, Arthur?' asked Charlie with a grin on his face.

Granddad chuckled. 'I'll leave that to you young folk. But I've decided that I'm going to move in with my new friend Sjaak. It'll be good to have a bit of company and we enjoy having a laugh together. We've found a lovely place to rent together, all on one floor so it conforms to your mother's feelings about being practical for someone of my supposed seniority, but it's modern and slick, no old-person detritus in sight.'

'That sounds absolutely perfect. And living with a good friend is the very best. And you know what happened when Charlie and I moved in together,' I teased.

Granddad laughed. 'That would be a surprising development. But I feel spritelier than ever at the thought of the new place. There's life in the old dog yet. And speaking of the pooch, I was wondering if you would agree to go with a joint custody arrangement. I reckon Ted has got used to being around you two, and he'd be most disappointed not to be able continue supervising the work at Oak Tree Cottage.'

Ted gave a grunt from the Ikea bag. He'd grown so used to being smuggled into the care home in that manner that he'd started taking naps in it.

'I think that's Ted's way of saying he approves of the plan. As do I,' I said. I checked my watch. 'I'm afraid we're going to have to love you and leave you for the time being, Granddad. We have an important appointment with a roofer. A house isn't a home without a roof. Or love,' I added, with a wink at Charlie. 'And as you're breaking out of Dodge, perhaps Ted could forgo his incognito method of travelling.'

'You rebel, Hutch,' said Charlie.

'You're a bad influence on me, Humph,' I responded lightly.

'The Terrible Twosome march again,' said Granddad.

'With our four-legged friend making a third,' I said.

I took Charlie's hand in mine, and we walked out of the building together, Ted trotting merrily at our heels, and headed home.

Acknowledgments

First thanks have to go to you, lovely reader, for choosing to pick up this book. I hope reading Freya and Charlie's story brings you as much joy as I got from writing it.

Writing can be a solitary occupation, so I'm grateful to my bookish friends who are wonderful cheerleaders and a true inspiration. I'm also very lucky to have the support of my superstar editor Jennie Rothwell and the rest of the fab One More Chapter team. Working with you all is a dream! Thank you as well to my brilliant agent Amanda Preston for always having my back.

And finally, thank you to my family for your love, encouragement, and belief in me. You are my shining light.

**Read on for an extract of *Take a Chance on Greece*, another
uplifting and funny romcom from Emily Kerr...**

When Lydia wakes up after a wild night out in Kefalonia
with a tattoo saying 'Awesome Andreas', she's mortified.
She doesn't remember meeting anyone called Andreas. And
after all, she's an accountant with a five-year plan. She's
definitely *not* a party girl.

Deciding to become more spontaneous, Lydia decides to
track down the mysterious Andreas, but the path to true
love is never simple. Perhaps Lydia is looking in the wrong
places, and the right man for her is just next door, if only
she'd take a chance on him . . .

Take a Chance on Greece: Chapter One

If I'm being completely honest, I think I was still a little drunk when we got on the airport shuttle bus, which could have been something to do with the ouzo Kat had persuaded us to down as we rushed to get packed. She'd claimed it was pretty much the same as mouthwash and would help freshen our morning-after-the-night-before breath. I'm not sure the shot delivered on Kat's promise, but the aniseed-tasting liquid had certainly cleared my sinuses as it burned its way down my throat, leaving my lips feeling weirdly numb.

'Hurry up, Lydia, you're keeping everyone waiting,' Amira called across the bus as I stumbled my way down the aisle, feeling strangely queasy and floaty at the same time. Was this what a hangover was like? If so, why did people subject themselves to it on a regular basis? It had been a big mistake to go beyond my usual personal limit of a glass of wine with a meal, but the girls had accused me of letting the side down – especially as I was the reason we'd flown out to Kefalonia for this trip in the first place – and I'd allowed myself to be peer-pressured into becoming the life and soul of the party. At least, I think that's what happened, but my memory of last night was more than a little patchy. I read in the newspaper once that even after only a few drinks, the brain can stop forming new memories, so perhaps here I was demonstrating that scientific study in practice. I didn't feel great about it. I remembered getting ready at the hotel, the three of us playfully squabbling over mirror space in our cramped room and posing for pictures on the balcony before we set off. I remembered enjoying our meal in the coastal town of Sami, especially the delicious honey-oozing pastries which the waiter presented us with when we'd paid the bill. And I also remembered Amira leading us along a seemingly endless street between tavernas, promising that there was an amazing bar at the end of it, while Kat and I tried to keep each other upright as our heels wobbled on the uneven surface. But after that, mostly nothing, until I was woken this morning by Kat chucking a glass of water on the back of my head as I lay face down on the bed, still clothed in last night's outfit. We'd been in too much of a packing rush to compare notes on the evening, but hopefully when it wasn't ridiculous o'clock in the morning, my brain would crank into gear and I'd be able to fill in the blanks.

The slight unease about not being able to account for every minute was adding to the booze-induced churning in my stomach and I was worried it might tip me over the edge. Despite letting their hair down just as much as I had, this morning Kat and Amira looked healthy and put together, whereas I felt like acid was swirling around my insides while tiny creatures held band practice in my skull. But then again, as the girls kept reminding me when they were nagging me about this holiday, they're far better at letting loose than I am, so maybe they'd built up a hangover immunity.

Even thinking about the word 'hangover' made me feel sick. A bubble of bile threatened to make its way up my oesophagus and I paused to take a few deep breaths, clutching the back of a complete stranger's seat so I didn't end up slumping onto their lap instead. This was mortifying. Why had I allowed myself to be talked into coming on this trip when I could have had a nice, quiet few days at home instead, ticking things off my to-do list while bingeing episodes of *Bake Off* and secretly imagining what it would be like to be one of the contestants? Actually, thinking about *Bake Off* and all the creamy, sugary concoctions they create was a seriously bad idea. I gulped.

'Uh-oh, she's turning green,' Kat announced to the entire bus as she thrust a sunhat under my chin. 'If you're going to vom, aim for that. We'll miss our flight if we get chucked off this thing.'

I forced myself to swallow as my cheeks glowed with embarrassment. I'm not sure what was worse, the effects of the hangover, or the humiliation of my fellow travellers judging me for my terrible state. We'd had to hustle hard to make the transfer bus, and I'd not even had time to change or check my appearance in the mirror before leaving, which was probably a good thing, because I had a horrible feeling that the remnants of last night's mascara had gone full panda eyes on me. It was also horribly obvious that I was still dressed in last night's going-out clothes, and while the girls would probably argue that my version of going-out garb was still pretty understated compared to their fabulous efforts, my attire of sparkly top, which was now rather crumpled, and too-tight-to-be-comfortable denim shorts, made me feel like I was doing the walk of shame down the bus aisle. The one thing I had managed to achieve before setting off was dowsing myself in perfume, but such was my delicate state at the moment, the flowery scent was making my eyes water.

I wanted to assure the other passengers that, despite appearances, normally I was a perfectly respectable human being who held down a sensible job and everything, but I wasn't sure I was capable of stringing the words together in the right order.

'All good,' I said, shakily, 'I'm definitely not going to throw up.' I hoped that saying the words out loud would make them come true.

Kat shoved the hat back on her head. 'Excellent. If you'd ruined my favourite hat, it would have sorely tested our friendship. Besides, I'm not sure it would have made a very good bucket, being made of straw and all. Smile for the camera.'

Before I could process her words, she'd whipped out her

phone and snapped a shot, which I knew was far too close up to be flattering.

'Jim is going to love this, his beautiful bride-to-be in all her hen-do glory.'

'Give me that.' I tried to grab the phone, hoping to delete the horrible picture, but also thinking that there might be some images on it which could fill in my memory blanks, but my dexterity and reaction speeds were not up to their usual standards. Yet another reason why I shouldn't have had those extra drinks last night. Kat slipped the phone out of my reach and winked at me. I silently prayed she wouldn't immediately upload the photo to Instagram as was her usual habit. Jim didn't really bother posting to social media, but he always seemed to be amazingly across what was on there, and that picture would definitely not fit into the guidelines of acceptable professional behaviour at the firm which he ran and I worked for. He was so diligent about not being seen to give preferential treatment to me, that he would be bound to make a point of speaking to me about it, regardless of what his boyfriend perspective on the picture might be. Actually, his boyfriend perspective would probably be similarly unimpressed. He wasn't keen on either of us making a spectacle of ourselves in any context.

'And I'm not a bride-to-be,' I added, for what felt like the hundredth time. I was beginning to think Kat was doing it deliberately to make a point. 'I don't know why you keep insisting on calling this my hen-do. Jim and I are just moving in together, we're not getting married.'

Kat pulled a face. 'Oh yeah, I forgot. He's decided not to

propose until he's done a full analysis to decide whether the costs of a wedding are offset by the tax benefits of marriage.' Her tone made it very clear that she did not agree with his logic.

'It makes sense. There's no point in being saddled with tons of debt for the rest of our lives.' I automatically defended Jim, even though I secretly still felt rather affronted by his pragmatic approach to our relationship. If there was one area to throw caution to the wind and go with the heart rather than the head, it was this. And then I felt disloyal for thinking that way. Jim had always been steady and dependable, I knew exactly where I was with him, and that was why he was so good for me, as he always reminded me.

'Careful consideration of decisions leads to no unexpected surprises.' I recited our mantra.

'Typical accountants,' muttered Amira. She was one to talk. As a doctor who spent most of her life picking up the pieces from other people's mistakes, she was nearly as risk-averse as Jim and I, but perhaps the holiday spirit had got to her too.

The bus lurched forwards as the driver decided he'd had enough of waiting for me to sit down and turned the engine on. Hot, petrol-scented fumes started pumping from the air-conditioning vents and the speakers crackled into life, blasting out a Greek pop song at full, painful, volume. It was a ridiculously cheesy tune, the kind of ditty which insinuates itself into your brain and remains playing on repeat for hours, even if you have no idea what the lyrics mean. It was definitely not hangover-appropriate. I fumbled in my handbag, trying to find my earplugs, but then the music changed key and the briefest flash of a memory sparked in my head as the singer crooned a high note. For a moment, the disgusting sensation of ickiness disappeared, to be replaced with something else altogether. It was more a recollection of a feeling of happiness and joy, rather than an image of an actual event, but that impression of utter contentment helped make my insides settle down a bit. I knew it was silly to rely on intuition rather than cold, hard facts, but I suddenly had a strong sense that last night's blank spaces had been filled with good experiences rather than bad.

That was enough to give me the strength to stagger the last few steps, reach up and stow my hand luggage in the overhead shelf. The girls had both bagged themselves window seats, so I was left with a choice of who to sit next to.

'Finally,' Kat said, moving her handbag so there was room for me. 'I thought you were going to spend the whole journey walking down the aisle. I suppose you've got to make the most of it for now until Jim pulls his finger out and puts a ring on it.'

I refused to rise to the bait, knowing there was nothing Kat enjoyed more than teasing people. I turned my back on her, plonking myself down next to Amira instead. In fact, I must have plonked a bit too heavily because I got a sharp pain in the small of my back when I landed on the chair.

'Ouch,' I winced, pulling the seat belt slack so I could

turn around to see if there was something sticking out of the seat. I ran my hand over the worn fabric, but couldn't feel anything sharp enough to have hurt me. Deciding I must have imagined it, I leaned back, but the pain started again.

I reached around and placed my hand against my back. Yes, it was definitely feeling tender and tight, as if I'd grazed it against something. I untucked my top and tried to feel my skin, but my fingers met with a layer of plastic which appeared to be stuck over the sore patch with some kind of tape.

'What the heck?' I muttered, trying to pick at the tape. I'd felt pretty grotty leaving the hotel without washing – 'No time for showers,' Kat had said – but now I felt even more grim, knowing that I'd managed to come out with some kind of makeshift plaster stuck to my lower back. This was not like me at all. The bus went over a pothole on a hairpin bend, making my nails slip and land in the centre of the painful bit. I winced and decided to stop pulling at the plastic and instead try to find out how I managed to get an injury. I closed my eyes and concentrated hard, trying to visualise the town we'd spent the evening in, focusing on different senses in case any of them ignited a memory. I could feel the rough stone of the buildings I'd brushed my fingers along as we'd made our way down the road between the pools of light from the streetlamps. I could hear the tinny sound of pop music mixed with the hubbub of different languages, voices raised over each other in a bid to be heard. And I could smell the scent of the sea in the air, and something else, something vaguely spicy, warm and comforting, closely followed by the tang of antiseptic. But try as I might to sharpen these flashes of sensation into something more tangible, the memories remained frustratingly elusive.

'My back's stinging. Did I scrape myself last night or fall over or something?' I asked Amira, lowering my voice in the hopes that Kat wouldn't overhear my question. I'd never live it down if she realised that the previous evening was pretty much a blackout for me. It was mortifying enough to have to ask in the first place.

Thankfully Amira looked concerned rather than amused.

'Not when you were with us. Are you OK, babe?'

I turned to face her square on. 'What do you mean, not when I was with you? Wasn't I with you all night?'

It was as if my stomach had fallen out of my body, leaving a horrible sense of dread behind in its place. I knew that statistically Kefalonia had a very low crime rate – it was one of the reasons I'd agreed to it as a destination – and I'd never felt anything but safe during our brief holiday here, but anything could have happened in my drunken state. I did another quick body scan, but thankfully the soreness on my back was the only niggle. I checked my purse, but my cash and cards were still safely in place. I reminded myself of the memory of a flash of happiness. Surely if anything terrible had happened, it would have overridden that?

Amira shrugged. 'I'll be honest, my memory is a tad patchy too, but there were definitely a few hours in the bar when we weren't all dancing together. You said you wanted to chill out at the hotel because your feet were sore. Maybe you bashed your back then.'

'But what about girl code? Never leave anyone behind,' I said indignantly. 'You know I'm a lightweight compared to you guys.'

'Sorry, Lyds, but you did insist you'd be fine sitting out for a bit and the hotel was only over the road and we watched you walk across to make sure you'd got there OK. If a bruise on your back is your biggest concern, then nothing really bad happened, did it?'

Kat cleared her throat from across the aisle.

'I hate to interrupt the heart-to-heart, ladies, but I've got a very important question to ask.' She paused and looked me squarely in the face. 'Lydia Evans, who is Andreas, what makes him awesome, and why do you now have his name tattooed on your lower back?'

Want to find out what happens next?
Take a Chance on Greece **is available now in ebook and paperback**

ONE MORE CHAPTER

YOUR NUMBER ONE STOP

FOR PAGETURNING BOOKS

One More Chapter is an
award-winning global
division of HarperCollins.

Sign up to our newsletter to get our
latest eBook deals and stay up to date
with our weekly Book Club!
<u>Subscribe here.</u>

Meet the team at
<u>www.onemorechapter.com</u>

Follow us!

 <u>@OneMoreChapter_</u>
 <u>@OneMoreChapter</u>
 <u>@onemorechapterhc</u>

Do you write unputdownable fiction?
We love to hear from new voices.
Find out how to submit your novel at
<u>www.onemorechapter.com/submissions</u>